THWARTED DESIRE

She placed a delicate kiss on his cheek.

Don't do it, he told himself. *Don't indulge. She does not understand what she does, perhaps not even its effect on a man.*

But her lips were so close, her scent was so intriguing, and he had only to reach out a little, turn his head just so.

No, he mustn't do it. He mustn't. Yet, slowly, he turned his head. And as his lips came in contact with hers, he thought his body might burst apart. He felt too much, desired too much, and the craving tore at him. Barely able to contain this woman's effect on him, he broke off the kiss. He knew he must put a stop to this immediately, or he would have to take back everything they had thus far discussed.

Unable to set her away from him completely, he pulled her into his embrace and hugged her. Her head fitted perfectly into the crook of his neck, he noted, as though she were made exactly for him.

He set her away from him, running his fingers down the smoothness of her cheek to her neck, on down toward her chest. "We should not do anything further," he said. "We must not. You do agree?"

She nodded. "I know. And yes, I agree."

More praise for Karen Kay

"Entrancing!"
—Cassie Edwards

"Enchanting . . . will capture your attention quickly and never let go!"
—*Huntress Reviews*

"A tour de force Native American romance."
—*Romantic Times*

the SPIRIT of the WOLF

KAREN KAY

BERKLEY SENSATION, NEW YORK

THE BERKLEY PUBLISHING GROUP
Published by the Penguin Group
Penguin Group (USA) Inc.
375 Hudson Street, New York, New York 10014, USA
Penguin Group (Canada), 90 Eglinton Avenue East, Suite 700, Toronto, Ontario M4P 2Y3, Canada
(a division of Pearson Penguin Canada Inc.)
Penguin Books Ltd., 80 Strand, London WC2R 0RL, England
Penguin Group Ireland, 25 St. Stephen's Green, Dublin 2, Ireland (a division of Penguin Books Ltd.)
Penguin Group (Australia), 250 Camberwell Road, Camberwell, Victoria 3124, Australia
(a division of Pearson Australia Group Pty. Ltd.)
Penguin Books India Pvt. Ltd., 11 Community Centre, Panchsheel Park, New Delhi—110 017, India
Penguin Group (NZ), Cnr. Airborne and Rosedale Roads, Albany, Auckland 1310, New Zealand
(a division of Pearson New Zealand Ltd.)
Penguin Books (South Africa) (Pty.) Ltd., 24 Sturdee Avenue, Rosebank, Johannesburg 2196,
South Africa

Penguin Books Ltd., Registered Offices: 80 Strand, London WC2R 0RL, England

This is a work of fiction. Names, characters, places, and incidents either are the product of the author's imagination or are used fictitiously, and any resemblance to actual persons, living or dead, business establishments, events, or locales is entirely coincidental. The publisher does not have any control over and does not assume any responsibility for author or third-party websites or their content.

THE SPIRIT OF THE WOLF

A Berkley Sensation Book / published by arrangement with the author

PRINTING HISTORY
Berkley Sensation edition / April 2006

Copyright © 2006 by Karen Kay Elstner-Bailey.
Cover art by Robert Papp.
Cover design by George Long.
Interior text design by Stacy Irwin.

All rights reserved.
No part of this book may be reproduced, scanned, or distributed in any printed or electronic form without permission. Please do not participate in or encourage piracy of copyrighted materials in violation of the author's rights. Purchase only authorized editions.
For information address: The Berkley Publishing Group,
a division of Penguin Group (USA) Inc.,
375 Hudson Street, New York, New York 10014.

ISBN: 0-425-20920-2

BERKLEY SENSATION®
Berkley Sensation Books are published by The Berkley Publishing Group,
a division of Penguin Group (USA) Inc.,
375 Hudson Street, New York, New York 10014.
BERKLEY SENSATION is a registered trademark of Penguin Group (USA) Inc.
The "B" design is a trademark belonging to Penguin Group (USA) Inc.

PRINTED IN THE UNITED STATES OF AMERICA

10 9 8 7 6 5 4 3 2 1

If you purchased this book without a cover, you should be aware that this book is stolen property. It was reported as "unsold and destroyed" to the publisher, and neither the author nor the publisher has received any payment for this "stripped book."

This book is dedicated to
Eric Dyer,
my friend,

and
Cheryl (Clark) Dyer,
whose golden beauty is renowned.

And to my husband, Paul.
I love you.

I would also like to acknowledge the following artists
for their continuing inspiration:

The music of
Blake Shelton
Robbie Robertson & The Red Road Ensemble
Drew Tretick
Jeff Carson
David Pomeranz
Brulé
Tracy Lawrence
Music Flex
Celine Dion

The paintings of
George Catlin
Karl Bodmer

THE GAME OF *COS-SOO*

To the Reader:

Cos-soo, sometimes called the game of the Bowl, was a common game known to the Indians on the plains—all tribes. A game of chance, it was played only by men, and the stakes were often desperate.

The rules of the *Cos-soo* were as follows: Players used a wooden bowl slightly less than a foot long, highly polished with a rim of about two inches. The "dice" were not dice as we might think of them, but were objects which were common on the plains at this time. These small objects would have been assigned certain value.

The highest value went to the large crow's claw—there was only one per game—which was painted red on one side and black on the other. When after a throw it was standing, it counted for twenty-five points (or sticks). The count was kept by sticks. It was also counted for five on its side if the red side was up—and so a total of thirty points would go to the large claw, if it were standing. Otherwise it counted for only five.

Next were four small crow's claws, also painted red on

one side and black on the other. They counted for five if landed on the red side, and nothing if on the black.

Next there were five plum stones. These were white on one side and black on the other. If the black side was up, it counted four; if the white side was up, it counted for nothing.

Then there were five pieces of blue china—they were small and round. Blue side up was worth three points; white side counted as nothing.

Farther down the line were five buttons. The eye side up counted for two each, the smooth side for nothing.

And last there were five brass tack heads. The sunken side counted for one, the raised side as nothing.

Each man kept his opponent's score, not his own, by means of handing his opponent a number of sticks equal to his throw. The sticks were kept in view so that all could see them. In the early 1800s Edwin Thompson Denig (a trader married to an Assiniboine woman) noted: "It has been observed in these pages in reference to their gambling that it is much fairer in its nature than the same as carried on by the whites and this is worthy of attention, inasmuch as it shows how the loser is propitiated so that the game may not result in quarrel or bloodshed . . ."

The game was often kept up for forty-eight to seventy-two hours without a break except for meals. And it was usually played until one or the other of the players was ruined totally.

Horses, guns, weapons, clothing, and women were all stakes in these games. Again, Edwin Thompson Denig observed, "We have known Indians to lose everything— horses, dogs, cooking utensils, lodge, wife, even to his wearing apparel . . ."

PROLOGUE

In a time long ago a Northwestern Indian tribe, one composed of five different tribal bands or clans, betrayed the god of Thunder. It happened in an age when food was plentiful, when starvation was unknown. Yet, the men of the tribe sought to kill more game than was needed.

The Thunderer's children thought to intervene on the animals' behalf, but little did they know that the tribe's greed had turned to lust. Ultimately, the tribal leaders and their followers killed the Thunderer's children, every one of them.

In retaliation for this evil deed, the Thunderer stole four beautiful women from the tribe, and sought to destroy every other member of it, all clans. It would have been accomplished, too, but for the Creator, who intervened.

"Nay, these people shall not die," the Creator decreed. Instead He sent the people of these tribal bands into the "mist." There, they would live a half existence. Neither alive nor dead, every individual would be cursed to live forever in the shadows, not real, not even ghosts.

But once a generation, a boy would be summoned as his clan's champion. Becoming real and taking a form of substance forever, the boy would set out into the real world, where he would be charged with the duty of undoing the spell which enslaved his people.

In 1816, there were four tribal bands left, their people still imprisoned in the mist. Swift Hawk, then ten years old, was chosen to represent the Burnt Chest Band of the tribe; Spirit Raven, also ten years of age, was next selected from the Fast Runner Band; Long Bow would represent the Black Fire Band; and Spotted Wolf, the Yellow Shawl Band.

The boys were to go out into the world, to be adopted by other Indian tribes. The champions were to grow, to learn, to watch, to come to know the enemies of their adopted tribe. For it was only through a special act of kindness and selflessness toward an enemy that the enchantment could be broken.

In 1835, Spirit Raven has less than a single year left to break the spell. Adopted by the Assiniboine Indians when he was still a lad, Spirit Raven is now known to his adopted brothers as Grey Coyote; Coyote, because of the form his spirit protector takes, and Grey because the Assiniboine have observed that black clouds and hard times follow the boy . . . always . . .

With so little time left to accomplish his mission, Grey Coyote is desperate.

And so begins our story . . .

Chapter 1

The Western American Plains
The early 1830s

The scent of sacred herbs, of sage and sweetgrass, hung low in the air. With a steady hand, the young man, naked, bathed his entire body in the hallowed smoke. At the same time, he sang the good songs, his voice lifting to the heavens.

> *"Hi-ya, hi-ya, hi-ya, haii.*
> *Hi-ya, hi-ya, hi-ya, haii."*

Night had fallen. In the distance, a wolf howled. Then came another wail, another and another until the song of the wolf mixed with the rhythm of the night.

Ancient voices, long dead, and the beat of many drums rang out over the plains. A nighthawk squawked. But the young man, although aware of these signs, paid them little heed.

The howling of his spirit protector, the little wolf, could be heard over the rest. It beckoned. It was a good thing.

At last, the young man was to communicate with the Creator; Grey Coyote was to have his vision.

Positioned high atop a lonely butte, Grey Coyote raised his arms to the heavens in silent invitation, his voice for the moment stilled. Then, as though the music of the evening surrounded him, he sang out,

> "Wakonda, *Creator, have pity on me.*
> *What I seek is not for myself.*
> *It is for my people.*
> Wakonda, *I have been charged with the duty of freeing*
> *my people from the land of the everlasting*
> *shadows.*
> Wakonda, *I am twenty-nine winters in age.*
> *And in all this time, I have not learned how to help my*
> *people.*
> Wakonda, *Creator, have pity on me."*

Grey Coyote waited. He could not see his protector, the little wolf, but he could still hear its yipping, off in the distance. Then its song came closer and closer, until its noise grew loud even to Grey Coyote's ears. But Grey Coyote did not draw away.

Rather, he reached out farther, that he might grasp hold of his protector; perhaps he might touch something tangible, something that would show him that this time he was walking the good path, the right path. But he felt nothing.

Disappointed, Grey Coyote fell to his knees.

And then it happened, taking place so slowly, that at first Grey Coyote did not recognize the spirit for what it was. The little wolf's howl had transformed from an eerie series of wails, to words. They were yipping, guttural words, it was true. But to Grey Coyote, never had a sound been sweeter.

He looked up, and there on a ledge before him was his vision, his protector. There, too, was a faceless, dark-haired, white man.

"Seek out this man," barked the little wolf. *"You will know him by his long, dark and stringy hair; you will recognize him also by his greasy, ugly appearance. Many are the things that this white man will do that will repulse you. But you must persevere, for when you have found him, you need only solve this riddle:*

Neither small nor large, nor wide, nor narrow, the white man possesses a thing that will propel you toward freedom. Though he will think it is possessed by him and though you must possess it, and it will possess you, only when you are free from it, yet act as it, will your people be released from the mist.

You alone must solve this, you alone must act on it, and if you do, your people go free. Fail to settle the riddle satisfactorily, fail to act, and your people remain enslaved. Further, if you err and do not solve this, you will live the rest of your life forever knowing that you did not prove yourself worthy.

"I have spoken."

The voice faded away, repeating these words over and over, *solve this, act on it, and your people go free,* until at last the spirit itself began to evaporate.

"Ogluksa, wait!" cried out Grey Coyote. "Spirit Protector, have pity on me. I am but a simple man. And I do not understand this riddle."

But the music had stopped. The ancient voices had stilled. Even the wolves in the distance no longer howled.

And though Grey Coyote cried out again, the spirit of the little wolf had gone. Grey Coyote was alone . . . again . . .

CHAPTER 2

The Minnetaree Village
A Permanent Indian Village of mud huts
on the Knife River
Upper Missouri Territory—in what is today
the State of North Dakota
Summer 1835

From the corner of his eye Grey Coyote watched the white man sneak a stick into line beside those that were already present, giving the white man eleven sticks instead of ten that he had won fairly.

So, decided Grey Coyote, *the white man has no honor*.

At the thought, Grey Coyote raised a single eyebrow and cast a glance across the few feet that separated him from the white man, the man the Minnetaree Indians called the scout, LaCroix. LaCroix was French, as were many of the white men in this country. His face was pale and bearded, his hair long, dark and scraggly. His breath stank of the white man's whisky, and his body smelled of dirt and grime.

But none of this bothered Grey Coyote. In truth, he was

smiling at the man, although the expression could hardly be called one of good humor. After a moment, Grey Coyote said, "Darkness has fallen again. We have been playing for longer than a full day now."

LaCroix grunted.

"As you know, we are both guests here, in my friend's lodge, in the Minnetaree village," continued Grey Coyote. "And I would hardly be the cause of a fight if I could avoid it, for it would bring shame to our host, Big Eagle."

Grunting again, LaCroix looked away. His gaze shifted from one object in the room to another, not centering on anything in particular, not even on the lovely white woman who reposed on one of their host's beds in a corner of the hut.

As discreetly as possible, Grey Coyote let his gaze rest for a moment on that golden-haired beauty. He had never before seen a white woman, and to say that Grey Coyote was surprised at her appearance would have been an understatement.

He would have assumed that the white man's woman would have been as unkempt, and perhaps as hairy as her male counterpart. But this simply was not so. The woman was uncommonly pretty. Slim, small and curvy, with golden hair that reached well to her waist, the woman's coloring reminded him of a pale sunset; golden, translucent, mysterious.

Her eyes were as tawny as her hair, like those of a mountain lion's. Even at this distance, and despite the ever-growing darkness in the one-room hut, Grey Coyote could discern their color. It was a rare shade to be found here on the plains, where the eye colors of dark brown and black dominated.

Warming to his subject, he noted discreetly that the

white woman's skin was also quite fair, unblemished. Her cheeks were rosy, as pale and pink as the prairie rose. To his eye, she was a beautiful sight.

But she paid no heed to the people sharing this hut, not sparing so much as a glance at another being, except perhaps the Indian maid who appeared to serve her. In truth, the white woman seemed lost in her own thoughts.

And perhaps this was best, thought Grey Coyote. From the looks of her, she might prove to be more than a mere distraction to him if he took a liking to her, something Grey Coyote could ill afford.

Slowly, Grey Coyote returned his attention to the matter at hand. The game of *Cos-soo*—an Indian man's game of chance—had been started a day ago, Grey Coyote being more than ready to gamble with this particular white man.

After all, LaCroix fit the description of the white man whom he sought. Perhaps this was the chance Grey Coyote awaited.

But to find the man cheating?

Clearing his throat, Grey Coyote spoke again, saying, "I admit it is dark, growing ever darker as we sit here. I concede, too, that a good many hours have passed since we decided to begin this game, but do not think that because of this my eyes are so tired that they do not see."

"What? What is it that *monsieur* insinuates?" asked LaCroix, his look incredulous.

Grey Coyote nodded toward LaCroix's sticks with his forehead. "I am keeping track of the number of your sticks." Grey Coyote again raised one of his eyebrows and said, "There should be ten sticks that you hold, for as you see, you received ten points for your roll. Remember, you had lost all of your other sticks in the previous roll."

"That is not true. I kept one stick that was left over from before. I should have eleven sticks, not ten."

Grey Coyote's stare was bold. "You lost the last bet."

LaCroix's eyes grew round, though he could still not match Grey Coyote's direct gaze. "Is it true? I thought that . . . *Oui, oui,*" he blurted out, his words being accompanied by a chuckle. "Ye are right. What was I thinking? I do not know how this other stick came to be here, for I had taken all my sticks away. Perhaps two sticks stuck together. *Oui*, I am sure that is it."

"*Hau, hau,*" said Grey Coyote, using the Assiniboine word for "yes." He continued, "Let us hope that no other sticks see fit to stick together." Grey Coyote again nodded toward LaCroix, and reaching across the playing space handed LaCroix fifty sticks. "These are for my last roll," said Grey Coyote.

"*Oui, oui,*" said LaCroix, who accepted the twigs and commenced to set them out along the ground beside the two men. Grey Coyote carefully watched the man at his work, not fooled by LaCroix's attempt at "sleight of hand."

He said, "Scout LaCroix, I gave you fifty sticks, the amount of my throw. But you have only set out twenty."

"But, *monsieur*, I have done this because it is the number of sticks that is appropriate for your roll. Do ye see? Ye rolled five burnt sides, which is four points each, or twenty."

Grey Coyote narrowed his brow. "You should look closely at the bowl, Scout LaCroix," said Grey Coyote. "Do you not see that the big claw stands on end, red side up? As you and I know, that is worth thirty."

"Is it standing? My mistake. I did not see the big claw stand on end." LaCroix leaned over, as though to peer into the polished, wooden bowl, a bowl that was used in the game to throw the dice. However, the man came so close to his target that he "accidentally" bumped into it. The big claw—the one dice that garnered the highest points—fell to a different position. "Oh, is a mistake. I am sorry, *monsieur*. But the claw, it does not appear to be on end. However, I will take yer word for it and will set out the extra thirty sticks if ye insist." His eyes didn't quite meet Grey Coyote's.

"Do not bother," said Grey Coyote after a long pause. And though LaCroix's actions more than alarmed him, Grey Coyote trained his features into a bland expression. He would let the incident pass. After all, it was not in his mind that he *had* to win everything that this man owned. All he needed was *the* possession, the one thing that would help Grey Coyote solve the riddle, though at present what that particular possession was, escaped him. And so he said evenly, "Pay more attention in the future."

"*Oui, oui, monsieur.* And now, if ye insist, ye may have another turn, since ye believed that the big claw stood on end."

Grey Coyote shrugged. "It is not necessary. I will give you the next roll."

"*Oui, oui,*" said LaCroix, and picking up the bowl with four fingers placed inside its immaculately polished rim, he threw the dice up by striking the bowl on the ground.

Maria Marietta Welsford sat in a corner of the Minnetaree mud hut, hardly aware of her surroundings. After having given her environment a quick glance to ensure that she was safe from molestation, she became once again lost in her own thoughts.

How long a journey would her return to England be? Would she arrive there in time to claim the family estate, Rosemead, an endowment she had thought was lost to her forever?

Of course she had responded at once to the solicitor's letter of two months ago, but how long would it take for correspondence from the American West to reach England? Would her reply arrive in time?

And what had happened to her uncle, the current Earl of Welsford? Was it true that he had disappeared?

It would seem to be so. For, according to the solicitor's note, upon her uncle's disappearance, legal queries had arisen, queries that had led to certain discoveries. Her uncle, the Earl of Welsford, was not, and had never been, the rightful inheritor of Rosemead, though all those years ago, the man had acted as though he were.

Worse, during his reign, Marietta's uncle had mismanaged the estate. He had accrued gambling debts, among other things. Creditors needed paying. But it now appeared that the funds for her uncle's endeavors could no longer be lawfully taken from the inheritance.

Truly, the current Earl of Welsford had overstepped his bounds.

To Marietta, it all seemed too fantastic to be true. After all these years, to learn that *she* was Rosemead's true inheritor? Indeed.

However, documentation had proved it true. Upon Marietta's eighteenth birthday, Rosemead had been endowed to her. Her uncle was never supposed to have been more than a trustee to the estate.

It was a daunting realization. *All those years ago, her uncle had not had the authority to do as he had done.*

It was well worth remembering.

Yet, it would all be for naught if she tarried now, if she did not hurry back to England. For she feared that if she did not return in a timely manner, the solicitors might be forced to conclude that she was dead.

At the thought, Marietta's stomach twisted uncomfortably. Rosemead, where lay all her memories of her parents, might go to someone outside the family.

It was not a pleasant thought; yet it could happen. For she had no brothers or sisters.

No, there was nothing else for it. She must hurry. As it was, a few months had already passed since the solicitor's letter had found her; the fact that it *had* found her, seeming to be a miracle.

Fortuitously, Captain William Clark of St. Louis had been acquainted with the party in which Marietta traveled. He had remembered Marietta and had passed the correspondence along to her via an Indian runner.

Yet, since that time, minutes, hours, days, flew by too quickly. She needed to hurry.

However, attempting to explain this to someone here in the American West, was rather like defining complicated mathematics to a child. Alas, in the Western wilderness there was no time clock. Events either happened at an even rate, or at a very, very slow pace, for to these Westerners, time was something held in great abundance.

If only she could travel on her own, she thought, or at the very least, hasten her guide. But neither action seemed possible. Her escort, Jacques LaCroix, appeared to manage his life in a tempo that was akin to sluggishness.

But at least Marietta possessed enough gold to buy her passage from the man. Unconsciously, she placed her hand over her purse, which was, for safety, resting on a string around her neck and tucked beneath her chemise.

The coin had come from Princess Sierra, Marietta's former mistress. Princess Sierra, a Spanish aristocrat from the northern provinces of Spain, upon learning of Marietta's inheritance, had generously bestowed upon her friend more than enough gold to see Marietta back to England.

A good friend she was, too. Was it not Princess Sierra, who, so many years ago, had rescued Marietta from obscurity? And at a time when Marietta had no one to turn to? Indeed, it was thanks to the princess that Marietta had never known poverty or hardship, something that might have been forced on her, had she remained under her uncle's thumb.

Still, despite this, it was not in Marietta's heart to forgive her uncle what he had done . . .

"Have a seat, Marietta." The Earl of Welsford, Marietta's uncle, indicated an empty seat, one positioned across from his massive desk.

Ten-year-old Marietta hobbled forward to do as he bid, sitting, and at once disappearing into the immense chair.

"As you know," the earl continued, "there are hard times upon us. Your father and mother did not provide for you as well as they might."

Marietta frowned. "But Papa always said that if anything ever happened to him, there was money enough to support me."

"The mere wishes of a dreamer," said the Earl of Welsford. "You must know that your doctor bills alone are such that your aunt and I have been forced into debt to pay them."

Marietta remained mute, but she knew that her uncle

lied. He gambled. If her family's money were gone, she was certain that it was this that had consumed it.

"Your aunt and I," continued the earl, "simply cannot continue to support you on the meager inheritance that your father left."

Marietta said nothing, but she became apprehensive.

"But come, don't look so downtrodden, girl. I have made arrangements for you." The Earl of Welsford smiled. "An opportunity has presented itself, and I was quick to take advantage of it, being the smart businessman that I am. What I mean to tell you is that starting next week, you will be in service to a princess, a royal princess. The arrangements have all been made."

"You have sold me into service?" Even at ten years of age, Marietta understood the implications of this. Mutinously, she glared at her uncle.

"But come, girl, there is no need to stare daggers at me. It is not as bad as all that. You will be serving royalty. Only those of gentle birth are allowed such a grand opportunity."

Marietta kept her tongue, but she was certain that the only one who had received any "opportunity" was her uncle.

However, the Earl of Welsford rose to his feet, towering over the diminutive, ten-year-old girl. He smiled, though there was more self-indulgence in that expression than good humor. "Marietta, Marietta," he said, "don't look like that. It's not the end of the world. The princess is your age. You'll be tutored along with her, as though you yourself were royalty. You'll be treated well."

"But I will be a servant."

"A servant to royalty, Marietta. Others should be so lucky."

"Then let someone else have the opportunity."

The earl, however, had merely smiled once more. "All must work for their keep, Marietta, even the tiniest ant. It is already done. The arrangements have been made. You will leave in a week's time. Now, that is all."

Marietta had never forgotten, nor forgiven.

It wasn't as if her life with the princess had ever been one of distress. Quite the contrary. But a person likes to think that she is the purveyor of her own deeds, and servitude, no matter its fancy trappings, is still servitude.

Yet, despite how it had begun, the princess had always been a stable influence over Marietta. And it was Princess Sierra now who had spurred Marietta into action, who had not only given her coin, but had found the Indian woman, Yellow Swan, to accompany Marietta on her journey to St. Louis.

However, for all her wonderful qualities, it was also because of Princess Sierra that Marietta now found herself stuck in the American West. From necessity, Marietta had accompanied Princess Sierra into the States in the princess's quest to find the man to whom she was married.

The princess had found him, and more. She had rediscovered true love.

Marietta was happy for her, for she truly loved her. In truth, she would still be with Princess Sierra, serving her and her husband, if not for that solicitor's letter. But now—

Crash!

The roar of thunder shook the ground at her feet, causing Marietta to reach out toward Yellow Swan, the young Indian woman who was not only her maid, but who had become her friend.

"Yellow Swan," said Marietta, "that . . . that lightning strike was close. Do you know anything about these huts? Are we safe here?" Marietta glanced quickly toward the young woman.

"We . . . safe," said Yellow Swan soothingly, and Marietta smiled, admiring the other woman.

Yellow Swan's friendship had truly been a blessing. Not only was Yellow Swan kindhearted, she was pretty, in an exotic sort of way. She had been stationed at the American Fur Company for some time, it appeared, and that time had lent her an unusual ability: She could hold a conversation, though stilted, in English. Plus, Yellow Swan was acquainted—at least a little—with the white man's ways.

But why Yellow Swan had even come to the fort owned by the American Fur Company, and why she had chosen to remain there—for she had not married any of the engagés—Marietta had never been able to ascertain.

One thing was certain, however. Yellow Swan was quite alone in the world, and when Princess Sierra had approached her—for the princess had been seeking someone to accompany Marietta—Yellow Swan had been quite happy about the arrangements.

Personally, Marietta suspected that Yellow Swan was hoping to reunite with family. It was the most that Marietta had ever learned from Yellow Swan: The woman searched for someone or several someones.

At that moment, Yellow Swan turned toward her, placing her hand over Marietta's. Though her eyes were wide, the maiden repeated, "We . . . safe. More safe than . . . if we . . . be . . . on plains."

"Yes, of that I'm certain," said Marietta. "But how secure is that?"

"Good," replied Yellow Swan. "Good . . . safe . . ."

Marietta shivered. "I hate thunderstorms. I have never been in one when there hasn't been something bad that's happened."

Yellow Swan gave Marietta a puzzled look, saying, "Then . . . white friend must not . . . seen . . . many."

"I have sat through plenty of thunderstorms. But always they are destructive. They kill trees, sometimes they kill animals, sometimes people."

Yellow Swan nodded. "*Han*. Very . . . bad."

"Yes," agreed Marietta. "Very bad." And then in a voice so low that it was barely audible, Marietta whispered, "My parents were killed in a lightning storm."

"Parents? Killed?"

Marietta flinched. She hadn't meant to say that last loud enough that Yellow Swan would overhear.

"What . . . happen?"

Marietta glanced away. And for all that she hadn't intended saying it, the words, like an avalanche, tumbled from her, and she said, "Many years ago, my father and mother were traveling in a carriage—it was late at night. They shouldn't have been out on the roads that night. But they were anxious to take me to a physician who was unable to travel to our home. It was an unusual thing to do, but they were afraid I wouldn't survive the night, you see. I have been told that I was young, and I was very sick.

"As they traveled, a storm came upon them. Lightning struck very close to the road. Too close. The horses bolted. The carriage overturned on a cliff. My parents were caught in the coach, whereas I . . . I was thrown free . . ."

Silently Yellow Swan pressed Marietta's hand.

"I still carry the scars of that accident."

"Mistress has . . . scars? I not . . . know . . . this word . . . scar . . ."

"They are a maiming, a distortion of the flesh . . ." She paused, and then in a whisper said, ". . . and of the heart." Turning back toward the young Indian maid, Marietta showed Yellow Swan the scar that ran up her forearm.

Yellow Swan nodded. "*Han*, Yellow Swan"—she pointed at herself—"understand . . . now."

Marietta nodded and glanced down at her clasped hands. "I couldn't walk for two years. I suppose that's what eventually drove my uncle to put me into service. I believe he thought I would be a burden to him for the rest of my life."

"Put . . . in . . . service?"

Marietta gazed up briefly at Yellow Swan. "Do you remember Princess Sierra?" she asked. "High Wolf's wife? The woman who introduced us?"

The Indian maiden nodded.

"For fourteen years I was her maid—a service that is rather like what you are with me, except that I was bound to the princess forever, or until she no longer had need of my service. The only difference between what I was and what you are to me, is that you are only traveling with me as far as St. Louis. You are also here at your own free will, something I was not allowed."

"Ahh . . ."

"Nevertheless," said Marietta, "the arrangement with the princess turned out well. Under Princess Sierra's care, I recovered fully, for the princess demanded little of me, except that I be her friend."

Again Yellow Swan nodded. "*Waste*, good." With her right hand, Yellow Swan made a quick gesture outward, away from her abdomen, the Indian sign for "good."

"In truth," said Marietta, "these last few weeks of travel

seem odd to me, since the princess isn't here with me. Strange, isn't it?"

"Strange?"

"Hmmm . . ." Marietta smiled. "But maybe it's not so odd. After all, the princess is the closest thing to family that I have. No mother, no father. Indeed, the princess has been . . . like a sister."

"It good. Good . . . friend."

"Yes. Of course, the princess couldn't accompany me on this journey, though. She has her own life here now."

A strained moment passed between the two women, one filled with silence. Then Yellow Swan sat up and said, "This one"—she pointed to herself—"also . . . be good . . . friend."

Marietta grinned at the maid. "You certainly are that to me. And I will be that to you, too."

Yellow Swan smiled.

In the distance, more thunder sounded, but it was so far away, it no longer seemed a threat. However, the clouds overhead must have opened up completely, for when the rain came, its downpour was furious. At once, moist air swept into the room.

Taking a whiff of the rain-soaked air, Marietta asked, "Will it rain inside the hut tonight?"

"*Hiya*, mistress . . . safe. No rain . . . here."

"Good. That is good." With a sigh, Marietta set her attention to other things, to the interior of the lodge. In Marietta's consideration, the Minnetaree dwelling looked to be no more than a mud or a clay hut. Nevertheless, it was really quite spacious, probably being about two hundred paces in diameter. It was also very clean. The floor, which was made of mud, was packed down so well that she doubted if a white dress trailed over it would show any signs of dirt.

All the Indians' things, their furniture and bags, were also put away neatly. In the center of the hut was a hearth in the form of a circle, sunk into the ground. It was here that a small fire had been built, and it appeared to Marietta as though that blaze were always lit. What was more, an earthen pot, containing some sort of soup, was suspended over that fire, the pot seeming to be always full, as well.

Next to that hearth sat her hired guide, Jacques LaCroix. After a week of rough travel and open-air sleeping—they had started at the American Fur Company and had followed the river south—this hut was to her like a godsend. And for that, she silently thanked Jacques LaCroix, for he had settled with their host, Big Eagle, for their sleeping arrangements.

Not that she trusted Jacques LaCroix overly much. A Frenchman, he had once been in the employ of the Hudson Bay Company but had abandoned that position years ago, giving up the low, but steady income of the Company for the life of a free trader.

LaCroix had come to her recommended by the gentleman who headed the American Fur Company. However, Princess Sierra's husband, High Wolf, hadn't trusted either of the men.

And so, neither did Marietta. However, when it became plain that Princess Sierra and High Wolf would not be able to conduct Marietta to St. Louis, Marietta had taken to looking elsewhere for a guide . . . and had found LaCroix.

In the beginning, she had hoped to pick her escort from a wide selection of men, for there were many white men who were employed by the American Fur Company. But the journey to St. Louis was a long one, and the steamship, the *Yellowstone*, had already left port, making Marietta's journey of necessity be over land and on foot.

In the end, Marietta had been given no choice, and when at last High Wolf, whose opinion Marietta did value, admitted that LaCroix, for all his faults, would probably be a safe-enough traveling companion, Marietta had made her decision.

She sighed, her glance taking in LaCroix. Currently he was lounging on a low seat while he shook some sort of wooden bowl. Across from him sat an Indian, a young Indian man, who, despite his savage dress of tanned skins, looked to be . . . handsome. That is, he might be if she could see more of his face. His mane hung over so much of his face, it was hard to form an exact opinion.

His hair, black as midnight, was quite long for a man, she noted, reaching straight to his waist. His cheeks, forehead and the center of his chin were painted red, while a lock of his hair had been pulled together in the center of his forehead, cut about nose-length and hung straight down to his nose. Two white beads hung over his eyes, attached there by a hair string.

He wore leggings of what looked to be deer hide, and a shirt of the same material that fell down almost to his knees. This shirt, which was tied in the center, emphasized a slim waistline. Over his shoulders was thrown a buffalo hide, devoid of hair and tanned in such a way that it looked to Marietta as though he wore a cape, much as a civilized man might don a redingote.

His fingers were long, giving the appearance of strength, and in his gaze, as he stared at Mr. LaCroix, was pure intention. There was also a look about the Indian . . . there in his eyes . . . that appeared . . . intelligent.

Was it that which kept drawing her glance? Or was it perhaps his aura of manliness? Whatever it was, that indefinable something made her stare at the man long after what she knew was right and proper.

But if he noticed her regard, he gave no indication of it. From her perspective, he didn't spare her so much as a glance.

Marietta drew in a deep breath, and bending toward Yellow Swan, who sat next to her on the floor, Marietta said, "Do you know what Jacques and that other man are doing? And how much longer they will be at it? I thought we would only be in this village a short while, but those two have been engaged at whatever that game is for well over a day."

"Han," replied Yellow Swan. "They . . . gamble. Some . . . times . . . takes long."

"Gamble?" Marietta sat up a little straighter and gave the two men a bit more of her attention. "I wonder what Jacques has to gamble with?" She said it almost to herself. "I haven't yet paid him the full amount he is demanding to take us back to the village of St. Louis."

Yellow Swan smiled. "Him have . . . knife. Him have . . . horses. Him have . . . gun."

Marietta gave her maid a quick glance. "But he will need all those items if he is to protect us on our journey back to St. Louis."

"Him also . . . have . . . umm . . . wife."

"A wife? Jacques has a wife?"

"Han." Yellow Swan pointed toward Marietta. "White woman."

"He's married to a white woman? That must be an unusual circumstance in this part of the country."

Yellow Swan giggled, but Marietta frowned. Again, using her thumb, Yellow Swan pointed at her.

"You," she repeated. "You . . . wife."

"I am not his wife. He is not my husband."

"*Hiya?* No? Then . . . why he . . . with you?"

"Because I have hired him to lead me . . . us . . . to St. Louis," said Marietta with a bit of exasperation in her voice. "That's all. There is nothing between Jacques and myself except gold and a desire on my part to return to St. Louis."

"Humph. "Yet . . . white woman . . . alone with . . . man not . . . husband? I thought he . . . you . . . I thought . . ."

"No." Marietta paused. "He is not my husband."

"Strange thing. Woman travel . . . with man . . . not husband. In this . . . country . . . when woman travel . . . with man . . . he is husband."

"Do you mean to tell me that in this country, just by the act of going from one place to another with someone, that person, if he be male, becomes your husband?"

"*Han.*" She nodded. "Or woman . . . have bad . . . hmmm . . . name."

Marietta shook her head. "Our societies are very much different, Yellow Swan," she said. "In my world, a woman may hire a man to guide her somewhere—and as long as she has a chaperone—you are my chaperone—no one thinks the less of her."

"Chaperone?"

"Like a grandmother, a guardian, a protector for a young girl when she is with a man."

"Ah, chaperone. *Han, han*, Yellow Swan can be . . . chaperone." Yellow Swan pointed to herself. "This one . . . think she with you . . . to cook . . . mend moccasins . . . help with . . . chores. Not realize . . . she chaperone."

"Oh, I see. There has been a misunderstanding between us," said Marietta. "No wonder you have looked at me strangely these past few nights when I have slept alone."

"Han."

"Well, please keep this well in mind. There is nothing between myself and Jacques LaCroix. Nothing. Truly."

"Han. Yellow Swan understand. White woman not married. Not worry . . . about . . . reputation."

Again, Marietta sighed. "Well," she said, "at least that's partially right. I don't worry about my reputation . . . here . . ." With a last fleeting glance at the two men, Marietta ran her hand over the smoothness of the hide beneath her. It was as soft as silk. "Yellow Swan," said Marietta, "will we sleep on this bed tonight? Last night we placed our blankets outside."

Yellow Swan nodded. *"Han.* This bed . . . ours . . . tonight. We in home . . . Big Eagle. Him . . . welcome us. If . . . we pull skin . . . around bed . . ." She gestured upward. "No eyes . . . see. Have much . . . privacy."

"Is that what this hide curtain is for?"

Again, Yellow Swan nodded. "Pull it . . . around . . . you undress . . . No one . . . see . . . We sleep."

"Good," said Marietta. "Good." And with one final flick of her gaze at the two men, Maria Marietta Welsford proceeded to do exactly that.

CHAPTER 3

Grey Coyote was not so caught up in the game of *Cos-soo* that he was unaware of exactly when the white woman arose. Without seeming to do so, he watched as she and the Indian woman—the one who appeared to accompany her—pulled the curtain around the bed.

Since he had begun this game with LaCroix, he had only seen the woman seated, and he was curious to note if, once she had stood to her full height, the white woman was as small and slender as she appeared to be. Grey Coyote was not disappointed. Despite the odd manner in which the woman was dressed—for he did not understand the white woman's style of clothing—he could clearly see that her breasts were full, her waist tiny.

And her hair, her glorious, golden hair, spilled down over her back and shoulders when she stood, as though her mane were a cascade of evening sunlight. It even shone, here in the firelight, as though it were imbued, for a moment, with a life of its own.

Despite himself, Grey Coyote was more than aware of his physical response to her beauty . . . a response he quickly quelled.

Staring at LaCroix, Grey Coyote asked, "Does your wife know that you gamble?"

"Monsieur?"

Grey Coyote nodded toward the women. "Your wife. Does she know the stakes involved in this game?"

"I am n—" The Frenchman stopped speaking suddenly. He frowned. "My wife does not interfere, *monsieur*. She is a good woman."

Grey Coyote nodded. "You are a lucky man."

"Oui. I am a lucky man. Very lucky." He smiled, the gesture emphasizing yellow and uneven teeth. "And so you should beware."

It was this last statement that set Grey Coyote to grinning, as well. *"Hau, hau,"* he said, "I am well warned."

"Oui, monsieur. Oui."

Thunder boomed outside. Lightning struck in the distance, only to crash into the ground much closer to hand. Water poured down from the heavens as though seeking vengeance. Darkness had spread across the land like a curtain, and the constant patter of the rain against the roof became a backdrop to the highly charged game that was taking place within the Minnetaree mud hut.

Here, inside that hut, while the white woman and her maid slept, excitement rose, for LaCroix was losing desperately—everything he had. Their host, Big Eagle, had spread word of the game throughout the village, and within a very short time, a crowd of people—twenty to thirty men and women—had swarmed around the players.

It was to be expected, for it was not often that men risked a game of *Cos-soo*, since one of the opponents would almost always end in ruin. Many of the villagers had begun placing their own bets on the outcome of the game, causing the tension in the room to reach fever pitch.

Would LaCroix go the entire distance? Would he lose everything? Or would he call a halt to it before the last of his possessions were taken from him?

Already he had lost most of his clothing, his knife, his powder horn, his rifle and his horses. Would he gamble away the only things he had left, two more horses, his whisky, his two women?

It was LaCroix's roll. Nary a sound, outside of the sparks from the fire, could be heard. Nervously, LaCroix clutched the wooden bowl as he spread his fingers around its polished rim. The tips of those fingers were white.

After a moment, Grey Coyote said, "From where I sit, Scout LaCroix, unless you have something else you would like to offer, the game is over."

LaCroix's lip turned up, and he snarled, "The game is not yet over, so do not rush me, *monsieur*. Ye do not see before ye a beaten man. I have other riches I have not yet tapped."

Grey Coyote nodded. "My mistake. Proceed."

LaCroix placed two sticks forward. "These represent my two horses. Good horse flesh."

Again Grey Coyote nodded.

This was it. LaCroix inhaled deeply, closed his eyes, and slammed the bowl on the ground several times, spinning it carefully.

A hushed quiet fell over the crowd. Bending, both men stared into the bowl.

"*Hau, hau,*" said Grey Coyote. "I see five burnt sides. That is four each, or twenty. Five eye sides up at two each, or ten;

four concaves up, at one each, or four. You must give me thirty-four sticks for your roll, and I will place them beside your others. But I see nothing else in this roll. Do you agree?"

"That is right," said LaCroix. "Is a good roll, what say ye?"

Counting out the number of sticks that LaCroix handed him, Grey Coyote set them next to the others that were accumulating in LaCroix's court, a total of only forty sticks. Said Grey Coyote, "It is, indeed, a good roll."

"It is yer turn, *monsieur*," said LaCroix, anxiety coloring his voice.

Slowly, as though unaware that he added to his opponent's tension, Grey Coyote took possession of the *Cos-soo* bowl. Then, more speedily, he banged the dish on the floor several times, he, too, turning the *Cos-soo* bowl round and round. There. It was done.

Both men bent over and peeped into the bowl.

At a glance, Grey Coyote sat back, reading off the amount of his roll to the crowd at large. "The big claw on end, or thirty; two red claws at five each, or ten. Three blue sides up, at three each, or nine. Four concaves up at one each, or four. It is a total of fifty-three sticks."

LaCroix's face fell. The crowd murmured in the background, and Grey Coyote carefully counted the sticks to give to LaCroix, watching to ensure that LaCroix set them all in Grey Coyote's court.

"*Monsieur* wins again."

Grey Coyote barely acknowledged the man. Instead, he paused, then in a low voice, he said, "I think we are finished, Scout LaCroix. You have nothing else of value to offer."

"That is not true, *monsieur*. I have yet a most prized possession."

Grey Coyote raised a single eyebrow. "And that is?"

"My wife, *monsieur*."

Grey Coyote didn't pretend to misunderstand the man, and though his heart skipped a beat at the very thought of the white woman, all he said was "I do not wish to have your wife, Scout LaCroix. Nor any woman."

"Not even the golden-haired wench?"

Thin-lipped, Grey Coyote hesitated.

And LaCroix, perhaps sensing the mood change, pressed his advantage. "What have ye to lose, *monsieur*? Is she not worth the last gamble?"

"She very well might be," said Grey Coyote. "But the manner of my life does not allow for a woman in it—not even one as fine as she is. Let us call an end to this game. Keep your woman."

LaCroix leaned forward. "What is this? Do ye try to make me think ye do not like white women?"

Grey Coyote shrugged, refusing to rise to the bait.

"Yet I seen ye lookin' at the wench."

"And who would not?" countered Grey Coyote, a little too quickly. "It is a rare thing to behold a white woman on the plains."

"Is it? I wonder . . . Ye speak English very well, *monsieur*. That means ye have some acquaintance with the white people. Are ye afraid of them?"

Grey Coyote scowled. He still would not take the bait that LaCroix so willingly offered; he was not to be roused into anger, nor bow to the need to justify himself.

And as for the woman, though Grey Coyote's body screamed with interest, he would pass up the opportunity. Indeed, it was his only choice; he, more than anyone, knew that his heart was not available to any woman; that his duty to his people prevented him taking a wife.

Hiya. No. Once this day, he had already had cause to suppress his physical desire, at least in relation to that woman. And this from a mere glance, and at a distance across the room. What would be his predicament were she to be in his constant presence?

He said, "I will not gamble for the woman, and I am not afraid of the white people. I have a relative who is white— he is a trader and married to my adopted sister."

LaCroix squinted. "And he taught ye English?"

Grey Coyote sat up straight. "He did."

"Well, my friend, I am afraid that it is not yer decision to make. Ye committed to this game, same as I. If I want to put up my wife as stakes, it is my decision to make, not yers."

Grey Coyote grimaced. What LaCroix said was true. By the rules of the game, once begun, *Cos-soo* was continued until one or the other of them was ruined. And LaCroix, being almost destroyed, claimed the right to either stop or continue to try to recoup his loses.

Grey Coyote said, "You are willing to lose such a fine woman?"

"I have already told ye that I am." LaCroix pushed forward a stick. "This," he continued, "represents my fine, white-skinned wife."

Briefly, Grey Coyote's gaze met that of LaCroix's. Then, with a simple nod, Grey Coyote accepted the bet.

LaCroix smiled and reached for the *Cos-soo* bowl. Whispering a prayer, the man breathed in deeply, then slammed the bowl on the floor, turning it this way and that.

At last, it was done.

The crowd's murmuring stopped. A hush fell over the room. Both men sat forward to inspect the contents of the bowl. Then with only a slight pause, to note the exact count of the roll, Grey Coyote called out, "The big claw is on end, which is thirty sticks. There are three red claws, or fifteen, a total of forty-five. No burnt sides up, no blue sides up, one eye up, or no points, and three concaves up, or three. A total of forty-eight sticks."

Grey Coyote counted out the stakes and handed them to LaCroix. It would be a difficult roll to beat, and secretly Grey Coyote thought his chances were slim.

"It is your roll, *monsieur*," said LaCroix unnecessarily.

"*Hau, hau,*" agreed Grey Coyote, and picking up the smoothly polished *Cos-soo* bowl, he, too, breathed out deeply. Then, pounding the bowl on the ground, and twisting it round and round, he let go, the bowl falling still.

In the background the fire crackled and the rain pattered down from the heavens. Both men, as well as most of the audience, leaned forward, peering into the dish.

Then, as though in a daze, LaCroix scooted so far forward, he might have fallen onto the bowl, unsettling it . . . as he had done once before this evening. But this time their host, Big Eagle, was there, and, catching hold of LaCroix, Big Eagle pulled the Frenchman back, away from the center.

"*Pardone,*" said LaCroix. "I felt suddenly dizzy."

Big Eagle said nothing, but in his gaze, there was censure. If LaCroix took note of it, however, he said nothing. Instead, he shook off his host's hold, and looking down into the bowl, called out, "The big claw is on end, or thirty points. There are no red claws, so there are no points there. Two burnt sides up at four each equals thirty-eight sticks." He paused. "There are no blue sides up, but there are five eye sides up, or ten sticks. It is a total of forty-eight."

Was it a draw?

No one spoke, not a word. Not even Grey Coyote, although with brow lifted, Grey Coyote fixed an unwavering gaze on LaCroix.

LaCroix cleared his throat, opened his mouth, but no words issued forth. It was left to Big Eagle to settle the matter, and stepping forward, he called out, "There are also three concaves up, at one each, thereby making the Assiniboine's roll fifty-one sticks. Grey Coyote wins the game, the horses, the rifle, the powder horn, the clothes, the white woman." He paused. "It is done."

Instantly, murmurings took root within the crowd.

"But I have another wife . . ." LaCroix jumped to his feet.

However, Big Eagle shook his head. "It is over. I will not allow Scout LaCroix to gamble his other wife," said Big Eagle. "Not tonight. Your luck has deserted you. You, Scout LaCroix, must take your loss like a man."

"But, with one more roll, I could—"

"I have spoken," said Big Eagle. Only the host had a right to interfere, and his declaration in his own home was law.

"But, *monsieur*, I—"

Big Eagle's gaze at the man was severe. For whether LaCroix knew it or not, he had this moment insulted this very proud man. To the Indian way of thinking, a man need only speak his request but once.

However, it appeared that Big Eagle was prepared to weather the abuse, and in a voice traced with sympathy, he said, "Take what little you have left. Take your last wife and be content that you still have her. Now, quickly, before the sun rises, you have much work to do. You must prepare your white wife for what is to come."

LaCroix hunched his shoulders, and with his gaze cast down over the bowl—which still held the last roll—he muttered, "I . . . I . . ." But for the moment LaCroix seemed at a loss for words.

At last Grey Coyote drew in a breath and stood to his feet, as well. *"Hau, hau,"* he said to the crowd, as he accepted their words and hands in congratulations.

But outside of the expected polite murmurings, Grey Coyote found that there was little happiness in him. In truth, it was on his mind to give the woman back to LaCroix.

Not that he wasn't tempted to keep her. But in his opinion, he was certain that the woman would be nothing if not pure distraction.

However, if he let the woman go, by the very rules of the game, he would have to hand back his other winnings to LaCroix. And this was a thing he was not at liberty to do . . .

. . . If LaCroix were the man from his vision—and Grey Coyote suspected he very well might be—then Grey Coyote had best tread carefully. To do otherwise would be as to sabotage his own vision.

Stepping toward LaCroix, Grey Coyote said, "I will leave this village at first light. Therefore," he directed, "you should awaken the white woman and prepare her for what is to come. You will also tie your horses next to mine. You may leave the other winnings here, next to the fire. I will see to them."

LaCroix nodded. "But, *monsieur* . . ."

"Hau, hau?"

"The woman . . . I should tell ye that . . ."

LaCroix paused, and Grey Coyote waited.

"I . . . I cannot . . ."

Their host, Big Eagle, suddenly loomed before them

both, and bestowing a wary look toward LaCroix, Big Eagle said, "Remember, Scout LaCroix, that you staked not only your possessions here tonight, but your honor, as well. Recollect also, my friend, that, while the white man might cheat another and suffer no repercussion within the white man's lodge, this is not so in Indian country. Here, a liar always comes to harm."

As the words were spoken, Grey Coyote stared hard at LaCroix. However, the man's reaction was difficult to interpret. True, LaCroix had tensed his shoulders, was breathing heavily and his eyes were flung down toward the floor. But when LaCroix looked up, screwed up his face, and said, "I will prepare her for ye, *monsieur*," there was nothing about the man to alert Grey Coyote.

LaCroix quietly stated, "But she will not like it."

However, Grey Coyote did not consider there might be a problem, unless it was the obvious one.

"Hiya," responded Grey Coyote. "I do not suspect that the woman will like the turn of events at all."

For a moment, LaCroix stared at Grey Coyote, as though it were on his tongue to say more. But at last, Grey Coyote's silence must have spoken for him, and without further incident LaCroix slouched forward, turned on his heel, and stepped from the lodge.

For the beat of a moment, Grey Coyote, frowning, watched the man walk away.

"Beware, my friend," said Big Eagle, who still reposed next to Grey Coyote. "I do not trust this man."

"Hau, hau. You speak with good reason." said Grey Coyote. "In truth, I fear I might acquire a knife in the back this night, instead of horses and a wife."

Big Eagle nodded. "And yet, all here were witness. All

here saw that it was not in your heart to gamble for the woman."

"*Hau, hau,* I regret this."

"But do not concern yourself," continued Big Eagle. "While you sleep, we will watch this white man; we will ensure that he will not do damage to you."

Grey Coyote gave a quick bob of his head, and holding up his right hand in a gesture of friendship, he murmured, "*Hau, kola,*" and turned away.

However, in his own mind, Grey Coyote knew that he was not concerned about LaCroix or what he might do. Compared to the turbulence of his thoughts, Grey Coyote considered the threat of death a minor detail.

No, what plagued Grey Coyote most was this: By the very edict of the riddle, once he had acquired the possessions of the man he sought, Grey Coyote was to communicate with the Creator by means of prayer, there to propose his speculations about the riddle. For if he guessed correctly, Grey Coyote had only to put this thought into action, and the curse would be lifted. But if he were wrong . . .

Neither small nor large, nor wide, nor narrow, the white man possesses a thing that will propel you toward freedom. Though he will think it is possessed by him and though you must possess it, and it will possess you, only when you are free from it, yet act as it, will your people be released from the mist.

Striding out of the hut, Grey Coyote stepped toward the river. There, at this hour, he was certain he could find a place where he might be alone with his Maker.

The night was black. Storm clouds raced across the sky like dark omens. No light shone aloft, though a grumble of thunder and a slash of lightning lit up the sky briefly, as though the heavens mocked him.

Always it was the same, Grey Coyote thought. Always the Thunderer followed him, taunted him. Indeed, so much was this so, that Grey Coyote's adopted people, the Assiniboine, had given Grey Coyote his name for that very observation: coyote, for his spirit protector; grey, for the turbulent clouds that stalked him.

Lifting his face to the sky, he called out, "Mock me, if you will, Thunderer. But I have still several moons in which to unravel this riddle. And I will best you." Then in a smaller voice, "I *will* best you."

The Thunderer chose not to answer, and Grey Coyote turned his attention to other, more important matters.

Neither small nor large, nor wide, nor narrow, the white man possesses a thing that will propel you toward freedom. Though he will think it is possessed by him and though you must possess it, and it will possess you, only when you are free from it, yet act as it, will your people be released from the mist.

What was it that LaCroix thought he owned, that was now in Grey Coyote's possession? What was it that, though Grey Coyote might own it, was not his?

Raising his arms up to the midnight sky, Grey Coyote began his vigil by singing a song of thanks to the Creator; it was also a song to entreat the Creator to hear his voice:

> "Wakonda, *have pity on me.*
> "Wakonda, *I come to you to make my guess.*
> "Wakonda, *have pity on me, for I do not fully*
>   *understand this riddle.*
> "Wakonda, *guide my thoughts.*"

Overhead, the clouds parted and for a moment, a star shown brightly. *Ah*, thought Grey Coyote, *the Creator listened*. Grey Coyote continued:

> "Wakonda, *each time I obtain the possessions of the one I pursue, you have allowed me to guess at this riddle. I will do so now.*
> "Wakonda, *I venture that the woman is the possession I seek, for LaCroix once owned her, but now I have her, yet I cannot own her, since no man can really own a woman. Yes, Creator, I guess that the answer is the woman.*"

Grey Coyote waited. The star still shone brightly; no thunder pealed in the sky. Barely daring to breathe, Grey Coyote recognized these as good signs. Indeed, if he were not mistaken, this meant he had thus far guessed correctly.

Now for the riddle's final catalyst: If the woman were, indeed, the correct possession, what action was required of Grey Coyote that he might end the curse? Briefly, he recalled the words of the Lost Clan's medicine man, White Claw:

"Show kindness and mercy to an enemy. Help them. Remember, had we done this to the thunder god's children so long ago, our fate would never have included an eternal curse."

But who was the enemy? wondered Grey Coyote. Surely it was not the white woman. How could a woman be his enemy?

Was it LaCroix? *Hau, hau.* It had to be LaCroix. After all, LaCroix was white. Had not the white traders cheated the Indians in trade? Did they not make the red man crazy

from the white man's water? Was not LaCroix also a liar?
And a liar, as all wise men know, is an enemy to all men.

Hau. Surely, LaCroix was the enemy. But what action
to take?

"*. . . only when you are free from it, yet act as it, will
your people be released from the mist.*"

How could one be free from a possession if one were
acting as it? Overhead, the clouds moved, signaling that
Grey Coyote must make a guess. Taking a deep breath, he
continued:

> "Wakonda, *my final conjecture concerns the action I
> must take to end my people's fate.*
> "Wakonda, *guide my words, as well as my actions, for
> I am but a simple man.*
> "Wakonda, *LaCroix is my enemy, to whom I must
> show kindness, to whom I must aid. Because the
> possession that concerns us is the woman, I
> conclude that I must return the white woman to
> LaCroix. For as any man knows, to take away one's
> wife is to steal a man's heart. Further, if I am to act
> as 'it,' or to act as the possession would act, would
> not the woman desire to stay with her husband?*"
> "Wakonda, *therefore, the action I should take will be
> to hand back the woman to LaCroix.*"

Grey Coyote waited. Nothing happened at first. Had he
done it? Had he ended the curse? His heart beat out a fast
cadence, and his hopes rose, for the star still shone
brightly.

But then, as quickly as the clouds had earlier moved
aside, they now stirred briskly in the opposite direction,

forming a curtain over the star, hiding it. The thunder rumbled, it spun, it roared, its noise sounding to Grey Coyote's ears like the mockery of laughter. And then, as swiftly as that, the star was gone.

Grey Coyote's arms fell to his sides, and silently he bowed his head.

He had failed. Once again, he had failed. Almost desperately, he whispered, "Wakonda, show me how to understand this riddle. For in all this time, I have never guessed it correctly." Raising his face upward to the heavens, he cried, "Wakonda, I ask you. How can any man act as that which he possesses?"

There was no answer, unless of course, one considered the wind a living entity. But at present, Grey Coyote was too distraught to hear its voice.

The Creator had gone, that's all that mattered, and Grey Coyote, despondent, turned away.

His thoughts were gloomy. And why not? In his opinion, his life was practically wasted.

Was this his fate? To drift from one white man's post to another? Always seeking the man who would fit the description from his vision?

As though in answer, it began to rain. Grey Coyote grimaced. Always, when he failed, the heavens spit rain; Grey Coyote assumed it was another of the Thunderer's quests to make nothing of him.

Stepping back to the Minnetaree village, Grey Coyote made his way to Big Eagle's lodge. Entering, he trod toward the fire, there to pick up the possessions he had won this night, for now that his theories were proved wrong, he would need to keep these hard-won possessions, if only to study them, that he might guess more accurately next time.

Looking up, Grey Coyote observed LaCroix, there against the far wall of the hut. Already, the man stood over the white woman, who was sound asleep. Grey Coyote watched LaCroix bend toward her sleeping form, awakening the woman.

Grey Coyote turned away from the sight, to allow the couple a moment alone in which to say their farewells. He left the lodge as silently as he had entered it.

Besides, there were many other things to be done for departure, more important things, indeed. For one, Grey Coyote should prepare the horses for the journey ahead—both her horse and his would need attending.

Stepping toward the four ponies he now owned—three having been LaCroix's, one his own—he loaded his possessions onto two of the ponies. These would act as pack horses while the other two could carry himself and the woman.

The woman . . .

The mere thought of her triggered a physical response, and a very male part of his body twitched as though in anticipation of what was to come. But Grey Coyote contained the reaction, reminding himself that she was his for but a moment. It was Grey Coyote's intention to take the woman to a white man's post as soon as he determined what part she played, if any, in his own drama.

Though it was fairly obvious to him that his speculation about her tonight was wrong, that she had nothing to do with resolving his own problem, he would study her until he was certain.

Then he would take her to a white man's post, and there, he would leave her, untouched, whole. It was the only honorable way to discharge his responsibility toward her. For though she would be considered his wife, he knew better than most that, until he resolved this riddle, his life would not allow for a female in it.

And so it was with some degree of chagrin that Grey Coyote heard the wind murmuring in his ear, *"The woman,"* it whispered. *"The woman, Marietta. She is the means . . ."*

"Wake up, *mademoiselle*. It is time to go."

Comfortable for the first time in many a night, Marietta turned over and yawned. Lazily, she stretched her arms above her head and peeped open an eye. Except for the fire, the room around her was pitched in complete darkness. But this she had come to expect. Since she had begun this journey, she and the others were almost always up and on the trail before first light.

However, she feared this day might be her toughest yet. From all appearances, the rain hadn't yet let up, for it was still pattering wildly against the mud hut. Hardly a thing a woman wanted to hear upon first awakening.

"Ohhh," she purred and stretched again. "Do I have to get up? This bed is so comfortable, I should like to stay here and rest more tonight. Could we not do it?"

"Non, mademoiselle, we must leave here at once. And do not speak so loudly. Others sleep. Here," said LaCroix in a whisper. "I have made ye a cup of coffee."

"That was kind of you," said Marietta, bringing the rawhide cover with her as she sat up. Reaching out toward LaCroix, she accepted the cup—a hollowed out horn—full of the steaming brew.

She took a sip of the stuff and winced. "Oh! It's quite bitter, isn't it?" she commented sleepily.

"Is good for you. Ye drink it while I get the horses ready."

"I will," said Marietta. "But have you made some of this brew for Yellow Swan? She should have some, too, since I think she might need it more than I. Look at her. She's still sleeping."

"*Oui, mademoiselle*, I will do that. But ye do not need to awaken her yet. As ye know, she does not require so long to prepare herself for the day as do ye. Now drink up."

"Yes," said Marietta. "I will." She took another sip of the coffee. "Hmmm. It rather grows on you, doesn't it?"

"*Oui*, drink."

Marietta did as told, and, one sip after another, she finished the entire brew, handing the cup back to a rather anxious-looking LaCroix.

"Get yerself dressed, *mademoiselle*. I will prepare the horses, and then I will return soon with more coffee for both yerself and Yellow Swan."

Marietta nodded. But it was odd. She felt suddenly spinny, as though the whole world careened out of control. Worse, she felt . . . drunk . . .

"Jacques." She reached out toward the man. "There is a peculiar feeling coming over me. You didn't . . . you didn't . . . Jacques, did you put something in that drink? Besides coffee?"

"*Oui, mademoiselle*. But only a dash of corn liquor and—"

"Corn liquor? But Jacques, why? I don't drink spirits, because I can't . . . because . . . because . . ."

". . . And a trace of laudanum," said LaCroix.

"Laudanum? But . . . I . . ."

Her words were becoming slurred. Her head spun, her eyes rolled back, and she was aware that she collapsed back against the bed. "Why . . . did . . . you?"

The last thing she remembered was the image of Jacques LaCroix leaning over her, saying, "Perhaps it was a bit more than a trace, *mademoiselle*."

And then he laughed.

CHAPTER 4

Black, rain-engorged clouds raced overhead as Grey Coyote set out from the village. Though it was early morning, the day was almost as dusky as night. Thunder rolled above him, water poured down from the heavens as though it meant to flood the land, and lightning forked through an ever-darkening sky.

Iho, this was no mere downpour. The Thunderer, god of the clouds and lightning, followed him. But this occurrence, though perhaps unusual for another, did not startle Grey Coyote. Indeed, for Grey Coyote, it was always the same. Since he had been ten winters old, the Thunderer had been his constant bedfellow.

Never a friend, the Thunderer taunted him, laughed at him, antagonized him. In an effort to end his clan's curse, many were the deeds that Grey Coyote had accomplished that would have been hailed as successful, were Grey Coyote a simpler man. But never had any of his accomplishments broken the spell. And each time he failed, the Thunderer jeered at him, mocked and ridiculed him.

No, the rain and thunderstorms followed him, blocked out his sun, left him always in the dark. However, these were such usual occurrences for Grey Coyote that on this day he paid neither god nor weather heed. In truth, the murkiness of the day matched his mood.

Grey Coyote was annoyed. Very annoyed. Not with the woman, who was draped in front and against him asleep. Rather, he was aggravated with himself.

Was the task set before him impossible? Was there no ending this spell?

Grey Coyote had only six or seven moons left in which to undo the curse that plagued his people. Already he was twenty-nine years of age, and by the very conditions of the enchantment itself, if he could not resolve the riddle by his thirtieth birthday, the opportunity to do so would pass. And if he missed this chance now, he would never again have another. Indeed, if he failed, he would be relegated to live his life forever humiliated.

Not that his life at present was a joy. Perhaps in his youth, Grey Coyote had been no stranger to sunshine-filled days, laughter and friendship. But as soon as he had come of age, his existence on this earth had been nothing if not a series of failed attempts and deep losses.

His was a lonely life, made more so because he would not inflict his travails upon anyone else. But then, Grey Coyote was also a scout, and scouts worked best alone . . . were even trained to take heart in their own company.

However, there were times . . .

In an effort to end this unproductive line of thought, Grey Coyote took a deep breath and inhaled the invigorating scent of wet skin and wet hair . . . feminine skin and hair. Like amber curls of sunshine, the woman's tresses fell back over his shoulder as, unconscious, the white woman leaned back against him. The touch of those locks against him was like a caress, and despite himself, Grey

Coyote was not of a mood to end it by setting her away from him.

Glancing down at the woman's oval face, he thought that perhaps she was prettier close-up than from a distance. Her lips were full—the color of a pale rose—her skin was unblemished and satiny, and her cheeks were alive with the hue of a crimson sunset.

He wondered if it had really been necessary to force the white man's liquor and drugs on her. Had she loved LaCroix so much? Or had she merely balked at the idea of her loyalties being transferred to another?

Whatever the case, LaCroix's actions had disturbed Grey Coyote. It was one thing to take "things" from a man, another to cart away an unwilling wife.

But what was done was done, he thought philosophically. Since it was too late to change it—not that he could—both he and the woman would have to abide by what was to be.

Yet, already it was as he had feared. Though only traveling for the better part of the morning, he was finding the woman more than a little distracting. Of course it didn't help that the feel of her skin was soft beneath his fingers, or that she smelled enticing, or that she was so scantily dressed.

Here was another matter for fruitful thought. He couldn't help observing again how odd was the white woman's form of apparel. In one of his bags he carried her clothes, and there were many of them. Not only a dress, but some stiff article that felt as though it were made of the most rigid rawhide. Plus, there was a lacy pair of clothing that looked much like the white man's pants; there were also mounds of other frilly articles, slips, delicate things that Grey Coyote could barely understand.

Where did the woman wear them all?

At present, perhaps because she had been taken while still abed, she wore only a thin, white slip of a garment, one which, beneath the heavy rain, accentuated her figure's every curve and valley. Grey Coyote could only wonder how LaCroix had expected her to keep warm.

Certainly, the style in which she was attired didn't help still his need, not when her buttocks bore in against him. Indeed, the feel of her before him was becoming pure torture, and to add to matters, the movement of the horse beneath him was luring Grey Coyote on toward a physical pleasure that he did not dare indulge.

Perhaps it would have been easier for him if he had been with a woman sometime in these past few months. But he had not.

And therein lay the problem. Physically Grey Coyote needed a woman, but emotionally he required peace. Though what peace he would find until he solved his riddle and freed his people, was seriously in question.

One thing, however, was certain. Every moment in these next few months was precious; he could little afford to do anything but endeavor to end the curse. And courting a woman had no place in his life.

Unless she were a part of this. And she could not very well be. His guess, which had involved her, had been incorrect.

Hunhe-hunhe, she was a mere distraction. Nothing more, nothing less. And the sooner he returned her to her own people, the better.

At the next trading post—which was less than a moon away—he would leave her there. In the meantime, he would do well to keep his honor, to behave himself and keep his distance from her, for she seemed to be made for temptation.

A temptation he would not indulge.

But even as he thought it, his arm tightened around her, and he pulled her in toward him. Taking a deep breath, he sighed.

Marietta became aware gradually that she was drenched, and she was getting wetter by the minute. Large raindrops hit her forehead, her neck and breast. Had she fallen under a waterfall or had the mud hut washed out to the river?

It was with a shock that she realized that she was leaning against another human being. Sharply, she drew in her breath, and without daring to move her head—which had fallen back on a muscular shoulder—she opened her eyes and peeped downward.

Sure enough, she was sitting astride a horse, and there was an arm around her middle . . . a buckskin-clad arm. Curiously, she studied the brown-tanned hand of her captor, noting the handsome, long fingers . . . fingers that held her tightly within their grasp.

This was not the hand of Jacques LaCroix.

Where was she?

Slowly, slowly, so as not to alert her host, she turned her head to the side, glancing upward at her captor's face.

She gasped aloud.

"Careful," said a male voice in English, his words colored with an unusual accent. He gazed down at her. "You might frighten the horses."

Horses?

Again, she chanced a glance upward. This time she sat upright and screamed.

It was an Indian holding her, one who was painted for war, or at least he might have been once upon a time. The paint was almost gone now—rivulets of it were running down his face.

She heard the man sigh before he said, on a note that held some little patience, "If you must wail like a child now that you are awake, I will have to place a cloth around your mouth. I fear that if you scream again, you will scare the horses."

Scare the horses? What about her?

Where was she? Who was this man? Where was LaCroix? Yellow Swan? What had happened?

She couldn't remember anything, except an early morning, Jacques LaCroix offering her coffee, and . . .

"He . . . he . . ." As the previous events fell quickly into place, she stumbled on her words, as though she feared to speak. But after a moment, she could no longer hold her tongue, and she said accusingly, "You . . . you drugged me."

"I have done no such thing," said the man, whose arm still remained around her, as though to steady her.

"No," she said, "but you managed to bribe my guide to do it for you, didn't you?"

"Hiya," said the man. "You are upset. That is to be expected, but do not accuse me of things that I have not done."

It was odd, she thought. The man's voice, sounding quietly bored, seemed to reach out to her, as though to calm her—but Marietta was a little beyond such tactics, and she said, "If not that, then why am I here?" She scooted forward as well as she could, trying to put distance between her hips and this man's. But the pony was small.

"Before he put you to sleep," said the man, "did your husband not tell you all that was to happen?"

"Husband?"

"Hau, husband."

Marietta shook her head as though to clear it. Had she gone to sleep only to awaken in a different time and place?

Shooting another glance behind her, to better see her enemy, her eyes met up with those that were the exact color of the blackest night. Her stomach dropped.

This was not simply *an* Indian. This was the man from the Minnetaree village . . . the same one who had been gambling with Jacques LaCroix . . . the man she had dared to think might be handsome . . .

And he had stolen her.

Still looking behind her, she murmured, "I remember you."

She witnessed his brief nod before he gave her a considering glance. "I am surprised."

"Surprised?" she asked, but she waited in vain for an explanation.

After several moments, however, he did say, "Perhaps your husband did not make his meaning understood."

Marietta opened her mouth to refute that word, "husband," but the Indian was continuing, and he said, "I won the game of *Cos-soo*. You were part of the winnings, and—"

"I was what?"

The man behind her drew in yet another long breath, as though he were weary of the whole affair. And then, in a voice he might have used to address a five-year-old, he said slowly, "Your husband told me that he . . . informed you of this before he gave you too much corn liquor."

"Before he . . . ?" She gulped. "Pardon me, Mister . . . Ah, I don't know your name."

But the Indian didn't answer the indirect question.

And Marietta tried once more. "Mister . . . ? You do have a name, don't you?"

The man still didn't reply, and Marietta attempted again to scoot forward.

At length, the man sat up, as though he were about to say something of importance, but he again hesitated, while Marietta held her breath. Then at last, he said, "A warrior does not speak his own name."

"Oh," said Marietta, glancing quickly behind her. "Then what am I to call you?"

He shrugged but didn't enlighten her.

Marietta closed her eyes and shook her very wet head. "Oh, this is perfect. Well, Mr."—she paused—"RainMaker-who-steals-women . . ."

As she looked behind her, she thought she saw him smile, but the gesture was so swiftly gone, she was not certain of it.

Another silence ensued. However, after a moment or two, she squared back her shoulders and said, "Well, Mr. Rainmaker, as I was saying, this may come as a shock to you, but I am not married. I have no husband."

Again, she chanced a quick glance behind her, but perhaps her look was too swift. She could discern no reaction from the man at all. And when he spoke, all he said was, "I am talking about the man who brought you to the Minnetaree village, the scout, LaCroix."

"Scout LaCroix? Oh, you must mean Jacques LaCroix, of course. He is not my husband."

"Yet you travel with him."

"Yes." She felt her ire rise. "Good Lord, is it a crime for a woman to travel with a man in this country? I *did* hire a maid to accompany me. I *employed* Jacques LaCroix to take me to a particular village. He is not my husband."

"But he is."

"No, he is not."

The man paused. "You do not understand," he said. "In this country, when a woman travels, she goes alone, with her husband, or with other women. To be with a man who is not her husband . . . alone . . . Her reputation will be marred."

"Yes, well, perhaps it is a good thing then that my birth does not originate from this country, and that I don't care about my reputation."

The man didn't utter a word, but by his silence, Marietta felt that he must certainly disapprove, and she felt compelled to say, "Mr. Rainmaker . . ."

"Grey Coyote," he said. "My name is Grey Coyote."

"Very good. Thank you." She nodded, her demeanor sweet, and one that might have spoken well for her had they been discussing no more than a harmless subject over a cup of tea and a tray of biscuits. "Now, Mr. Coyote," she continued, "understand, I was not alone. Yellow Swan, my maid, accompanied me. Also, where I come from, a woman may travel anywhere she pleases, and she may even hire a guide to take her to places, particularly if she does not know the lay of the land. And this is what I did. I engaged Jacques LaCroix, paid him money—gold—to bring me to St. Louis . . . a town farther south of here. That is all there is to it. Jacques LaCroix is no more my husband than you are." She paused, as if for emphasis. "And yet I am traveling with you."

The rain began to fall a little harder, drowning out whatever the man might say. But despite this, she thought she heard Grey Coyote state, "I am your husband."

"What was that?" she said, looking again behind her.

Patiently, as though women were a breed apart from man, Grey Coyote repeated slowly, "I am your husband."

"You are what?" she asked, squinting against the down-pour. "Did . . . did you say you *are* my husband?"

"That I am," he validated. "By winning you in the game of the bowl, I have become your husband."

Marietta sat as perfectly still as she was able, which was a feat, seeing as how she rode astride a pony. Briefly, she wondered, *Had she been dropped into some dramatic side show? Some badly written play?*

The rain seemed to splatter everywhere—on her, on him, on the pony, on the ground—and she was beginning to feel particularly cold, but for a reason she could not quite name, she was not of a mind to let this man know about the dis-comfort. At last, she pulled her thoughts together and said, "You can't possibly be my husband. I barely know you."

"Yet I won you in the game, and until I can decide what I must do with you, I am your protector, which makes me your husband."

"No," said Marietta. "That makes you my protector—and nothing more."

"*Hiya,*" said the man. "It is you who does not under-stand. A husband is a protector. And this I must be until I can take you to your own people."

That last had the effect of causing Marietta to sit up straight. *Take her to her own people? Was there hope for her, after all?* "You . . . you . . . ," she mumbled, "do you mean that you will take me to St. Louis?"

"I do not know what this St. Louis is."

"I told you. It is a village that lies south of here. It is a white man's village, and it is situated on the western side of the Mississippi River."

"Humph."

"Then you are taking me there?"

"*Hiya.* No."

"But . . . I thought you said . . ."

"I am en route to a trader's post, where I will leave you. It is not far from here, and it is not called St. Louis."

"I see," said Marietta, slumping back against her backrest, which was the man himself. Suddenly, she sat up straight again. "But . . ."

"I will take you no farther."

She didn't answer. *A trader's post? Something off the beaten track? She could very well be stuck there for months and months.*

As they continued onward, the rain let up slightly, but a wind had started to blow, and Marietta felt herself growing colder yet. Goose bumps appeared on her arms, and involuntarily, she shivered, her teeth rattling. And when he tightened his arm around her—almost as involuntary an action as hers had been—she said, "Is it necessary that we wander in this rain and wind? Couldn't we stop, seek some shelter?"

"Humph," said the man. "The rain does not hurt a man, and it does many good things. If you look behind you, you will see that the rain wipes away our trail so that it would be very hard to follow. And this might be a good thing, for I think that your husband may be a poor loser."

"He is not my husband," she reiterated. "And, since we're on the subject, neither are you."

They both fell silent.

After a while, however, he said, "The rain is good also for the life that is all around us. The rain is food."

Marietta blew out a breath. *Perfect. She was captured by a man who thought rain was food. What were they to eat? River water?*

She said, "If you call this food, sir, I think you may have

a strange idea of it. Rain is simply water. True, it is necessary for life, but it is hardly filling."

"And yet," he countered, "it must be food, for a man cannot live without it."

Marietta pressed her lips together. "It is not the same thing, and you know it. It is . . . water. It is not something one can chew. It is necessary, but . . ."

Again, she didn't finish the thought, mostly because to her own ears, she was beginning to sound shrewish. Meanwhile, she and Grey Coyote fell into a rather protracted silence, during which Marietta tried to recall what had happened between herself and her guide.

Had LaCroix tried to explain this fate to her? If he had, she certainly didn't recall it. No, her last memory before awakening to find herself in the arms of this man had been that of Jacques LaCroix's face swimming in her vision.

Sighing, she calmed herself. It could be worse. At least the Indian did not appear to be antagonistic, nor did he believe that she was his captive. Perhaps it might be safe to assume that if she kept asking, she might be able to persuade him to help her.

To this end, she said, "You say you won me in this game with LaCroix?"

"*Hau, hau,*" he answered.

"Yes," she said. "I can see, given your understanding of the situation, how you might reason that you now . . . ah . . . own me."

"*Waste.*"

"What does that word mean?"

"Good. It is good."

"Ah . . . But Mr. Coyote, I am English; I am not Indian, and am not subject to your rules. To my knowledge, the English are not a people to be bought and sold in an Indian game of chance. Besides, this is America—many people come here to be free, free to live their lives as they see fit."

He didn't respond.

"And if this be the case, that we are free," she continued, "then you don't really own me and—"

"But you are not in your own country. You are in my country, and here, if we are to travel together, we must be married," he interrupted. "It is to be regretted that this is difficult for you to accept, but I will try to make it as easy for you as I can until I can take you to the traders. Once there, we will part, and you will once again be as free as the wind."

Marietta shot a glance behind her. She said, "But how do I know that you will make it easy for me?"

"You will have to trust me."

"Really? How do I know that I can trust you?" She turned slightly so that she could watch him as she spoke. "I don't know you. I don't even remember how I came to be here. How am I supposed to believe you? For all I know, you might have stolen me from Jacques LaCroix. It certainly seems to be a custom in this country."

"I did not steal you."

But she was not prepared to give quarter, and she said, "Or you could have actually encouraged LaCroix to drug me so that you could cart me away without my screaming or alerting anyone to what you were doing."

He said nothing to this, simply tightened his arm around her and drew her back against him.

"Well?" she asked after a while, wiggling around in his arms. "What do you have to say to that?"

She felt him shrug. "You are free to believe what you will."

"But—"

"However," he cut her off, "your observation is poor, if you think this."

"And I might think it."

But he seemed to pay no attention to her, and he continued, "If I meant to capture you, you would be tied and gagged. Do you see that you are not?"

"Immaterial."

"I would have also taken you to my sleeping robes by now."

"Your what?"

"A captured woman—and particularly a pretty one—is never left with her virginity—if she had it before her capture."

Had he called her pretty? The compliment caused a warmth to stir within Marietta, enough so that she didn't quite catch the rest of that sentence. However, too soon the entire meaning of his words penetrated, and she said, "You mean you . . . a woman who is captured . . . Mr. Coyote, did you . . . ?"

"To you? I have not. Because you are now under my protection, I have not taken that which is considered mine to take."

"And . . . and . . . do you . . . I mean . . . is it . . . Will you?" She didn't look at him.

"A wife has many rights," said Grey Coyote. "Among them is the license to name her time and place, as well as her prerogative to say 'no.' And a man should try to abide by it."

"Oh, I see," she said. "But a captured woman has no rights?"

"None."

"Ah. And a man should try to abide by what his wife says?"

"*Hiya*, not necessarily. But it is a good idea if a man likes to have peace in his home, and he generally does."

"Fair enough. Then I order you to take me to St. Louis."

"*Hiya.*"

"What does that word, '*hiya*,' mean?"

"To the Assiniboine, it means 'no.'"

"Assiniboine. You are an Assiniboine Indian?"

Again, she felt him nod. And she, herself, wished she had spent more time learning about these American Indian tribes.

"Sir, you tell me I am your wife."

"*Hau.*"

"And does a wife have any influence on where she and her husband travel?"

He didn't respond.

"Well?"

He frowned. "It is the man who decides where the family goes, and when."

"But the woman must have *some* influence."

"Sometimes she does."

"Well, Mr. Coyote, tell me," said Marietta. "What must I do to influence you to take me to the village of St. Louis?"

He didn't respond.

"Sir?"

At last he roused himself and said, "There is nothing you can do. My mind is already set as to where we will go."

She turned in toward him, and in doing so, her breasts brushed against him, sending a shot of excitement up her spine. But she ignored it, certain it was only their unusual situation that caused it, and she said, "Surely there is something I could do to sway you to my cause. You see, a trader's post is far away from where I need to go . . . and I have some urgency to return to St. Louis."

Again, he remained silent.

And whether she should or not, she plundered on. "If you would like gold, I could pay you, as I had paid Mr. LaCroix."

"Humph!" He snorted. "I have no need of the white man's gold."

She turned her face outward, toward the environment. "Mr. Coyote," she said, speaking as though she consulted the wind. "I am desperate to gain the village of St. Louis. There must be something you desire from me. Something I could give you if you will only take me to that place."

She heard, or perhaps she felt his low groan. But all he said was, "Perhaps there is one thing you could do for me," he said.

"Oh?" she countered, hope rising within her. "What is that?"

It took him a while to answer, but at last he said, "You could perform your wifely duties for me . . ."

CHAPTER 5

"My what?"

"Your wifely duties," repeated Grey Coyote, his tone of voice the same as if he spoke to an infant.

But Marietta was not the meek foundling that this man might assume her to be. Perhaps she needed to demonstrate what she was made of, for if he expected her to . . .

Glancing down, she noticed that she was, indeed, not far from the ground. With a sudden move, she swung her leg over the back of the animal and jumped.

However, she had not accounted for that arm around her middle. Grey Coyote caught her before she hit the ground.

"Omph!" She hung along the side of the pony. "That hurt."

Grey Coyote shook his head at her, but he smiled.

She, however, glared up at him. Then, as though she weren't dangling delicately from the side of the horse, she said heatedly, "Would you let me go?"

"*Hau,*" he said, "if you really want to hurt yourself."

"*That* was not my intention."

"Ahhh." He drew out the word. "Then it must have been your plan to leap down and set up camp?"

She sent him a sardonic look, but, for all that, said sweetly, "Of course."

"It is not in my mind that we camp here." With a quick motion, Grey Coyote pulled her back onto the horse, setting her upright and seating her in a sidesaddle fashion against him. He said, "We will stop when I have put a good distance between us and the Minnetaree village."

She squirmed in his arms, but if her fidgeting bothered him, he showed no sign of it.

At last she glanced up at him . . . a mistake. From this position, the man was much too close, the musky scent of his skin was altogether too pleasant, and despite his rain-soaked appearance, Grey Coyote was considerably too handsome for *her* own good.

Perhaps that was why there was a tinge of desperation in her voice when she said, "Please, Mr. Coyote, it is very important to me that I make my way to St. Louis with all due haste. There are things that I must do, things I must see to, and I . . ." Abruptly, she stopped. What was she thinking? This man cared nothing for her concerns.

He gazed at her curiously, as though encouraging her to continue. However, instead of speaking immediately, she clenched her jaw.

Then, with brows narrowed, as though in preparation for a good fight, she cleared her throat and said, "Now, Mr. Coyote, I am more than willing to help you, but there are some things a woman cannot do, and I will not . . . well, you know what it is that I can't . . . I won't . . ."

He frowned. "*Hiya*, I do *not* know. What is it that you cannot do?"

She gestured toward him, toward his mid-section. "That . . . that . . . well, you know . . ."

Puzzled, he glanced down, then back up at her.

"That . . . that"—she stumbled—"lovemaking . . . thing. I will not—"

"Hau, hau," he said, smiling slightly. "At last I understand. However, when I spoke of wifely duties, I did not mean that we engage in sex."

That he had spoken the actual word in relation to her almost unseated her, but once again he steadied her before she could slip off the pony. *And* he held her firmly.

Shooting him as casual a glance as she could, she said, "Well, if not . . . that . . . what did you mean?"

He speared her with a searching glance before saying, "I would like you to clean the game that I bring to camp. To gut it, cook it and do other things. Gather wood for the campfire. Light the fire when we camp, mend torn clothing. Tan hides. Patch moccasins. Dry meat. Gather berries . . . all those things that a wife is expected to do."

"Oh," said Marietta. It sounded like hard work to her, although harmless . . . at least compared to what she had thought. However, there was a problem. What did she know about cleaning game, or gathering firewood, tanning hides, or for that matter, cooking over a fire? She had been a lady's maid for a royal princess, not a scullery maid. She said, "I am skilled in mending clothing, but I am not a cook or a gatherer."

"Humph!" He pinned her with a gaze. "You were on the trail with the scout, LaCroix," Grey Coyote pointed out. "Surely you—"

"Do you remember me telling you that I had a maid with me? Yellow Swan was her name, and she did all those things for me. And I'm afraid I had my attention on other matters, things very important to me. So I didn't pay heed to what she was doing, nor am I certain I would have learned completely from it, even if I had."

"Humph!" was again all Grey Coyote said. But in his gaze was curiosity.

"However," continued Marietta, "if you would be so kind as to take me to St. Louis," she was quick to say, "I would try to help you," Her eyes, anxious now to please, sought out the dark orbs of his.

"Hmmm . . ." He eyed her carefully. "Say the name of that village again."

"What? St. Louis?"

"*Hau.* It is a white man's village?"

"It is."

"Perhaps . . ."

"Oh, sir, if you would take me there—"

His glance at her was sullen. "I might . . . if I do not find what I seek at once, and if it is in a direct line to that which I travel. And if—"

"Oh, sir, I would be—"

"And *if* you can prove yourself to be of use to me on the trail."

"On the trail . . . ? Oh, I see. Yes, yes, I would do all I can. Truly I would. And what I don't know, I could learn. I have been told that I acquire skills quickly."

Grey Coyote raised an eyebrow, though he didn't utter a sound. He gazed at her oddly, and despite the heavy downpour and its inevitable result, he seemed to peer at her in a way that pierced deeper than mere flesh.

Had he found her wanting? Did he realize that her promises stemmed from hope rather than ability?

Flustered, Marietta said, "Honestly, I promise you that I am a quick study." She gulped, and holding her breath, waited for his next words.

But she waited in vain. Aside from the thunder that continued to rumble overhead and the occasional crash of lightning in the distance, there was no reply . . .

The fresh, crisp air that follows in the wake of a storm rang in the sunset. They had left three of their horses hobbled at the foot of a butte and had begun the climb to the top of that jutting mound. Though they had chosen to traverse up the most gently sloped side of this small mesa, it was still a steep incline.

The butte was certainly an interesting sight, thought Marietta, for it seemed to pop up out of the prairie as if by accident. All the rest of the land around it was flat. Beautiful, mysterious land, yes. But flat.

The rain had stopped hours ago, leaving its signature on the plains by bathing the land in the glow of a multicolored rainbow and a dusky, crimson sky. The rainbow sat south of them, Grey Coyote having pointed it out to her earlier.

At present, Marietta sat atop their little steed while Grey Coyote led the pony up the slope. This was a very difficult thing for her. Not that she was exerting herself in any way, but rather, what was hard was trying *not* to notice Grey Coyote. He had removed his cloak and shirt, having long ago draped both of them around her. That this left him standing before her in no more than leggings, breechcloth and moccasins shouldn't have taken her attention. Yet it did.

His style of dress was savage, wild. She tried to tell herself this was so, as if only by downgrading him could she find relief. But in the end, it didn't matter what she did or what she thought. He was a magnificent sight.

Every muscle of his back seemed to be proportionately placed, all centering down to a narrow waist. His leggings and breechcloth were tied around his waist, though both fell down indecently low on his hips. She tried to avoid looking there, for it tended to lead her gaze downward toward his tight buttocks.

His had a tall, slender build, she noted, perhaps six feet in height, and his long hair fell in dark strands across his back. In one hand, he carried a lance, and around his shoulder, and falling down low over his backside was his sheath, full of arrows, as well as his bow.

His thighs and calves were tightly encased in buckskin. The snug leather emphasized every lean muscle, as well, and as he climbed up the butte, she watched the strain of his muscles. On his feet were moccasins, which seemed to make little sound over the ground, even as he stepped from rock to rock. Only the pounding of the pony's hoofs interrupted an otherwise balmy, silent journey.

This man thought he was her husband. The idea seemed suddenly erotic. And she wondered fleetingly if she truly wished this man to think of her in a platonic way.

Hastily, she pulled herself up on this particular line of thought. It was unproductive, for regardless of what happened here, she was merely passing through this country.

Yet, it did no harm to look, did it?

How she wished that Princess Sierra were here right now. If she were, Marietta would confide in her, share her thoughts, perhaps discuss the ways of men. But the princess wasn't here. Marietta would have to decide these things on her own.

And decide she did.

As the two of them wound their way up the incline, Marietta's thoughts began to drift to other things, and she found herself wondering about Grey Coyote's reasoning. Surely their trail didn't require them to climb up and over this butte, did it? Couldn't they go around it? Or was there some other reason for their trek?

At last, they reached the top of the little mesa, and as soon as they did so, Marietta was no longer left in doubt as to what was in Grey Coyote's mind. It *wasn't* from necessity that they were here. Indeed not. Grey Coyote had come here from choice.

Standing quite still, he gazed at the sunset that was laid out before them. As though only now remembering her, he looked behind him, and shooting her a quick glance, Grey Coyote motioned, indicating that she should slip down from the pony.

Wasn't he going to help her down? Disappointment washed over her. It was too bad, for she had begun to think of Grey Coyote as a savage sort of gentleman.

"Sir," she said, "do you mean not to help me down?"

Grey Coyote spun back toward her, and she at once wished she had remained silent. It was one thing to ride next to the man with scant inches of clothing between them; it was another to bear witness to the wide expanse of the man's muscular and naked chest. Perhaps she would do well to hand him back his shirt.

She gulped instead.

Frowning up at her, he asked, "Help you down? Do you have an affliction that does not allow you to jump to the ground on your own?"

She bit her lip. "No," she said, "I can jump."

His frown deepened.

"It is only," she continued, "that in my society, a gentleman helps a lady down from her mount. It is considered good manners."

Grey Coyote nodded. "And so you think I am ill-mannered?"

"Well . . ."

"This is not a custom in my country," he said. "Here, most women would be offended if I offered help. Here, a woman might wonder why I was assisting her instead of attending to my duty to guard her."

"Really?"

"*Hau, hau*, it is so. She might even be angered if I tried to aid her, for in her mind, for me to do this, would be as to say that she was not worthy of defending."

"Truly?" inquired Marietta, gazing off at the panorama of beauty. "It's strange, isn't it?"

"Strange?"

"How different are some of our customs," she said, and bringing her attention back to the matter at hand, she started to vault down from the pony. But she had only begun when he was there in front of her.

Tossing her a lighthearted grin, he said, "Let me help you."

She laughed.

Looking up at her, he stopped cold, staring at her as though she had sent a poisoned arrow to his heart. His smile faded, and time seemed to have developed a warp, for she could have sworn it stood still.

But he recovered swiftly enough, and without further hesitation, his hands came around her waist, and he lifted her easily from the pony. On the descent, she rubbed against him, the action sending a jolt of energy surging through her body.

Briefly, he held her against him, and then, with a

chuckle and a shake of his head, he said, "I never realized how clever is the white man."

"Oh?"

"*Hau, hau,* it is so."

"And what makes you say that?"

He grinned. "A red man would need a very big reason to hold a woman such. But the white man excuses himself with manners. *Hau, hau.* I think the white man is very clever, indeed."

Marietta, too, grinned, saying, "Indeed," and gazing up at him, she stepped out of his arms.

For a fleeting moment, their eyes met, held. Then, unexpectedly, he turned away.

To her surprise, she felt suddenly bereft. "Mr. Coyote," she said, stepping up to him, "did I say something to offend you."

"*Hiya,* you did not," he answered. "In truth, I am uncertain that you could do something that *would* offend me. But I came here to see this." He gestured toward the western side of the prairie, where the sun was announcing its departure by means of a glorious, golden sunset.

Marietta gazed that way, also, and saw that the sun, which had been hidden from them most of the day, was practically screaming at them now. As they watched, the sun sent streaks of light upward through clouds, clouds that were awash in various shades of golds, reds, pinks, blues and grays. Moreover, the sky itself was painting the once brown-drab prairie, transforming it into shades of amber and scarlet, the land appearing as though it were a gigantic mirror, set afire in color.

Then the oddest thing happened. Coming down onto his knees and lifting his hands to the sky, Grey Coyote began to sing.

Watching, Marietta stood aghast. The moment was strange, yes, for Marietta was not accustomed to men opening their arms and breaking out into song. But oddly enough, the event was also stunning, and she hardly dared breathe, afraid she would disturb its unusual charm.

In due time, she allowed herself to take a breath, and as she did so, she gazed toward the west. From here, she thought, one might very well be able to see forever. In truth, so much space was there, she felt as though her soul expanded.

It was then that it came to her. Grey Coyote was praying . . . He had climbed all this way to do no more than communicate with his Creator. Was he even now thanking the Lord for the beauty set here before them?

Watching, Marietta was aware that her throat felt tight, and worse, that there was a tear forming in her eye. Not because of him. No, more likely it was because of the enchantment of the prairie, or maybe even the crisp feel of the pure air. Or perhaps it was no more than the incessant wind, which was even now blowing directly in her face.

How odd, she thought, to discover such beauty here; here where there was nothing but the earth, the sky, the winds. Unforeseen, unexpected, the beauty seemed to take hold of her.

"It reminds me of you," said Grey Coyote after a moment, and Marietta was awakened to the knowledge that it had been several moments ago that he had stopped singing.

"What was that?" she asked. "What did you say?"

"The sunset," he said, pointing outward toward the west. "It is golden like your hair, red like your cheeks, pink like your lips. You should be called Little Sunset, I think. Even now, your hair reflects the colors, looking as though it is set afire."

The praise was simply said, yet it was one of the most excellent compliments she had ever received. Certain she was blushing, Marietta turned away. In a moment, she said, "Thank you. That was kind of you."

"Perhaps," he said. "But it is also true."

Marietta didn't know why, but she could not look at Grey Coyote right now. To do so might break whatever enchantment she felt. Instead, she said, "You were praying."

"*Hau*. I was praying. Were you not also doing so?"

"I . . . I . . . No."

He gave her a queer look. "Do the white people not pray?"

"Of course we pray."

"*Hau*. Then why do you not pray now?"

"Now? But why should I?"

He gave her another one of those odd looks. He said, "Were you never taught to give thanks every morning for the new day, and every evening for the day past?"

"I . . . No. We . . . ah . . . we pray differently where I come from."

"Differently?"

"We pray only when there is great need, or perhaps only on Sunday."

"Only then? Only in great need? Every Sunday? Do you never simply thank the Creator for the beauty He has created?"

"I . . . perhaps in my own way. Sometimes before I go to sleep at night I will give thanks, but I also ask for His grace to see me through the night."

Grey Coyote nodded. "It is good." He arose, his movements so elegant, it was uncanny. He said, "Come, we must continue our trek, for it is no longer safe for us to travel in the country of my enemies during the day. Today was an exception because the rain hid us. The night will hide us also."

Marietta glanced up into his eyes. "I didn't know you were in the land of your enemies."

He didn't respond.

"Who are your enemies?"

"The Crow, the Blackfeet, the Gros Ventre, although I have friends amongst the Gros Ventre, as you saw last night. However, someone from their village may try to follow me."

"The Gros Ventre? You mean the ones that live in the mud huts?"

He nodded.

"But I thought those Indians were called the Minnetarees."

He shrugged. "Gros Ventre is their French name. There are the Gros Ventre of the Plains and the Gros Ventre of the River. Those that are by the river are also called the Minnetarees. But they are the same tribe."

"I see," she said. "These are all your enemies?"

"It is so."

"Then what we are doing is really rather dangerous?"

He nodded. "*Hau.* But if we journey through the night, and are careful, we should meet with no trouble . . . unless the Gros Ventre or your husband follow us—"

"LaCroix is not my husband," she reiterated.

However, Grey Coyote didn't respond.

After a while, Marietta found herself asking, "Isn't it more difficult to travel at night—I mean, you can't see very far in the dark, and what if we accidentally disturb someone . . . else?"

"I can see well enough in the dark," he answered. "There are usually stars or a moon to guide us. And I will

not make the mistake of running into . . . someone else."
He grinned good-naturedly at her, and it was Marietta's
turn to stare hard at him. It was the first time Grey Coyote
had openly smiled at her, and something about it caught
her attention. True, the gesture transformed his hard face,
making him appear almost boyish. But there was another
thing about him . . . an energy, if you will, that she couldn't
quite name . . .

But he had turned away and had bent down, unfastening
the hobbles from around the pony's legs. For a moment,
she watched his powerful fingers at work, recalling their
feel upon her waist only a few moments ago. Strange how
a simple action like this could seem so utterly erotic.

But then he was finished, and without looking at her, he
opened up one of the bags that he had hung over his pony's
back. And from there he extracted something . . .

Why, it looked like a blue-and-white garment of some
kind, and . . . was that a corset? And . . .

"My dress," she supplied. "You have my dress," she said
again, stepping toward him.

Almost shyly, he offered the garment to her. "The nights
are often cold here," he said, his gaze looking anywhere
but at her. "You may need these, as well as my shirt and
robe."

She accepted the gift from him. "Yes," she said, "yes, I
will need it. Thank you." And spinning away from him and
using the pony as a shield, she stuffed the corset into a bag
and threw the dress over her head, settling its length down
over her waist and her chemise. She drew in the dress's
waist with its buttons and ties, and then began the long process of fastening the material-covered buttons down its
back. But it was hard work.

"Mr. Coyote," she said, after a moment. "Might you

help me? I can't seem to reach all these buttons." Her back was to him, but when she cast a quick look over her shoulder, she was amazed to glimpse an expression of the utmost apprehension on his face.

She smiled to herself. Was he as affected by her as she was by him?

However, she did truly need his assistance, and when he didn't immediately rush to her aid, Marietta glanced again over her shoulder, said, "Sir?" and watched as he cautiously approached her.

With one arm bent, and reaching down over her back, she gestured toward the buttons. "They are here, at the top of my dress."

And then she felt his fingers on the dress, working over the buttons. It took a much longer time than she would have expected; once or twice, when his touch grazed the delicate skin at her neck, shivers raced along her spine.

She gulped.

But at last, she heard Grey Coyote cough, as though to clear his throat, and stepping away from her, he said, "It is finished. Now, come."

"Very well," she agreed, turning around for his inspection. "How do I look?"

He didn't say a word. Indeed, he gazed at her as though he barely believed she had to ask.

But he was her only mirror, and Marietta repeated, "Do I look all right? Everything in the right place?"

Grey Coyote nodded, appearing most strained in doing so. However, after a moment, he seemed to have collected his wits about him, and said once more, "Come."

"Yes," she responded. "I will." And together, with the pony following after them, they wound their way back down the bluff.

But before they left that spot completely, Marietta glanced back at the top of the rise affectionately, looking for the place where they had stood. What was it about that spot? Their time there? If she weren't mistaken, there, on top of that lonely butte, something had touched her heart . . .

CHAPTER 6

They traveled south and west, riding through the soft, balmy night. She noted that Grey Coyote seemed to take his direction from the North Star, since she observed his examination of it several times. *So that was how Indians found their way.*

As if by mutual consent, Marietta rode her own mount now, noting with some surprise that the animal had already been primed for this purpose: Her pony was equipped with buckskin reins and a blanket for a saddle.

Strange how the thought of escaping from this man now seemed ridiculous. Was it only this morning that she had accused him of stealing her?

Perhaps he had done so, but she didn't really care anymore. Though she had been in his presence for only a few hours, already she felt as though she could trust him.

Would he take her to St. Louis? Could she use feminine wiles to her advantage? He had said, maybe—if she performed well on their travels. But would she perform well? After all, what did she know about camp life?

Glancing ahead, toward Grey Coyote, she observed

that he must have increased his pace, for he was leaving her behind.

"C'mon, pony," she whispered to the mustang. "Let's not let him get too far ahead."

And soon, with very little effort, both were racing their mounts over the land. On the one hand, it was frightening. Dusky shadows fell over the earth; she couldn't see where she was going, and images of prairie dog holes danced in her imagination.

On the other hand, the open spaces of the prairie seemed to urge a person to let go. Not of anything in particular, but to simply let go. And the peacefulness of the prairie, the expanses of the space, as though it were urging one to be free, pressed in on her. And despite herself, she felt unfettered.

As she looked up, the stars above her were everywhere. Indeed, from her position, their numbers looked to be so great, that she thought if she were to account for their total with a slash on a blackboard for each star, those slashes might well fill an entire room.

Marietta's pony jostled beneath her, and she petted its neck, bending down and saying, "What a good pony you are. You run like the wind." At her words, the animal seemed to glow with pride, appearing to step even more surefootedly over uneven ground.

There was a constant wind in this place, Marietta noted. But this was summer, and it was not a cold wind that blew at her, though at this time of night, the breeze did tend to chill. However, she had her dress, Grey Coyote's shirt and his cloak to warm her, so it was not as if this were a hardship.

Glancing upward, she decided that the time was probably around midnight or perhaps later. And if that were the case, then they had been riding hard for well over five hours. Yet she was hardly tired. Indeed, glancing off toward the north, Marietta espied a series of lights, columns of dancing lights. Now green, now blue, now yellow.

Had this just started? She didn't recall seeing this earlier. Why, the whole northern sky was alight with streams of light—light that looked as though it played in the heavens.

Were these the northern lights? They seemed unreal but fantastic. As she watched them, she felt childlike and as though she were privy to a treat.

Grey Coyote slowed to let her pony come up alongside of his own, and he caught hold of its reins, unnecessarily pointing out the lights to her. She nodded, smiling at him, then gazed at the lights again.

But some sixth sense had her looking back at him, and when she did, she was startled to realize that he hadn't taken his eyes from *her.*

"Is something amiss?" she whispered.

Grey Coyote, however, didn't respond to the question, and after a while, he simply turned away, setting his pony once again into dashing across the moonlit fields. Marietta followed, but at a more leisurely, thoughtful pace.

Was he as caught up with her as she seemed to be with him?

A wind rushed in her face, as though it tried to speak. But what it said, if it did say something, she could not interpret.

Hours passed, and still Grey Coyote hurried onward, as though he had wagered himself against the coming sunrise. It was only in that extreme darkness before dawn that Grey Coyote at last called a halt to their march. Sighing deeply, still atop her mount, Marietta began to relax, looking forward to a restful sleep.

* * *

There had been no sleep, however. None for her, for Grey
Coyote or for their horses, either—not even a few hours. In
truth, after a too-brief meal of pounded, dried meat with fat
and berries added—a meal she had once heard called
pemmican—she and Grey Coyote shifted mounts—so as
not to overly tire any one pony—and had once again set out
across the prairie.

They had traveled all morning, not taking the slightest
rest. Many were the times when it had been in Marietta's
mind to ask for respite, but each time she had formed the
question on her lips, she had at the same moment thought
better of it. After all, if her goal were St. Louis—and it
was—the faster they traveled, the better.

But finally—and it must have been close to noon, for the
sun had been straight overhead—they had stopped. However,
that time was long past now. Grey Coyote was gone, too, having taken the horses and saying he would return shortly.

That had been several hours ago.

Marietta, meanwhile, had collected the smallest sticks
that she could find; her task, to light a fire.

Clink, clink, clink.

The sound of the flintstone and the iron pyrite, as she
beat them against each other, was beginning to grate on her
nerves. After these last few hours' work—and doing nothing but this same thing over and over—it seemed to her as
if the entire process was impossible. She had never made a
fire this way, and it didn't look as though she would be
lighting one now, either.

Straightening up, she raised the flap of their shelter's
entrance and glanced around the little gulch where they
had settled, looking for any sign that would indicate that
Grey Coyote had returned. But nothing met her gaze except the now-familiar landscape of their little gully.

It was a pretty place. On one side of the ravine ran a gurgling stream, and next to that stream grew a few short scrub trees, clinging to the shoreline. Each bush threw out delicate patches of shade, as well, though so flimsy was that shade, it did little to give human comfort.

Their little abode was interesting, also, since Grey Coyote had fashioned the structure so that it blended into the environment. Indeed, he had done this so well that their little lodge "disappeared" to the eye.

Marietta wasn't certain how he had accomplished that, either. One moment, he had been working over it, the next, she could barely find it.

She remembered earlier watching him position two boulders close together and had seen him throw his robe between and over those two stones. The action had created their "ceiling," of sorts. Marietta had seen him make a smoke hole at one end of the shelter, and over the entire thing he had laid grasses and plants and bushes, placing them around their dwelling, as though he landscaped the entire thing.

Then she had lost interest in the activity, had glanced away, and the next thing she knew, she could barely detect that a shelter was even there.

However, for all that the dwelling was temporary, it was really quite comfortable, she thought as she glanced around it now. Over the ground Grey Coyote had placed a buffalo robe—their "rug" or "floor"—and beside her were bags full of berries and fruit, as well as some roots, pemmican and water.

These, too, had been left by Grey Coyote, who had then informed her that she was to stay within the protection of their hideaway during his absence. And so saying, Grey Coyote had gathered the horses together and had trudged off. He had mentioned that he would be looking for a place to keep the horses, some location distant from where they were camped, for if left grazing next to their little niche, the animals would announce their presence.

Marietta had questioned Grey Coyote about the wisdom of doing this, certain that if left on their own, the animals would either return to the wild or be stolen. But Grey Coyote had shrugged, saying he would hobble them, but if they were stolen, it was no loss. Ponies abounded on the plains, he said; he could always get more.

She did not quite understand his attitude. Did the man care nothing for his possessions?

But no amount of arguing could persuade Grey Coyote to do otherwise than what he thought best.

Clink, clink, clink. The sound of her efforts filled the small space.

"You will never light the fire that way."

Marietta jumped. The low voice came from behind her, within the shelter itself. Where had the man come from?

Pressing her hand to her chest, she let out a breath. "Mr. Coyote," she said, "you frightened me. Not only did I not hear your approach"—she glanced around the interior— "but how did you come to be here?"

"I did not intend that you would hear me, and there are ways," he said, staring down at the array of small sticks she had gathered together. He crouched down beside her. "Where did you find this tinder?"

"I took it from the ground."

Grey Coyote picked up one of the sticks and examined it. "The storm must have blown these off the tree last night." He bent the stick. "Do you see that it is still green?"

"Yes, well, green wood will burn."

"With difficulty, and with much smoke," he countered.

"Besides, even with dry twigs, one would never start a fire this way."

Marietta, who had been sitting forward on her knees, flopped down, sitting back on her rump. She brought her knees up to her chest, placing her arms around them, and said, "Very well. Then tell me how it *is* done."

"Surely you have lit a fire before this."

"No, not in this manner, I have not. Where I come from we have matches."

Grey Coyote nodded. "I have seen these, for my sister's husband keeps them. They are a source of great mystery to the red man. But here on the plains," he said, "a man must learn to light a fire another way. One does not often find matches in nature."

"No, I don't suppose one would." She gave him a shy glance. "Are you going to show me how it is done?"

"*Hau, hau.* I could do this." Glancing at her, he gave her a wink.

And Marietta, seeing it, stared at him. *Had he meant to wink at her? Was he flirting with her?*

"What we will need," he began, "is something dry and small—"

"But these branches I gathered are small."

"Scrawnier yet," he said. "What is required is something like dried grass or moss, which we have here in plenty. Watch." Pushing aside the buffalo robe, he pulled up some brown grass, taking it in his hand and pinching it until it resembled dried flakes. These he placed on top of a small, flat stone.

She watched his hands yet again at work, and swallowing hard, she recalled their feel on her skin when he had helped to button her dress.

But he was continuing to speak, and she gave him her

attention easily enough, as he said, "Now rub the stones together, over this grass."

She took up the flintstone and pyrite to do as he said, rubbing the two together.

Several tiny sparks fell down to the flakes. At the same time, Grey Coyote bent low and blew on those hot specks, adding more grass, until the whole thing began to flame. To this he added tiny bits of dry wood.

"Do you see how it is done?" he asked, gesturing toward the fire and looking up at Marietta, who still sat next to him. "First one must feed the fire with dry grass, then blow on the sparks until they ignite, then add little chips of wood. It does require some patience, but not much."

A tiny flare shot up from the mixture.

"Now we need a place for our fire, for we will require it to be a little bigger than this small stone. Perhaps we can pull back the buffalo robe and make a bigger fire here at the entrance, since there is a smoke hole here."

She nodded.

"Watch." He sat up, pushed away the buffalo robe, and set the stone and the gentle blaze on the ground. "Now we gradually add more wood," he continued. "It must be dry wood, for if it is green, it will send up smoke and alert our enemies that we are here."

Again, she nodded.

He glanced up at her, his gaze soft. "Do you think you could keep the fire alive while I find more wood that is dry?" he asked.

"I think so."

"Hau, hau." Crawling out of their refuge, he was gone but a few moments. When he returned, he carried boughs and offshoots, and only a few larger pieces of wood.

She said, "But the wood you've brought will burn through quickly."

"Then we will keep feeding it. What we need is a small fire, nothing large. A fire can be seen at great distances on the prairie. The trick is to make the blaze small, and one that is smokeless . . . almost impossible to detect."

"I see," she said, and the both of them fell silent, watching the fire. Occasionally one or the other of them would feed pieces of wood to burn.

After a short time, however, he asked, "Are you hungry?"

Almost without pause, she responded, "I am."

"Then come," he said, "the fire is good. It will keep. I have brought us fresh meat."

"Fresh meat?"

"Two rabbits," he said. "Follow me, for I left their carcasses outside our shelter. You can help me skin and clean them, and we will have a good meal."

Marietta noisily sucked in her breath, causing Grey Coyote to arch a brow. He said, "Is something wrong?"

"No, no," she responded. "It's only that I have never skinned and cleaned a rabbit before."

He nodded. "Do not worry. They are gutted much like anything else."

"No," she said, "you do not understand. I have never skinned or gutted anything in my life. I was a lady's maid, and something like this was never required of me."

This seemed to surprise him, and he frowned at her. But he said not a word of censure. Instead, he crawled out of their sanctum, and without standing up, held out a hand to her and motioned her to come after.

Leaving their tiny lodge, she came down on her hands and knees beside him, where he knelt next to the rabbits.

But Grey Coyote didn't immediately set to skinning the game. Instead, he placed his hand on the still bodies of the rabbits. Then with head bent, he said, "Thank you for giving your life to us, my brothers. Your sacrifice will mean our survival. Thank you, Creator, for this food."

It was a simple prayer, but only when it was uttered did Grey Coyote pick up the game, and, coming up onto his feet, he set off toward the stream.

Marietta followed, uncertain that she was ready for this. It was one thing to eat meat; it was another to behold the animal from which that meat came.

Once at the rivulet, Grey Coyote squatted beside the flowing water, and, gesturing toward her, urged her to come closer. Again, she did as asked.

"I did not realize how new this is for you," he said, unsheathing his knife.

Marietta drew back from the weapon, but all he said was, "A good tool is necessary if one is to skin the game well."

Turning the handle of the dagger, he offered its hilt to her. When she hesitated, he encouraged her, with a few simple hand motions, to take it.

Gingerly she grabbed hold of the object, but as she did so, her fingers came into contact with his. At once, a charge, like lightning, raced over her spine, and without hesitation, her eyes sought out his.

Had he felt that?

He was, indeed, staring back at her, and his gaze was intense. But again, he said not a word to her about it, and Marietta slowly let out her breath.

At last, when he chose to speak, his words were soft, as he said, "The first thing that one must know about hunting and cleaning game is to realize that all life must eat in order to live. To survive, one must take from nature. But it does not also follow that life must be taken without thought. Life is precious to all; all life has a spirit, otherwise it would not be alive. And all life has a right to live."

She nodded.

He continued, "And so if one is to take a life, no matter if it be plant or animal, the need must be great. And once the deed has been done, one must always thank the animal or plant that was killed, for that creature has given of himself that we might survive. That is why prayer is necessary. Do you understand?"

"I do," she said gently, "although I have never heard of doing this before now."

He lifted his shoulders and said simply, "I know. My Assiniboine sister is married to a white man."

Then, turning his attention again to the game, he handed one of the rabbits to her and stated, "We begin here." From his belt, he grabbed hold of yet another blade. With this, he ran its sharp edge from the anus of the animal up toward the head, and as he did so, he cut along its belly.

While she watched, Grey Coyote gutted the animal, pulling the skin from the body and washing the meat off in the creek. He even pulled off any remaining fur. Then, without a word to her, he reached for the rabbit that she was supposed to be skinning, and he did the same to it.

"Now," he said, when it was done at last. "We shall find two long sticks and put the meat on those, place them in the fire, and we shall have a good meal."

Marietta nodded. She offered him back his knife.

But he shook his head. "Do you have a good blade?"

"Ah, no, I don't."

"Then you should keep that one. Here." From the cord around his waist, he untied one of the buckskin sheaths, handing her its casing. "Keep the dagger in there. It will help to ensure it is kept sharp."

"Yes," she said, glancing down at the sheath. It was a beautiful piece of work that he loaned her, soft to the touch and decorated all over with red, green and yellow beads. She ran her fingers over those beads.

"Come," he said after a while, getting to his feet. Once standing, he reached out toward her.

With some little anxiety, Marietta stared at that proffered hand. She knew what would happen if she touched it. Awareness of him would swamp her. Sensation would engulf her. After all, it took little to recall what had happened to her with the merest of his touches only moments ago.

Looking up at him, her gaze caught onto his. *Good heavens,* she thought, *he appeared as apprehensive as she felt.*

Perhaps that's what decided her. At last, placing her hand in his, she allowed him to help her to her feet. And if her breasts tingled because of it, and if that place between her legs most private ached for a moment, she decided to do as she believed he had done earlier; she would ignore his effect on her.

CHAPTER 7

Gradually, a cool, thunder-free summer night descended upon them, its balmy breeze carrying with it the fragrance of wild flowers, dry grass and the fresh scent that always accompanies a babbling brook. The constant chirping of the crickets and locusts were broken here and there by the ceaseless wafting of the wind, as well as the shrill call of a nighthawk; in the distance, a wolf howled while a coyote yelped.

Ever alert for danger, Grey Coyote sat across from the white woman, the small fire that they had built blazing between them. As its smoky aroma enveloped his senses, Grey Coyote listened to the sounds of the night, attentive to any clamor or movement that was not a part of nature. Yet, despite this, he was terribly conscious of every gesture the woman made, every nuance of her expression.

He should speak to her. He knew he should. But though he searched his mind for a topic of conversation, he could think of nothing to say.

Grey Coyote wished he were more skilled in carrying on a discussion, yet as he sat with Little Sunset, it was as though an old crow had stolen away his tongue.

What was wrong with him? There were many things he could say and probably should say. Truly, the very least he could do was converse with the woman.

Yet, he did not.

Was it because of her beauty? Was it this that made him hesitate?

"Other men will want a pretty wife for their own," came Grandfather White Elk's voice from out of the past. *"Always some man will covet her; there may be fights, jealousy, you may wonder if she is true to you. Peace will become a stranger in your home. Choose wisely when the time comes for you to marry, grandson, and know that ofttimes, it is best to take a plain-looking woman as your bride."*

Yet, that advice, though good, was of no use to Grey Coyote. What was done was done, and since he could not undo it, and since he and the woman were to be together for several weeks, it would behoove them both to come to some sort of understanding.

He opened his mouth. Then, realizing he had no idea how to start, he closed it. Once more he tried. Again, he shut his mouth and remained silent.

At last, because there was nothing else for it, he plunged in and asked, "What awaits you in the village of St. Louis?"

"What?" she asked in return, her golden eyes staring up at him as though he had startled her.

He repeated, "Is there someone who awaits you in the village of St. Louis?"

"Someone, who . . . Oh, no, no one waits for me," she said. "It is only that I will be able to engage a boat there, which will bear me home."

"Hau, hau." He bobbed his head in understanding. "Where is your home?"

"England," she said, as if it were a holy place. "But England is far from here. However, though it is distant, it is the place where my heart belongs."

"England," he repeated. "I have never heard of this village."

"Oh, it is not a village. Not as you think of villages," she said. "It is a country."

"*Hau, hau.* I understand that word, 'country.' Tell me," he said, "is your country as beautiful as mine?"

"Oh, yes," she responded. "But it is very different than yours. Here, there is a rugged beauty; here, there is sun and wind and heat, and open spaces. England is more a land of rolling, green hills filled with wild flowers and forests. The sky is blue, the clouds are white and dainty. The moors are quiet, the villages quaint, and there are lazy afternoons that beg one to do no more than lounge."

Again, he nodded. "You must love this place. I can hear the admiration of it in your voice. It will be good when you return to it again."

"Yes," she said. "Yes, it has been many years since I last saw her shores . . . fourteen to be exact."

"Ahhhh," he said, drawing out the word. "And that is why you are content to hurry across my country without pausing to get to know her? So that you might see your home again soon?"

"Yes," she agreed, although at the same time a frown marred her brow. "However," she continued, "there is another, more vital reason why I am most anxious to return. You see, I . . ." She paused midsentence, sending him a surreptitious glance.

Then, straightening, she continued, "But enough about me. What of you? Why are you here, traveling alone in a country that is hostile to you?"

Although more than aware that she had censored her thoughts, he chose to let the incident pass without comment, and he said, "I am on an errand for my people."

"Oh?"

"*Hau, hau.*" He nodded. "I am charged with a duty, and I seek a white man—one who looks much like the scout, LaCroix—for this man holds something that is important to my people."

"Really?" she asked, as though in speculation. "Is that why you let Mr. LaCroix gamble away everything that he owned?"

Her voice carried a note of disapproval. Grey Coyote, hearing it, sent her a frown. He said, "The scout LaCroix knew what the wager held; he understood what he had to lose. Besides, he remained in custody of a few of his things even in the end."

"Oh?" Even that softly spoken word conveyed reproach.

But Grey Coyote chose not to react to her. Instead, he poked at the fire; a log fell, sparks shooting up from it.

After a time, she said, "So you are charged with a duty?"

"I am."

"And it weighs on you?"

Again he met her question with silence. In essence, there were some things a man did not discuss.

"You needn't answer," she said after a while. "I can tell that it sits heavily on you. May I ask what this duty is that you must perform?"

Over the light from the crackling flames, his eyes met the burnished embers of hers. For a moment, he did nothing but behold the loveliness that was hers alone. And then, knowing what he must say, he uttered simply, "I cannot speak of it."

She held his gaze, saying nothing, and she stared at him for so long that the quiet noise of the evening began to intrude on them.

"It appears," she said after several moments, "as though we neither one are as yet able to trust the other with our deepest, most heartfelt secrets."

He inclined his head slightly. "It may be so," he agreed. "However, perhaps our distrust is natural. We have but met."

She placed her head to the side, as if by that angle, she could better study him. "I would say yes and no to that," she uttered softly, and then, having delivered this peculiar assertion, she turned her attention elsewhere.

He frowned. "I do not understand."

"No," she said, "I don't expect that you do." She sighed. "I barely grasp it myself."

Grey Coyote chose to say nothing, though he watched her closely. After a moment, she said, "It is odd. Yesterday I found myself in the charge of a stranger, going Lord only knows where, possibly even captured by him, with only his word to tell me what had happened. And here I am. Though I am not headed in the direction that I must, I yet find that I . . ."

He remained silent; intent, but silent.

She cleared her throat. "By rights," she continued, "I should assume that this man is my enemy."

Again he bent his head in agreement.

"But the problem is that I *don't* think that way." As she lifted her gaze to his, her eyes were big, round. "And that's what is so strange," she said. "Though I hardly know you, Mr. Coyote, though I should fight you and fend you away—perhaps even order you to take me where I please—I . . . I trust you."

Across the fire, their eyes met, held. She whispered, "Mr. Coyote, do you know why this is?"

"Perhaps . . ." His voice caught. Annoyed at this obvious show of weakness, he cleared his throat. "Perhaps, despite our differences, our hearts speak to one another in the same language. It is possible."

"Perhaps." She said the word softly. "Mr. Coyote, what do you mean by 'our hearts'?"

"Kindness, maybe," he explained diligently, "or perhaps a sort of sympathy, something that beckons us. To be guided by one's heart is different than to be led, and perhaps fooled, by one's head. It is an instinct, a sense. And it is never felt for oneself, alone. One is tended in a direction toward another because one feels . . . something . . ."

"Well said," she remarked. "Well said. Then when you say 'heart,' you were not referring to . . ." Suddenly she stopped speaking; she looked away from him.

But he was curious, and he said, "Referring to . . . ?"

Her face became a deep shade of crimson, which caused his study of her to deepen, and he said, again, "Referring to . . . ?"

"Nothing. It is not important." She sighed, but still, she didn't look at him.

He drew his brows together. *Was she also having difficulty because of who he was? Was it possible that they were both experiencing a similar rush of feeling?*

He swallowed, then remarked, "Of course, you are probably aware that I am attracted to you. It is possible that this concerns you, and if it does, be assured that I mean you no dishonor."

Her eyes went wide. "Oh, no, no, I know that . . ." Her voice faded away.

"I have given you my word that you are safe with me. After all, I intend to leave you at the trading post as soon as—"

"Unless I can convince you to take me to St. Louis." She flashed him a grin.

He, however, raised an eyebrow at that. "Do you think that suggestion is a wise idea?" he asked. "My taking you to St. Louis?"

"Well, naturally. Why not?"

"Because when two people are alone," he explained, "male and female, there can build between them an affinity that is hard to break." Across the smoldering remains of the fire, he scrutinized her features, finding them . . . pleasing. He continued, "What you ask of me could be . . . difficult for me."

She was silent. Then, with her attention still focused elsewhere, she asked, "Difficult because of the attraction?"

He nodded.

"Then you have decided not to take me to St. Louis?"

"*Hiya,* I have not yet made that decision. I am only telling you the factors that I must take into consideration."

"I see," she said, then she dropped off again into silence. The fire crackled merrily, as though unaware of any tension between these two.

In due time, however, he continued to speak, saying, "Perhaps now that we may talk openly to one another, you might be of assistance to me with this problem. It is good that we may speak of it. Hear me on this. For though you are by rights my wife, and I your husband, until I complete the task set before me, I am not a free man. And perhaps I never will be a free man. Know, therefore, that a true marriage to me . . . is impossible."

She remained mute.

And he went on to say, "Thus, so that we both continue to be honorable to each other, let us make a pact between us that from this day forward, no matter how our hearts might tend us, we agree we will not be swayed. To do so could distract me from what I must do. It might do so to you, also."

Her glance was focused on the ground when she said, "You speak as if we were of long acquaintance and in danger of losing our hearts to one another, Mr. Coyote. And yet we have barely known one another a day."

"*Hau,* that is true. I understand why you say this, and it is possible that you do not share the same problem that befalls me," he said. "But when I held your hand this day . . ." He stopped. Though he realized they needed to speak about and around this subject, this particular line of thought was not one he wished to pursue.

Yet she coaxed, "Yes?"

He swallowed hard. "I cannot state more."

"Cannot?"

He shrugged, jerking his chin to the left. "My wife, you are the first white woman I have ever seen, that I have ever known," he explained. "By the very laws of nature, I should treat you with respect because you are so different from me. I should admire you, should even withhold the things that my tongue speaks now, for I fear if we are not careful, you could divert me from the mission that rules my life. Possibly this is true for you, too. And yet, even knowing this, here I am, telling you that I find you . . . beautiful."

She caught her lip between delicate, white teeth, and he stared intently at those lips until he realized what he was doing. Quickly, he looked away.

"Thank you," she said. "That was kind of you to say."

"Perhaps," he responded. "But I did not mean it to be kind. I spoke of this because I believe it is true, and because I wish you to be aware of it. Together, if we agree, we can ensure that we will keep each other's honor."

He brought his gaze back to hers, watching her as she sucked in a quivering breath, as though her emotions were involved. At the thought, his stomach twisted.

Then all at once, she said, "If that be the case, perhaps it would be best if you simply took me straight to the village of St. Louis, rather than risk spending more time with me by going on to the trading post, and then traveling farther to St. Louis."

"Perhaps," he said. "But know that there is another reason why I am choosing the path to the white man's trading post."

"And that is?"

"The man that I seek might be there. And if he is, I must find him."

"Oh," she said. "I hadn't thought of that."

Observing her closely, with the firelight throwing her features into shadow and light, he truly thought she was the most exquisite creature of his acquaintance. However, all he said was, "We have had a good talk, and since we are husband and wife, we are allowed this. But I think the time has come for sleep. You should go to sleep now. I have set a buffalo robe toward the back of our lodge for that purpose. I will stay here at the front of our abode and keep watch."

"Yes, yes, of course, you are right. I should sleep. It is late, after all," she said, and she came up onto her knees. But before she crawled to the back of their tiny hideaway, before she wrapped herself up in the warmth of the buffalo robe, she leaned over, said, "Thank you. I appreciate your consideration," and placed a delicate kiss on his cheek.

Grey Coyote felt like all his blood seemed to dive and pool below his navel, so great was his reaction to her.

Don't do it, he told himself. *Don't indulge. She does not understand what she does, perhaps not even its effect on a man.*

But her lips were so close, her scent was so intriguing, and he had only to reach out a little, turn his head just so.

No, he mustn't do it. He mustn't.

Yet, he wondered if he would be quite male if he did not. Slowly, he turned his head.

And as his lips came in contact with hers, he thought his body might burst apart from all the energy that flooded through him. Suddenly a simple touching of lips to lips was not enough. His hands came up to frame her face, and his mouth slanted hungrily over hers, tasting, licking, kissing, not once, not twice, but over and over again.

He felt her cheeks, running his fingers gently down to her neck, over her shoulders. Her skin was an added inducement, he thought, for it was soft as a doe's, and all at once he yearned to feel every part of her.

But it was too much for him. He felt too much, he desired too much, and the craving tore at him.

Barely able to contain this woman's effect on him, he broke off the kiss. He knew he must put a stop to this immediately, or he would have to take back everything they had thus far discussed.

Unable to set her away from him completely, he pulled her into his embrace and hugged her, much as he had been dreaming of hugging her all evening. Her head fitted perfectly into the crook of his neck, he noted, as though she were made exactly for him.

And he couldn't help but whisper in her ear. "Perhaps now is not the time to tell you that I desire you, and have done so from the moment I first saw you. It is this that I fight."

"Yes," she said as softly as he. "Perhaps now is not the time."

He set her away from him, running his fingers down the smoothness of her cheek to her neck, on down toward her chest. He said, "But we should not do anything further. You know this. I know this. We must not. You do agree?"

Again, she nodded. "I know. And yes, I agree. After all, our time together will be short."

However, no sooner had the words been spoken than they rushed into one another's arms.

All thought fled. The only consideration in Grey Coyote's mind was how good it felt. Her arms had entwined themselves around his neck, pulling him down to her. His arms had fastened around her waist, bringing her in so close, he feared she might feel the imprint of his passion.

And the sweet scent of her . . . His head reeled.

It felt good to hug, too good. It felt good to have her arms around him, also. He whispered, "It is up to the man to think reasonably, to call a halt to the passion of the moment; for a woman, once pushed too far, can be convinced of most anything. Therefore, it is my responsibility to say that we must stop." He set her away from him, but he did not relinquish his touch of her. His hands had dropped to her waist while his throat worked convulsively.

Again, she agreed, nodding. But her gaze was centered on the ground. And when she raised her eyes to his, his heart soared, for he recognized the passion that stared back at him. He groaned.

But that's all he did, fearful that if he took any further action, or if he even said another word, he would betray all he had thus far settled. He dropped his hands.

After a moment, she said, "You are right. I should go to bed. I will do so now." But her attempt seemed halfhearted, and when she made a move to leave, she brushed in against him, her breasts rubbing against his own.

He sucked in his breath, and she looked at him. A simple action, yet potent. Their gazes clung together, as though, each knowing this was all they could share, they would commit the act of love with a look alone.

She swallowed. He did the same. Then she said, "Good night," touching him on the breast.

And then . . . rapture.

Suddenly, they were wrapped in each other's arms, and they kissed and kissed, as though the action might allow them to crawl into each other's skin. Neither came up for a breath. Neither had any thought of stopping the assault.

It went on and on. His hands came up to cup her face in his palms, then down, down, he felt her, down to her neck, down to her waist.

To his horror, his hands shook. But luckily, she seemed unaware of it. Or perhaps if she did know, she chose to make no mention of it.

Still they kissed, their tongues mating in the time-honored dance of love. His fingers tangled with the buttons at the back of her dress, although he seemed unable to undo a single one of them. Coming up for air, he gasped, and in a last ditch effort to control himself, said, "If you can stop me, do so, for I seem to have lost my will to do anything but make love to you."

She made a high-pitched sound, deep in her throat, and whispered, "Mr. Coyote, I fear that you cannot depend on me for this. You will have to think for us both."

He inhaled noisily. But when he spoke, all he said was, "If it be so, then you must know that I want to make love to you."

She swallowed hard, and at the sound of it, his heart tripped over itself, and when she said "I, too," his body throbbed maddeningly, his spirits soared.

Barely daring to question his good fortune, Grey Coyote's fingers stumbled over those material-covered buttons at the back of her dress yet again, and he managed to undo . . . none of them . . . It took her steady hands to reach back and undo the buttons herself.

It was over in a few moments, but in that short time period, he had managed to kiss every part of her fragrant skin, there at her neck, at her throat, and he made several daring forays downward to the cloth that covered her breasts. All the while his hands massaged the sides of her waist, up and down, over and over.

But though the dress fell to her waist, she was still almost fully clothed. Beneath her outer garment was yet another, a white dress. And beneath that, another article of clothing. But her fingers were nimble, and soon it was done.

Her clothing fell forward, exposing her snow-white breasts to the air and to his hungry eyes. For a moment, he forgot to breathe.

Was this real? Was he dreaming? Had his luck changed?

For, although he was no stranger to the act of love—having lain with several of the widows of his tribe—he had never dared to court a maiden, knowing that he could not give a woman the things that she desired most: a home, a steady food supply, children. Thus, his sexual experience had been relegated to a casual night, here and there. Never had his heart been involved.

But this was different, and he realized its difference at once. This *was* a meeting not only of the heart, but of the soul. Odd that it would be a white woman who would affect him so.

He took in a deep breath, letting go of it slowly, as though afraid that any quick action on his part might cause her to disappear. At last, however, he found his voice and discovered he was able to say, simply, "You are beautiful."

She smiled up at him, and in that look was so much affection—innocent, yet provocative affection—that he thought he might quietly go out of his mind.

Then he did what seemed the most natural thing to do. He tenderly caressed her breasts. He then bent toward her, trailing impassioned kisses from her forehead, down to her cheeks, down farther to her ear, her neck, and finally to each rosy tip.

She moaned and then threw back her shoulders as though to offer herself more fully to his ministrations. His body answered hers in an entirely male way. He pulled her dress past her waist and then took it completely off her, leaving only the transparent white material of her gown covering her. This, too, found its way to her feet quickly. He knelt down and massaged each foot in its turn, as he pulled off her shoes and hose.

Then glancing up, he was enamored by the sight of her completely naked form. Emotion choked at him, but aware of what they both needed, he pressed her onto her back and came up over her. His fingers trailed up and down, over every quivering bit of her flesh, found unerringly, too, that moist, wet place between her legs.

As his touch feasted on her there, her hips swayed against him in a sweet, gentle rhythm. It was an exquisite bit of pure heaven, and he said, "I think, my wife, that you are ready for me."

"Yes," she said, "I think so, too. Although . . ."

He frowned down at her.

". . . Although shouldn't you remove *your* clothes?"

He gulped. His own state of dress had escaped his notice.

Reaching toward his waist, he untied his breechcloth, letting loose his engorged manhood. At her gasp, he felt a pleasure wash over him, for surely, she complimented him. And then he positioned himself over her.

Yet, though he could barely hold himself back, before he took the next step, he needed to ask, "Forgive the question, my wife. I mean no insult. But had you and Scout LaCroix been physically intimate?"

Again, she moaned, but this time it did not sound as though it were from pleasure. And she said, "Please believe me. LaCroix was not my husband."

He nodded. "But did he—"

"Please, go no further."

Grey Coyote swallowed, and feeling as guilty as a young lad having been caught doing some wrongdoing, he became still. True, he had asked her to stop him if she were able, but he had never dreamed he would come so far before she would demand a withdrawal.

He dropped his hands, and setting her away from him, he reached for his breechcloth.

"What are you doing?" she asked. "Why have you stopped?"

He cleared his throat. "You said to go no further. I will respect that."

"Oh, no, no," she replied easily, relaxing back against the buffalo robe. "You misunderstood. I meant not to speak to me further of Jacques LaCroix. Please believe me, I speak true when I tell you that he lied to you. He was not, is not, has never been, my husband. I have never been married to anyone. In truth, I have never been with a man before."

Again, Grey Coyote swallowed. "Never?"

She shook her head. "Never."

His breathing stopped, his throat tightened. This woman was a virgin?

If it were possible, his spirits flew straight to the heavens, for it took no genius to realize that he would be her first. Would he also be her only?

He refused to follow that line of thought, and pulling together his musings, he said, "I think we will proceed slowly."

"Yes," she agreed, nodding. "But not too slowly."

Again, he swallowed hard, and then he came down over her, pressed his lips to hers, and with one slow push after another, he joined himself with her physically.

Ah, the warmth that welcomed him, the pleasure of her inner recess. He shuddered, and his sigh against her was deeply felt.

Everything about her was right, he thought, from her feminine scent, to her naked form, to her very soul. Forget that they had been together for so short a time. It was as though they were old friends, as though this were merely a reacquainting of the heart. And he wondered, had he been born that he might live and experience this moment?

He pushed himself upward, still sheathed within her tightness, and proceeded to love her, but perhaps in a slower, more controlled way than that to which he was accustomed.

After all, she deserved to reach her pleasure, even this, her first time.

As Marietta traded kiss for kiss, embrace for embrace, she couldn't remember ever wanting anything more. Why? Surely this wasn't love.

It couldn't be, since it was not as if what happened here

would change the course of her life. No, the pattern of her life was set, had been set years ago. Why then did she feel such longing, such joy?

Oh, if only she had someone to confide in, someone to tell her deepest longings to. But the princess was far away, as was Yellow Swan.

No, she would have to decide these things for herself. She would have to trust herself, her own judgment. And oh, dear Lord, being in this man's arms was . . . sweet.

It was too bad, she thought, that they would not have more time to share with one another. But the die was already cast, her role in life set. Besides, there were some things more important than love.

Love? There it was again. And it didn't belong here. What was probably a more correct statement of fact would be to say that what she felt was lust.

But Grey Coyote had intimated that theirs was a matter of the heart, an instinct, if you please. Was it true that their hearts had spoken to each other?

Perhaps it was so. Certainly she couldn't credit their coming together from Grey Coyote's words of undying love—there hadn't been any.

Yet, she could not deny that there was something about this man that made her want to . . . enrich him, to contribute to his welfare. Did this mean he had touched her heart?

On its own, an image of this man in prayer, up there on the butte, came to her. Was it only yesterday?

Why was that moment magical?

She sighed. She simply didn't know, and there was no other feminine presence here to guide her. She was on her own.

"Hmmm," she moaned as pleasure rocked her body,

making further thought impossible. The sensation took her by surprise, for she hadn't expected it. True, Marietta was more than aware that a man might find ultimate pleasure in the act of love. But a woman?

Wasn't it a woman's lot to enjoy kisses and hugs only? Wasn't that what the ladies in Princess Sierra's court had whispered?

Marietta moaned again as pleasure swept through her. Perhaps it wasn't true.

Grey Coyote broke into her thoughts, however, and whispered in her ear, "Wrap your legs around me and let yourself go. Though this is your first time, this act should bring you much joy. Spread your legs and give yourself to me. I will not betray you. Remember, I am your husband."

His voice, so soft and husky against her ear, sent a wave of heat along her nerve endings. She whimpered lightly, and beside herself, she strained against him, all the while opening herself to him. And though it was true that she spread her legs more fully, it was also a fact that she opened *herself* up to him, becoming, perhaps, a part of him spiritually, and he, most likely, of her.

Then a pleasure spread through her, the source of it originating at the junction of her legs. Her attention became absorbed by it and it alone.

The pleasure of it built, as well; it rose, it crescendoed, until all at once, an uncontrollable physical elation swept through her body, sending radiating warmth to every part of her. She wiggled against the tide of it, and against him, straining for more, and she wondered, had he felt it, too?

Perhaps so. For at that very instant, she felt him release within her, and she caught her breath.

It was like being endowed with a bit of paradise.

Who would have thought that here, in this dangerous, savage environment, was a bit of heaven?

But their lovemaking wasn't over. Not yet. As they bore against one another, their gazes locked, and together, wrapped in one another's arms, they tripped over the edge of heaven, again and again and again.

At last, exhausted, they fell against each other, her body cradling his. And it was a very long time, indeed, before either of them moved. Longer still before either of them spoke.

Gradually, she fell into a blissful sleep. And if her dreams were filled with images of herself and Grey Coyote flitting through space as though they were one, she was to be forgiven. For at this moment in time, so close was she to him, she felt as if she were him . . .

CHAPTER 8

Sometime in the night, a male voice commanded her to "turn over."

Yawning, she peeped open an eye. It was still a very dark night outside their shelter, and she queried, "Turn over?"

"Hmm," Grey Coyote said. "How am I to rub your back if you don't?"

"You are going to rub my back?"

"Hau," he said. "But you sound shocked. Has no one ever done this for you?"

She shook her head. "No," she said. "Never."

"Then I am pleased to know that I will be the one to impart yet another new experience for you this night."

"Yes," she agreed, as she obliged him by rolling over.

"Hmmm" was all he said in response, and then his hands were spreading themselves all over her nude body. From the top of her shoulders, down to her buttocks, and even then, no place was left untouched. He massaged her there, in the junction between her legs, and she caught her breath.

Dear Lord, it was pure enchantment. As his hands found

the knots in her muscles and gently assisted them to let go, Marietta did, also. She closed her eyes, content.

"Hmm," she groaned as his hands worked over her buttocks, his fingers finding again that place most feminine and wet. His massage didn't stop there, however. He continued rubbing her, her legs, her calves, her feet. She closed her eyes, sighing deeply.

Then up again came his touch, his fingers finding again her moist recess, and as he touched her there, she felt again that rousing sensation in the pit of her stomach.

Before she could roll over to accommodate him, he had joined with her, there at her back. It was unusual, she thought, committing the love act this way. And yet it was so erotic, she found herself meeting her pleasure almost at once. He followed her, spilling his seed into her, and again, wrapped in one another's arms, they fell into an exhausted sleep.

The pattern, however, had been set, and they made love over and over the night and morning through, as though on the morrow they might find that this had all been no more than a lovely, passionate dream.

As she drifted off to sleep, the last thing she remembered was a kiss on her neck, followed by masculine arms wrapping themselves around her. She curled herself into those arms, and strangely, she was aware that this was, perhaps, the happiest moment of her life.

How odd, she thought sleepily.

Yes, indeed. How odd.

She awoke, blanketed with warmth and fully content, though very much alone. Was it as she feared? Had it all been a dream? She sat up, bringing the buffalo robe with her, and scooting forward toward the opening of their little nook, she peeped outside.

Grey Coyote was sitting quietly before her, facing her, about five or six feet away, and he was skinning what looked to be a recently killed deer. As she brought her face into prominence in the entryway, he glanced up at her, and his entire countenance broke into a most engaging smile.

"You are awake at last," he said.

"Yes," she agreed. Curiously, she glanced toward the sky, noting that the sun was directly overhead. To her horror, she realized that she had slept well into the noon hour. Is this what happened to a woman when she found a lover? She said, "It is late. You should have roused me."

He shook his head. "Sometimes beauty needs its sleep."

She grinned at that, then said, "I will dress and help you with your chores."

"Must you?"

"Must I what? Help you?"

"Must you dress?"

She giggled slightly. "Yes," she said. "I'm afraid I must."

He gave her a quick shake of his head, then quietly muttered, "Shame."

She beamed back at him but disappeared nonetheless into their shelter, where she quickly pulled on her clothes.

What she really needed, she decided as she glanced down at the evidence of her recently surrendered virginity, was a bath. She stopped. For a moment, if a moment only, shame engulfed her.

She had given away her virginity to a man she did not intend to marry. He might call her his wife, but she had not lost sight of the reality of the situation.

What did that make her? A woman of the world, or was she still simply herself?

Oh, if only there were a way to confide in a sister, a friend or a mother . . . someone who could guide her. But there was no one.

Marietta sighed. Well, right or wrong, intuition told her that she could trust this man; he would have to be her teacher. This decided, she promised herself that she would enjoy every minute of that instruction.

Smiling, she glanced down at herself. Oh, dear, she really did need that bath. Lucky for her, they were camped near a stream.

Scooting again toward their shelter's entrance, she opened the flap slightly and said, "Mr. Coyote?"

"Who is this Mr. Coyote?" he mimicked, but he smiled at her all the same. "Am I not your husband?"

She grimaced. "Perhaps. Now, Mr. Coyote, I need a bath."

"You say *perhaps* that I am your husband?" Again, he smiled at her, but apparently, he didn't intend to pursue the subject. Instead, he nodded toward the stream. "A bath would be a very good thing. And we have much water. Come"—he gestured toward her—"if you are quick about it, I will scrub your back."

"Would you really?" she called, as she crept toward the far end of their shelter. Once there she removed her dress, hose and shoes, which left her clothed in only her chemise and drawers. In these, she decided, she would swim, washing them and herself at the same time.

She crawled out of their shelter and then, looking over her shoulder, she cast Grey Coyote a quick glance and said, "I'll race you."

It was a silly challenge where neither one cared who

won or lost. But once she had voiced the dare, there was no taking it back, and she tore over the dry grasses and sharp stones on the ground.

She would be darned if she backed down, and she gave the race her all. Of course, Grey Coyote beat her. She hadn't expected to truly *win* the race.

He caught her at the edge of the stream, and laughing, she fell into his arms. He accepted her gladly, it seemed, for he hugged her to him, bending down to press kisses to her cheeks, her neck, the top of her head, and finally to her lips.

"Good morning," he said.

"And a very good morning to you, too." She laughed up at him.

Taking her by the hand, he led her to the stream's bank, the cool sand refreshing upon the soles of her feet.

"Hmmm," she said, "the sand feels good."

He nodded. "The water, also. Come," and he attempted to pull her into the stream along with him.

But he had no more than waded into the water, when she pulled back. "Oh, no," she voiced to him, letting go of his hand. "That water is cold." She shivered, as if for emphasis.

"I thought you desired a bath."

"I do."

"Then you should dive in," he said, "and let your body adjust itself all at once."

"Oh, no, not me."

"Then it is your intention to bathe on the side of the stream?" A smile pulled at the side of his mouth.

"No," she said, "I would simply like to take my time and adjust to the water's coolness . . . gradually. That is all."

"*A-a.*" He smirked. "Then I had best go back to my

chores, since I think you may stand here until perhaps the sun goes down."

She grinned at him and said, "Now, behave. I will not be that long. Besides, you're one to talk. I don't see *you* diving into the water. Why, even *I* could stand in cool water up to my ankles. Have you bathed today?"

"*Hau, hau.* I have. And I bathe in the cold water every morning, even in the dead of winter."

"I don't believe you."

"*Ecenci*, and yet it is so. All Assiniboine men bathe thusly, and first thing in the morning."

She smiled saucily at him. "Prove it."

He chuckled but hardly hesitated as he stepped out of the flow of the stream, shrugged off his moccasins, untied his breechcloth, throwing it to the side. Then, grinning at her, he ran straight at the water, executing a perfect dive that sent little droplets spraying everywhere.

She stepped back, but not soon enough. Cold water splashed at her, wetting her from head to foot. She shivered.

"Brrrr, it is cold."

"*A-a*, feels good."

Using the tips of his fingers, he sprinkled her yet again.

"Oh, don't do that."

He grinned. "Don't do what? This?" He repeated the action.

"You know very well that I asked you *not* to do that."

"Me? What?" He did it yet again.

"You're doing this on purpose, aren't you?"

"*Sece*, perhaps. But how am I to scrub your back if you do not come into the water?"

"Could you not scrub my back as I sit here on the shore?"

He grinned, shaking his head. "You merely delay the inevitable. Come now, the water is not that bad." Diving below the surface, he swam toward her, emerging before her at the shoreline.

He stood up, in all his naked glory, letting the water rush down his body, as though it, too, adored him. A hard, muscular chest and broad shoulders, tapering to a narrow waist, met her hungry glance. Tight abdominal muscles and stomach, muscular legs, which were curiously devoid of hair. In truth, except for the top of his head and the sprinkling of hair cushioning his sex, Grey Coyote's body sported little hair, if any. This included his chest, arms, legs, even his face.

He held a hand out to her, and she stepped toward him as though summoned.

"Are you not going to remove your underclothes?" he asked.

Immediately she felt her face flood with color. It was one thing to lie nude with this man upon a bed of buffalo robes. In truth, within the heat of passion, it was, indeed, most pleasant.

It was quite another, however, to disrobe with Grey Coyote's watchful gaze upon her, here in the bright light of day.

He tilted his head, his look at her short of a leer. He said, "It is a little late for modesty."

"I beg to differ. It is never too late for modesty."

"But I have seen all of you."

"That was different."

He didn't respond, simply grinned at her. "Then come," he said, holding out a hand to her. "Perhaps you may wash your clothes, as well."

She smiled. "Yes, that was my thought, also." Reaching out toward him, she took hold of his hand and executed a cautious step toward the water.

But he didn't pull her into its depths, as she had feared

that he might. Rather he bore with her as she let herself become gradually used to its coolness, seeming to her as if he had all the time in the world to spend with her.

She asked, "Are we safe here? I know that you have spoken of the problem of our going into enemy territory. Are we there yet?"

"It is a good question," he said. "It shows your awareness of the environment, and that is good."

"Well, thank you."

He nodded but continued, "We border the territory of my enemies, although once I passed down from the Minnetaree village, I have been treading more and more into enemy country, thus the need to hurry to our shelter."

"Then you have camped here before?"

He nodded once again.

"So we are safe here?"

"For the present. I have not sensed the presence of anyone close to our camp. And to be safe, while you slept, I set man-traps and holes all around our camping area, as a precaution. I have also been out to hunt this morning—as you saw—and when I was searching for game, I found no recent signs of an enemy."

She nodded. "That is good."

"It *is* good. However, I am afraid there may be no one else to see such beauty as this except myself and perhaps a stray buffalo bull that may wander into our camp, much to his demise. But do not worry, I do not think you would interest a buffalo bull overly much."

"No, I suspect not." She smiled.

"Come." He led her farther down into the water. "I will wash your back."

She nodded and took a cautious step forward, sinking down into the water almost to her waist.

He immediately drew her chemise down over her arms, and then off of her, doing the same with her drawers, tossing both articles of clothing toward the shore.

She heard his rapid intake of breath.

"Is something wrong?"

"*Hiya.* Nothing is wrong. It is only that I do not know the white man well, and in particular, before you I had never seen a white woman. The rosy color of your breasts beckons me. And I think I shall never tire of the sight."

She sighed. "I don't imagine you will, because . . ." She sent him a speculative look.

"Because?"

She sighed, glancing around the little gully, their short-lived paradise. "Because our time together is short," she said. Then, perhaps out of pure curiosity, she added, "I don't imagine you would consider coming to England with me, would you?"

His lips thinned, and his glance danced off hers as he said, "Must we talk about this now?"

"No, we don't have to speak of it now, but . . ."

He brought up his hand to run the backs of his fingers down her cheek. "But?"

She bit her lip. "You must realize," she said, "that if you don't come with me to England, or if I don't stay here—which I cannot do—that our time together is destined to end . . . very soon."

He nodded. "I know."

"But if you were to come with me . . ." She stared up at him as though, if she could, she would read his thoughts. Then tentatively, ignoring the thought that even if he did come with her, theirs would be a difficult life, she asked, "Could you?"

"You know that I cannot. I am charged with a task of extreme importance. In truth, all my actions, even here in our camp, must contain an element of some urgency."

She pressed her lips together, glancing away from him.

Though neither one wished it, it appeared that now was the time for them to speak of this. Fixing a finger under her chin, he drew her face around to his and said, "Do not despair. It is said by even the wisest of the wise that we must sometimes lose those things we love most. What is important is not what is lost, but what we do with the time that we have now, no matter how brief that may be."

"Yes," she said. "Yes, you are right, but . . . have you considered . . . ? What if you were to finish your task before I leave?"

He shook his head, sighing. "For nineteen winters of my life I have fitted myself to complete this task. It has ruled my life, for it is of great consequence to my people. I have tried over and over again to accomplish what I must. Many things have I attempted. But in all this time, I have not been able to master that which I must."

She bobbed her head up and down absentmindedly. "I understand," she said. "What you're saying is that it is doubtful that you will finish this task before I leave?"

"*Hau.*"

"Which means that you will have to stay here."

"*Hau.*"

She raised her chin. "If that be the case, then it does seem that we are fated to part, my husband, for you must know that I cannot stay here."

Again, he nodded, then said, "I have understood that from the first time you mentioned it to me. But now I must ask you something else."

"Yes?"

"When that time comes," he said, "that moment when

we must leave one another, I would ask that you throw me away."

"What do you mean? Throw you away?"

"In the Assiniboine camp this is how a couple parts. She takes a stick. It represents her husband. She throws it away. This action rids both man and woman of their marriage, leaving each free to pursue other interests . . . or not . . ."

"I see. But what if I am unable to do it, or do not wish to? Couldn't you do the same to me?"

"*Hau.* It is so. But I do not think that I ever would."

Sadly, she cast her glance away from his. "It would appear that neither one of us wishes to part." She paused. "Come to England with me. Help me do what I must. Then we will return here, and you can follow the path that you must. If you do this, don't you see, I would be here with you."

He shook his head. "I have only until my thirtieth year to complete my task. I am now twenty-nine winters old. It is summer. Winter will soon be upon us. I have very little time left in which to accomplish much."

"Oh, I see." She nodded. "Yes, yes, I understand the problem now."

"But perhaps," he suggested, "you could stay with me until either I solve the mystery, or turn thirty, and then—"

"I cannot stay here," she reiterated, sending her glance, once again, off to the side of him. "I, too, must act quickly."

He didn't respond, and they stood there together, wet, cold, and worlds apart. At last a chilly breeze roused them, and he was the first to speak, saying, "Then come. As I said before, it is destined that one must sometimes lose that which gives him pleasure."

"Yes," she said. "I suppose that is true."

"*Hau,*" he agreed. "Many people have the rest of their lives to come to know one another; we have only several days, or perhaps a moon. But do not lose hope. The passage of time does not govern the intensity of the heart. One can as easily feel strongly about another in the breath of a moment, as within a hundred winters."

"That is true."

"And if this be so," he continued, "then let us, by our actions today, do those things that will remain in our hearts always. In that way, though we may be apart, forever we will have our memories."

She swallowed on an ever-tightening throat.

And he carried on, saying, "When that time comes, and you throw me away, it will signify that you are free to live a good life elsewhere, one without me. And perhaps, I, too."

She nodded. At the moment, words failed her.

"You will do it?" he asked.

Once again, she inclined her head. Then whispered softly, "I will. But not until that time comes."

"*Hau.* Not until then."

This said, he took her in his arms, holding her tightly, as though he feared that she might disappear this very minute. He sighed, and slowly, one muscle at a time, he began to enact his earlier promise, and with his fingers, he gently worked over the muscles of her back.

"Hmm," she hummed. "That feels good."

"*Hau,*" he said. "It does."

Smiling, she turned into his arms, inviting him to massage the front of her as well. And as he gladly complied, she pushed her fingers through the long length of his dark mane.

"I love the feel of your hair," she said. And then, "Why do you wear it so long?"

"It is a symbol of manliness—or womanliness, as well, depending upon to whom you speak. Long hair is much prized by all my people. It can have great power. And one only cuts his hair if there is a death of a loved one. Do you not like it?"

"I love it," she said, running each lock through her fingers more passionately. "I love it."

As I love you.

Silently, she gasped. No, that was all wrong. The thought had been a mistake.

She didn't love this man. She couldn't love this man. Her entire life, her whole future was destined to be lived elsewhere.

While she could admit that she *did* feel something for Grey Coyote, wasn't the emotion she felt merely that afforded them because of their being alone with one another? And for an extended period of time?

Yes, that was all this was. It had to be.

But, screamed another, moral, part of her, if she didn't love him, what was she doing here? Like this? Had the far West somehow made a loose woman of her?

She sighed at the sense of moral obligation. One would think that a person would be permitted to have at least one skeleton in the closet, one adventure in life. After all, it wasn't as if it was *that* bad. Both she and Grey Coyote referred to one another as husband and wife.

Indeed, he truly believed it.

And so it was that on this particular thought, Marietta quickly came to a decision: She would have her adventure; she would have her skeleton. Alas, she would have her memories. For, in truth, she could never remember a time when she had been happier.

Thus, having settled this conflict within herself, she stepped forward, closed the distance between them, and suggested, "Is it your idea to repeat much of what we did last night? Now?" Smiling up at him, she drew her fingertips down his chest, emphasizing her point.

"It is, my wife. Though I fear you may be sore from our lovemaking last night. Are you?"

She nodded. "A little."

"Then come, there is time enough for more of the same. Let us bathe now and heal that part of you with the mud from Mother Earth. But do not be deceived. When you are healed, it is my intention that we repeat last night again and again and again."

She grinned up at him. "And I think, husband, that I will give you little complaint."

He, too, smiled, and they beamed at one another, her heart, even his, there for the taking, there within a heated gaze. True, their passion might be temporary; in fact, it might end tomorrow, but neither of these things would make the intensity of the moment less.

Indeed not . . .

CHAPTER 9

Their little camp had become a flurry of activity, and it was a good thing that Grey Coyote had secured their gully against an enemy, for it would be here that they would pause for a few days. Days that would be filled with the chore of drying meat and making pemmican.

"We will be traveling deep into enemy territory," Grey Coyote had explained. "We will not be availed of the luxury of lighting a fire along the way."

Lighting a fire was a luxury? One would never know it, Marietta thought, the way she struggled with the chore.

Grey Coyote continued to speak. "*Kakel*, thus, although I do not like to wait, for there is urgency in my duty, we must take these few days to prepare our food. But I can only allow two or three, perhaps four days at the most."

Marietta readily agreed. This suited her, and she was quick to let Grey Coyote know, as well.

And so today, their third day together, Grey Coyote had taken to the hunt early, informing Marietta that she was to remain inside their hideaway until he returned. Since she bore many chores involving the pounding of various berries, this was no hardship.

Grey Coyote returned before noon, carrying the carcass of a deer over his back. Marietta watched from their shelter's entryway as Grey Coyote lowered the animal to the ground. In truth, she never tired of looking at the man, for his physique was most pleasing.

Crawling out from the shelter, she said, "Good morning, Husband." Odd, how the term "husband" fit him well. Strange also how natural it sounded on her lips, as well.

"*Hau, hau*," he replied, pulling her into his arms. He gave her a sound hug.

She said, "It never ceases to amaze me."

"What is that, my wife?"

"How is it that you can carry a deer for miles and miles, and do not seem to tire?"

He shrugged. "Perhaps it is because I have done so all the days of my life. I know of no Indian man who cannot do it."

She merely shook her head. "And still, for me, you are the only one I know who can."

"Perhaps the white man has a more leisurely life."

"Maybe," she said. "Well, come. Before we start skinning the deer, you should take yourself down to the stream and bathe, for you smell of deer and blood."

He sniffed at himself, pulling at his shirt. "You do not like it?"

"There are other scents I prefer."

He grinned, but nonetheless, turning, headed toward their little stream. She watched him with a greatly adoring gaze. Then, sighing, she returned to her chores.

Soon both she and Grey Coyote were hard at work.

It would be Grey Coyote's duty to clean and gut the animal, while Marietta set to striking up the fire and fixing the tripod that would hold the meat for smoking. It would also be her task to dig out the marrow from the various bones of the deer, for this yellowish fat looked and tasted much like butter, and when it was pounded, along with berries and dried meat, it made a fine pemmican.

At the moment, however, she had ceased her work, for Grey Coyote had come to her, and at present, he was bent over her, painting her face.

To herself, she grinned, for it seemed that Grey Coyote regarded her with a bit of awe. His hands shook at his task, and his fingers were unsteady. Though she dare not smile openly, as Marietta watched him, she was thoroughly charmed.

"Tell me again," she said, barely moving her lips. "Why is it that you are painting me?"

He paused, his midnight eyes looking deeply into her own. For a moment, they shared an affectionate glance. "Because your skin is fair and will burn under the sun. Therefore, you need protection. Also because it is my duty as your husband to do this for you."

"Ahhh. An Assiniboine husband performs this custom for his wife as a matter of course?"

Grey Coyote nodded. "Every day. Unless there is no sun."

"I see. And what does an Assiniboine wife do for her husband in return? Does she paint his face as well?"

Grey Coyote drew himself up as straight as he could, given his position, and said, "No man requires a woman to paint his face." He frowned at her, his countenance mock-serious. And though he smiled, he asked, "Do you mean to insult me?"

"No," she said, not wishing to offend. "I was just curious."

This seemed to placate him easily enough, and though his hands still trembled at his task—reminding her again that he treated her as though she were a fine jewel—he at last completed the chore.

Sitting back, Grey Coyote surveyed his handiwork, and said, "Since you have asked, I should tell you that instead of painting a man's face, an Indian woman takes care of her man by cleaning the meat, sewing him good, sturdy clothes, putting together their lodge, and many other things. An Assiniboine wife is very tireless in her work, and when a man returns from the hunt with game, she will settle her man into their lodge and bring him pipe and food. She will even remove his moccasins and rub his feet."

"Really?"

He bobbed his head. "She will also slick down his pony and take the game he procured, will dress it and cook it. It is a good time for a man. An Assiniboine husband anticipates these leisure activities with his wife with much joy."

"Does he now?"

"*Hau.*"

"It's really a lot of work for a woman," Marietta said with a smirk. "You should know this."

"It is true. And a good woman is the object of much affection, as you are with me."

She grinned.

"But tell me," he continued, "does a white woman do no work?"

Marietta shrugged. "She does much work, as does her husband."

He nodded. "It is the same for the Indian. There are women's chores and men's chores. And when in camp with others, the two never cross. Now here, I help you with many of the chores that are traditionally considered the tasks of the woman. I do this because there is no one else here, and because you do not know our ways. But were I in an encampment of my people, if I were to be caught doing these things for you, I would be laughed at—even called a woman, perhaps even rejected from the society to which I belong."

Marietta tossed her head and tut-tutted.

Still, he continued, "But a good Assiniboine wife does not object to her work. If she is a good woman, she takes much pride in her tasks, and would shoo a man away with a stick if he tried to help her."

"Truly?"

"It is so. She would accuse him of trying to make her lazy. Her mother and grandmother, if they were also good women, would taunt her; they would call her lazy, and this no woman of good merit could stand."

Marietta smiled at him. "Well, Husband, if we are ever in an Indian encampment, I will be certain to bring you your pipe and food, and rub your feet."

"But only if I return with game."

"Only then?"

"It is so. If I fail to bring home food for the family, the Assiniboine wife will ignore her man and will leave him alone, sometimes not even returning that night to sleep with him."

"Honestly?"

"I speak true."

"All right, then, if we are ever in an Indian encampment and you bring home game, I will collect your pipe and food for you, and will rub your feet . . . most adoringly," she added.

It caused him to grin. "Do not tell me this, Wife, if you do not mean to keep your promise, for I will hold you to it."

"I'll do it." She frowned. "*If* we are ever together in an Indian encampment. But do you think that will ever happen?"

He gave her a rather crafty smile. "We will see."

"Humph."

"And I will remember to hold you to it."

She smiled at him. "Do that."

Two days had passed. Two days of rapturous bliss, the daylight hours being filled with the chores of pounding berries, smoking meat and pemmican making; the evenings fueled by passion, quiet conversations and teasing embraces.

It was a little past noon on this, their fifth day together. Grey Coyote was sitting across from her in their shelter, a small fire between them; he had been sewing together a pair of extra moccasins for their journey, when, at last finished, he put away his handiwork and looking up, stared at her.

He said, "The time has come for us to make final preparations to go."

Go? Leave their paradise? So soon?

Their gazes met, locked, and though neither one spoke what might have been in their hearts, each knew what was on the other's mind. Still she managed to smile and say, "This is good."

He nodded.

In the silence that ensued, each one of them carefully avoided looking at the other. In due time, however, Grey Coyote said, "There is one more thing that I will require before we journey to the trading post. But only the one."

"Oh?" she said. "What is that?"

"Arrows," he said. "I will need a few more arrows. We will need to travel to a place that is good for this, a forest in the hills. After I have procured the right kind of wood, the arrows are not difficult to make. But I must find the right kind of wood."

"That is good," she said. "And then we will be ready to travel onward?"

"It is so."

"And is this forest very far out of our way?"

"A little," he said, "but, though time is precious, this must be done if I am to defend us properly."

"Ah," she acknowledged, "does that mean that we leave today?"

"*Hau,* except that from now until we reach the trading post, we will of necessity travel only at night."

"Is it safer to travel that way?"

"*Hau.* It is summertime. A time for warring parties, for young men seeking revenge, and for young men looking to count *coup* so that they may court the girl of their choice. It is not a good time to be traveling on the open prairie."

"I see."

"Therefore we will go forward at night only, and even in doing this, we will need to disguise ourselves and be very careful."

"All right," she said. "Then I should make preparations to leave tonight?"

"Yes."

She nodded. "What kind of wood do you require for your arrows?"

"The Juneberry or the chokecherry are the best wood for this," he said.

"Did you say the Juneberry or the chokecherry?"

"*Hau.*"

"But . . . I don't understand, why do we have to travel to find this wood? There are Juneberry and chokecherry trees here. I have been picking berries from them."

"*Hau.*"

"Did you not know? I am glad that I asked, for now we are saved a needless trip. Perhaps we could spend the extra time here in our camp? Hmm," she went on, "although probably not, since time is of the essence."

He didn't respond. And she went on to say, "You see? Your requirements are right here."

"And so it might seem to you," said Grey Coyote at last. "But in making an arrow, one must consider other things."

"Other things? Like what?"

"Look around you, outside our small dwelling, and tell me what you see," he said.

Although Marietta saw little point in the exercise, she pushed back the entrance flap and glanced here and there. "Well, there's lots of space," she said, "much brown grass, a few scrub trees . . . but mostly there are Juneberry trees," she emphasized.

"Exactly," he said. "Exactly."

"Exactly what? If they're Juneberry trees . . ." She shook her head.

"Look again."

She sighed.

"You must glance around you and discover what you do not see."

"Look at what I don't see?"

"*Hau.*"

"But I don't see anything else."

"Exactly."

Marietta frowned. "I don't understand."

"There is nothing else here, and that is what you must observe closely."

She groaned.

But he paid her little mind and said, "Do you notice that there are but few trees here, and even they are having a hard time in this soil?"

"Yes?"

"Tell me. From what you see here, would you say that this land needs these trees?"

"Well . . ."

"Why take what these saplings offer when they are required to remain here for the overall good and survival of the land?"

"Because they're convenient?"

"Ahhhh," he said. "You say they are convenient. But think again. If you do this, if you take the lives of these young trees, what will you leave for your children, and their children?"

Unconsciously, Marietta wrinkled her brow. "Does it matter?"

Grey Coyote jerked his chin to the left. "Of course it matters. Others will come after you. If you leave nothing but waste for those who follow, you are ignoring your greatest duty."

"But—"

"Is it good and right to steal from your grandchildren to satisfy yourself today?"

"I . . . But look at all that is here. The land is for use. Other trees will grow here eventually. I don't see that—"

"Will other trees grow?"

She hesitated, and he pressed forward, "The forest I seek

is near here and it is overcrowded. There are bushes and trees there that are in competition, and some will not live. Some are already dead. It is there that I will find what I need to make the arrows. If I take from here, I will hurt the land."

"But . . . I thought that you needed to arrive at the trading post in a timely manner."

"I do."

She tilted her head to the side. "Well?"

"And because I hurry, this would justify stealing from my grandchildren?"

Marietta didn't answer. In truth, this was the first time this argument had ever been proposed to her.

"*Hiya,*" he said, when she remained subdued. "I cannot take what I need from these young trees and bushes," he said. "We will go to the forest I mentioned. The way is not far."

Marietta frowned. "But, Grey Coyote, I protest this. It's senseless. You have a duty. I have a duty. Between us, we have so little time. Please consider fashioning your arrows here, while I continue to make food. Besides, we're only talking about a tree."

"Ahhhh." He elongated the sound. "And is the spirit of the tree less than that of a man?"

"Of course it is."

"Is it?" he asked. "Who says it is? You? Man? Did you ask the tree if it thinks its spirit is less than yours?"

She pulled a face. "Ask the tree?"

"Is it not life? Does it not obey all the laws of life? That it does not speak as we do does not mean that it is not alive, or is less a spirit, or that it doesn't in some way communicate."

"But—"

"Look around you again."

She did so, though with some impatience.

He asked, "Do you see that this land is parched?"

"Yes."

"Yet, despite these conditions, these bushes and saplings that you observe here are young and healthy. While they might make good arrows for me, why take their lives when there are others that will die anyway in another forest?"

But Marietta hadn't given up, and she opened her mouth to speak.

Grey Coyote, however, cut her off, saying, "I must also answer another question before I act. If I use these saplings and bushes now, what will I leave this land? Have I helped the Creator make this earth a better place for others, or am I destroying His creation?"

"But—"

"If I must destroy a life," he said, "and I must, then, let it be a life that is already dead or dying."

Marietta squinted up at Grey Coyote. Though only in company with this man for a few days, she was amazed to discover how different was their attitude toward this subject, which bordered, actually, on the mundane. She was also amazed to discover how much she was learning . . .

"Mr. Coyote—"

He frowned at her, though the look was cushioned with a slight chuckle. "Who is Mr. Coyote?"

She smiled. *"Husband . . ."*

"That is better."

"Husband, if you do this, aren't you then playing God?"

"Perhaps I am," he said, "but there is no justification that can make this right. As the wise men of my tribe have said, none survives alone. While it is necessary to kill for food or shelter, remember that all life has the right of survival. And all life is interdependent."

Marietta shot the man a twisted smile. No harsh words had been spoken, it was true. Indeed, his voice had been, as usual, soft, calm. Yet he had won his argument all the same.

Apparently, they were to travel to this forest.

She said, "All right. I will go. You mentioned that we will need even more preparation for this journey?"

"*Hau, hau.* Though we have food enough, we should sew another pair of moccasins for you, and extra clothes— clothes that will not tear as yours do, for the manner in which we will be traveling will be rather harsh. Perhaps we should also have an extra robe for you, since the nights are cool. The deerskins we have already will do for this purpose. Tonight, when the moon rises, we will leave."

She nodded. "Tonight, then," she said. "But do you think we have time to make all of these things today?"

"I will help."

"Even with your help, I think the things you mentioned require much work."

"They will not be fancy."

"Still . . ."

"Come, let us set to doing this," he said, pulling one of the deer hides toward him. "But remember," he cautioned, "if we are ever in camp with others . . ."

"I know. I know. Women have their chores, men have theirs. I have not forgotten."

"You learn quickly," he replied, smiling at her, and bending, he lightly touched his lips to hers.

Somewhere on the Western Plains

Was it man, or bear? It growled like a bear when it spoke. It moved like a bear when it walked. It smelled of something rank and offensive; its body, even its face was covered in hair. But there were two distinguishing features that gave clue to its origin: It wore clothes, boots, and hat, though its hair was long, lice-infected and unkempt.

At present, it slunk toward a hunter, who, caught up in disengaging a wolf trap, didn't see or didn't hear the creature. However, after a moment, the stench of the beast gave warning.

The hunter stopped still. He sniffed the air. He listened.

"Who goes there?" he called.

There was no answer. Then, like a thunderbolt, the brute struck, the surprise, as well as the beast's strength, overpowering the slimmer constitution of the hunter.

A gnarly hand jerked up a knife, then down it plunged, down into the hunter's heart, stabbing the man once, then again and again.

It was over in a matter of minutes.

Letting go of the body, the creature kicked the hunter aside and grabbed up the hunter's wolf pelts. The beast then slung the furs—which were tied onto a ropelike string—over its shoulder.

"Blazing wolfer," the creature muttered, its speech more growl than human. "Deserved what 'cha got. This'n here's my woods, wolfer. No one hunts here but me. Reckon these is mine. A fine penny they'll fetch fer me, too."

The beast spit, first on the hunter, then on the ground. The brute snarled, as well, and with no concern given to the hunter's body, to the spirit of the man or to a decent burial, the beast crashed away through the undergrowth, heading toward the closest known trading post.

CHAPTER 10

It was early evening, that time of day when the sun has set, yet the west is still awash in the shimmering golds and pinks of dusk; straight overhead, however, the sky was the exact shade of the deepest blue. In the east a lone star rose over the horizon, while the high-pitched singsong of the crickets and locusts grew loud, replacing the more melodious chirping of the lark sparrow, the lonespur and robin. A lone dove cooed in the distance.

Grey Coyote was en route to the coulee where he had hobbled the ponies. Moisture hung heavily in the air as he trod over known ground. The fragrant scents of dry grass and wild flowers had settled densely over the land, perfuming the landscape with an aroma that was sweet, but weighty.

It happened suddenly. One moment the western sky was alight with end-of-the-day images, the next it was pitch black, thick with moisture-ladened storm clouds dominating the landscape. Overhead the thunder roared.

Though it was not uncommon for bad weather to suddenly come upon the unwary prairie traveler, Grey Coyote knew this was no ordinary storm. For five days Grey Coyote had experienced a reprieve of sorts from those things that haunted him; for five days he had heard nothing from the Thunderer.

But it appeared that his moment of respite was fleeting. Indeed, his archenemy was back.

All at once, a windstorm kicked up around him, and like a blast from a white man's gun, a fast-whirling prairie wind knocked Grey Coyote off his feet. No rifle was fired, yet Grey Coyote ached as though he had been shot, and many times.

Flat on his back, unable for the moment to rise, Grey Coyote had no option but to look up into the sky.

There, images had formed above him . . . two images. One was familiar—the man from his vision, the man with unkempt, unclean and straggly hair. The other likeness was that of a white trapper.

The trapper lay dead. But the beast—his appearance ugly and more bearlike than human—hovered over his victim like some wild monster, glad of its conquest.

And then came the familiar refrain:

Neither small nor large, nor wide, nor narrow, the white man possesses a thing that will propel you toward freedom. Though he will think it is possessed by him and though you must possess it, and it will possess you, only when you are free from it, yet act as it, will your people be released from the mist.

You alone must solve this, you alone must act on it, and if you do, your people go free.

What did this mean? Why was he, Grey Coyote, being given a vision now, when he had not sought one?

And then the answer came to him: The white man was near. Grey Coyote's moment, his chance to end the curse was close at hand.

But was that all? Was it not also a warning from the Creator? An alarm raised to show Grey Coyote that he must be prepared? That the one he sought was capable of inhuman acts?

Hau. Grey Coyote feared it was so.

The images faded, allowing Grey Coyote to rise up onto his feet. For a moment, he stood stock-still, his face upturned toward the heavens. Then lifting his arms, he began to sing.

> *Haiye, haiye, hai-ha.*
> *Haiye, haiye, hai-ha.*

It was a song of thanksgiving, a song sent to the Creator in acknowledgment. It was also a promise to the Creator— and to himself.

He would be prepared.

Grey Coyote had done what he must. Nevertheless, he dragged his feet all the way back to camp, his spirits burdened beyond comfort, for he dreaded the confrontation with his wife, which he knew would be forthcoming. But there was nothing for it. He had done what had to be done.

He had let the ponies go. He'd had no choice.

After the warning from the Creator, Grey Coyote knew he must proceed with caution. Where this white man was, he did not know; where this white man might stage an attack, he did not know.

But one thing was clear, it was time to leave, to travel again over the prairie. But safely.

Ponies, unfortunately, were a signal to war parties, as well as to the white hunters and mountain men; ponies, therefore, to a lone rider were dangerous. If Grey Coyote were to ensure that he and Little Sunset traversed this next part of their journey without incident—surprising the enemy instead of being surprised—then they must cross this land not as travelers, but as scouts.

Nevertheless, Little Sunset was not going to be happy, and it would be his responsibility to bring her to understanding, if he could. But her viewpoint, he feared, would be very different from his own, and he groped for the words to bridge the gap between their realities.

Alas, if only he could confide the deepest secrets of his soul, his task might be easier. But he could not; he alone must solve the riddle. Indeed, so much was this true, he feared that to share his plight with another could cause the forfeiture of his entire life's work.

So it was with these somber thoughts that he stepped into camp. Little Sunset, however, unaware of what plagued him, welcomed him heartily. Throwing back their shelter's entrance flap, she crawled out from it and happily pushed herself to her feet. Running toward him and smiling, she threw herself into his arms, grinning and saying, "You were gone so long. I worried."

He smiled back at her. "*Haye-haye,* this is a good greeting. Perhaps I should be gone for a long time each and every day."

"Maybe." She looked around him, toward his back, then at each side of him. "Where are the ponies?" she asked.

He sighed but didn't answer.

However, she seemed not to notice and went on to say, "I have prepared all of our things for the horses to carry, our robes, everything, and we have much pemmican ready."

Grey Coyote hesitated once more, his silence long and

drawn out. At last, however, knowing he had to respond in some fashion, he said, "The ponies are gone."

"Gone?"

"Hau."

"Did someone steal them?"

"Hiya."

"No? Then did they come loose from their hobbles and wander away?"

"Hiya."

She looked puzzled. "What happened?"

He breathed deeply. "I let them go."

She drew away from him slightly. "You what?"

Grey Coyote didn't elaborate all at once. But then, knowing he must again say something, he stated, "We are entering enemy country," as though this explained everything.

"Yes?"

He jerked his head to the left, then said, "When one is in enemy territory, and alone, one must be careful. If we bring the horses, we cannot predict that we will be able to safely cross the prairie."

"Oh. But . . ." She hesitated, and her voice was colored with confusion. Tentatively, she stepped out of his arms. She was frowning. "But I thought you went to collect them."

"It had been my intention to do so," he said, "but I fear I underestimated the danger on the prairie at this time of year. And so I have changed my mind. Circumstances now demand that we travel in a way so that we will be as invisible as possible."

"But the ponies were our only means of transportation, weren't they?"

He sighed. "We have other means."

"We do?"

"Hau." He pointed toward her feet. "You stand on them."

He watched as enlightenment dawned, and he waited for her answer, though he knew her reply would not bode him well. But at length, all she asked was, "We're going to walk?"

"Walk, crawl . . . and creep a little, too."

Her eyes wide, and with her mouth slightly open, she gaped at him.

Meanwhile, he went on to explain. "We will have to travel as scouts, since there is no one but myself to defend us."

"Scouts?"

He nodded. "Wolves of the plains. It is possible to roam the prairie unharmed when one is alone. But not on horseback, and not during the day. We will travel at night only, resting during the day. We will disguise ourselves, and we will arrive unscathed at our destination. I will show you how this is done."

She continued to gape at him, but after a short while, said, "But others travel on horseback . . ."

"They are safe to do so, only as long as they go in large numbers and have the means and manpower to protect themselves. I, however, as you might remember, have few arrows left. Thus, we must be extremely diligent."

"But . . . but . . . I thought . . . who will carry all of our things?"

He sighed, giving himself a moment in which to think. This next was probably what he most dreaded relating to her. After all, had he not observed that she was unfamiliar with the wilds, as well as being unacquainted with necessary precautions? Nevertheless, with jaw clenched, he plunged ahead and said, "We will carry our things, or maybe I should say . . . you will, for I will need to remain free of encumbrances in case we meet an enemy."

The silence that met this statement was perhaps telling. But when she spoke, all she asked was, "I? I will carry them?"

"Our load is not heavy."

She tilted her head. "I beg your pardon. Your robe is very heavy."

He nodded. "Yes, you are right. We will have to cache my robe before we go, along with anything else you cannot bring with you. We will cache my lance, as well, for as a scout, I will not be able to bring it with me."

"But that would mean that you would be even less able to defend us, and you will be cold at night. Besides, we have done all this preparation. Maybe you have not noticed, but I am not very strong."

"I have observed this," he said. "However, the food is not heavy."

"But extra moccasins, extra clothes for me, plus an extra robe for me? Do you forget that we went to the trouble to make it?"

"I will carry your robe."

"Can you? I thought you said that you had to remain 'unencumbered' in case we meet an enemy."

"That does not suggest that I will not tote a parfleche bag over my shoulder," he said. "In that we may place your robe."

She inhaled deeply and hesitated, her brow furrowed as though she were thoroughly absorbed in thought. After a time, however, she screwed up her face, stared him straight in the eye and said, "Are you still planning a trip into a forest to obtain wood for arrows?"

"I am."

"Might I ask how far it is to this forest?"

He shrugged. "It is perhaps a half moon away, maybe less."

"A half moon?"

"Hau."

He waited for her to say more, but when she did not, he reached out a hand to her and said, "Scouting only sounds difficult to you because you are not familiar with it. Once I describe what we do, and you have done it, you might like it."

But it would appear that she did not favor hearing anything he had to say. At least not right now. She turned her face away from him.

He rocked back on his feet, brought his arms to his sides and said, "I understand you're upset, but this is the way in which we must travel. Something has happened that makes me believe I must be more cautious than usual. I bear a lifelong enemy who I have reason to believe is close by. I must not be surprised by him. Besides, it is summer, a time of war parties, revenge and a warrior's thoughts of love. If we are attacked, I will defend us, but if we are ambushed, I will probably be killed and you taken captive, or perhaps, depending on the situation, you, too, might be killed."

She listened, bobbing her head as though in agreement, but she was silent for so long, Grey Coyote began to wonder if she had heard him. At length, however, she said, "I see your problem."

Grey Coyote, thinking she at last understood what was at stake, said, *"Ito,* come, let us gather our things. I will cache my robe, my lance and anything else we cannot carry."

But she pulled away from him and asked, "How far is it from the forest to the trading post?"

He thought a moment. "Less than a half moon," he said. "Perhaps three, maybe four days."

"That is all?"

"Hau."

"Very well," she said. "Let me ask you this also: If we were to head straight to the trading post from here, how long would it take us to arrive there?"

"From here?"

"Yes."

"But I cannot go there first," he said. "The trading post is also within enemy territory, and if I am to ensure our safety, I must make more arrows before we go there. That post is not considered a secure place."

"I do understand," she said, "but please indulge me. How long would it take?"

He thought a moment, then said, "We would travel eight, nine, perhaps ten days."

"I see," she acknowledged, taking a step back away from him. "Much less than if we journey to the forest first."

"That is true, but—"

"Well, that's that, then, isn't it?"

Grey Coyote relaxed . . . too soon, for she continued, saying, "Why didn't you tell me this earlier?"

"I have only just realized that we must be extra cautious. Plus I did not want to upset you."

"But you knew I would be upset?"

"I did."

"I think . . . I . . . I don't know what to say. I'm surprised . . . badly surprised."

"I understand," he said. "It is possible that you look on this as a hardship, for it would appear to me that the white woman in general is not used to walking. But you will soon become accustomed to it."

"Will I?" she asked. "And white women do walk," she defended, "but not hundreds of miles . . . and carrying things, as well."

Having no response to make to this, he remained silent.

"Well, as far as I'm concerned," she said, "if we don't go by horseback, we don't go at all. Perhaps we should stay here for the rest of our lives."

He decided to ignore her comment. Instead, he said while looking at her carefully, "That would be good to stay here forever . . . if we both did not have a duty to perform. You know we must go."

She exhaled on a sigh. "Yes, yes, I do know that," she said. "My duty . . . and yours . . . And you're right. We cannot really stay here. It was just . . ." She shrugged.

He nodded. "A dream?"

She turned her face aside but said nothing.

"*Ito,* come, it is good that you have grasped what is at stake," he said. "I understand, too, that you have been—"

"Do you? Do you understand me, really?"

Eyeing her cautiously, he turned reticent.

"Fourteen years ago," she continued, "I was sent away from home and put in the service of another. Fourteen years ago, my life changed. I no longer had a home to call my own; my parents were dead," she explained. "But now I discover that I should never have been sent away. It was all a mistake."

His brow narrowed, but he remained silent.

"Don't you see?" she asked. "For the first time in years, I have an opportunity to set the past straight. Something that has always been mine is awaiting me. I have only to reach out and take it. But the chance to do so is fleeting. I must act quickly, and I must act now."

He stirred uneasily.

"So, Mr. Coyote, if you truly understand what is happening with me, and you mean what you say with all your heart, then you will know why I must now insist that, Mother Nature aside, you must use the wood that is here for your arrows. As far as I am concerned, your need has become very great, indeed."

Grey Coyote didn't respond. *Never did the gap between them seem wider.*

In his own mind, he tried to understand that she was upset. Though he had explained it to her earlier, he realized that *she* did not share his viewpoints about life, or about the earth and the care that a man must show Nature. For if his wife did comprehend this fully, she would know that what she asked of him was a sacrilege.

Little Sunset continued to speak. "To my way of thinking, you have two choices. The first being this: Use the material here to make your arrows and then take me to the trading post; the second would be to leave the wood here for Nature to use, but bring back the horses so that we can journey to your woods in a timely manner."

He swallowed hard, knowing what he must say. "I can do neither," he said.

She spun away from him, presenting him with the loveliest of profiles, which he did admire, but . . .

"Of course," she continued, "there's always the third possibility."

"A third? And that is?"

Crossing both arms across her chest, she glanced at him over her shoulder and said, "Get the horses back and then take me once again to the Minnetaree village. It must be only a short distance from here, isn't it? Perhaps Mr.

LaCroix is still there, and if he is, maybe I could convince him to proceed as we had originally planned. That way I will only have lost a few days—wonderful days," she added, "but only a few."

Grey Coyote shook his head. Again she did not understand. He could not go back; he could only go forward. He said, "If there is one thing of which I am certain, it is that Scout LaCroix will be gone."

"Gone?" she questioned, turning to face him. "But we've only been here a short while. Why do you think he would be gone?"

"Because his presence was not welcome in that village," said Grey Coyote. "He has, in trade, cheated those people. It was my host, alone, who would bear his company, and my host, once he saw that Scout LaCroix was cheating at the game of *Cos-soo*, was not happy. No, Scout LaCroix will be gone."

"Then I could hire someone else."

"That you could do," said Grey Coyote. "But there is a problem."

"Oh? And that is?"

"I cannot take you there."

Her glance up at him was a grimace. "But it would only put you out of your way by a few days, wouldn't it?"

He shook his head slightly. "I cannot go back."

"Of course you could."

"*Hiya,*" he said. "I, too, must act quickly. I, too, have little time left. And there is reason for me to believe that the means to the end is near. Therefore, I must move ahead."

"Oh, I see," she acknowledged, frowning. She sighed, then said, as though to herself, "Then there's only one thing left to do. I don't like it, I might perish in the undertaking, but . . ." She took another deep breath, then glancing up at him, said, "I must go . . . If not with you"—she spoke softly—"then on my own."

He stared at her, hard. "You are right. You might perish if you do this."

But her response was odd, for she smiled at him, although her look held little happiness. She said, "But, Mr. Coyote, that decision is up to me to make."

"That is true . . ."

"Good."

"Usually. But because you are my wife, I cannot let you do this. I am responsible for you."

"No," she said. "No, you are not."

When he was about to continue, she held up her hand, and said, "Mr. Coyote, I know that in these past few days, we have considered ourselves married. You have thought it, as I have, too. And I have enjoyed it . . . very much."

"I, too," he said, reaching out and running the back of his fingers over her cheek.

But again she gazed away from him, ending the contact. Straightening her shoulders, she continued, "We have always known, no matter how much we didn't wish to think of it, that there would come a time when we would have to part, for we have been well aware that each of us follows a different path in life."

"That is true," he agreed, stretching out his hand once again to let his fingers trace the slim outline of her neck.

This time she let his touch remain, though she drew in a shaky breath. "And, we have also known that the time we have allotted to share with each other is short." She glanced up into his eyes, and at that moment, her look was uncertain, but it was also determined, as she continued,

"Mr. Coyote, what I'm saying is that I think the time has come for us to part."

"*Hau*, I know this is the direction of your thoughts."

"Yes. Just as I cannot force you to do something that is not in your nature, you cannot force me to do something against mine, either. If I miss the opportunity presented me, it will never be available to me again. And I'm not sure I could live with myself, knowing that I failed."

He nodded slowly. "I understand this very well."

"Good, then if you do, you will agree that I must return to the Minnetaree village at all possible speed, for that is where I may hire a guide."

"*Hau*," he said, dropping his hand. "I do understand. But come, let us talk of this some more before you do something you might regret. You are upset, and that is never a good time to make an important decision."

"I disagree. It is a fine time to make a decision."

"But you do not know this land," he countered. "Nor are you aware of the safe ways to cross it. Stay with me, and once I have completed my task, I will take you to this village of St. Louis. Perhaps it will not be as quickly as you would like. But I will see you there."

She nodded. "And how long will that take? How many months—or moons—would be required to get me there?"

"I do not know."

"And that is the problem," she said, her gaze at him serious. "I thank you kindly for your offer, but I feel I must decline. Think, if I return to the Minnetaree village now, I have the chance to arrive in St. Louis within the month, because we would travel by boat. From there I would be able to hire a ship returning to England and be home in the shortest time possible. This is important to me."

He didn't respond, simply looked at her.

She added, "It is *very* important to me."

For the first time, it became very real to Grey Coyote that this, indeed, might be their last time together. If he could not convince her to go with him—and it appeared that he could not—they would have to part, here, tonight.

She continued to speak, "In truth, we are not far from the Minnetaree village, are we? It is possible that I could make it back there on my own, is it not? Particularly if I travel by night? You could show me how."

Grey Coyote considered his choices while he hesitated, then said, "It is possible, but—"

"Then you must see that you have no other choice but to let me go. Honestly, in my mind, you are under no responsibility to me. In a way, I was forced on you. And you have been a gentleman about it. But the time has come for you to let me go."

Grey Coyote tilted his head, staring at her intently.

She continued, "Please, Mr. Coyote. I am pleading. We traveled here safely enough, and out in the open. I have been in this country long enough now that think I can return there without a problem."

He frowned. "It is possible . . ."

She swallowed hard, and reaching out, she touched him.

It was true that his buckskin shirt stood between his bare skin and her fingers, but it didn't matter: Her mere touch brought him excitement. But she said, "Let me take some of this food that we've prepared, and . . . It's only a few days' journey, isn't it?"

He took hold of her hand, bending down to touch his lips to each finger, and he said, "Perhaps three."

She sucked in her breath, but if her response was because of his kisses or due to what he said, he might never know. The look in her eyes, however, softened, but all she said was, "Only three?" She stared straight up at him. "If that is so, then I truly think I can do this."

He grimaced, squeezing her hand. "I do not like it . . ."

"I know. But you will let me go, won't you? You are aware that I have to do this. I have to try."

Again, he paused. However, at length, he finally conceded her point and said, "*Hokake*, you may go, but only once I have shown you how to travel at night."

She let out her breath. "I will learn. I will learn quickly. And thank you."

He nodded. "It is decided, then. I will whistle for my pony, for he has probably not gone far, and we will load him with provisions for you. Then I will show you what to do when you travel. But you must give me your complete attention."

"I will." She smiled and chuckled slightly, though the sound of it did border on a sob. "Thank you again, Grey Coyote," she said. "You won't regret it. After all, you'll be free of me; free to go your own way, without having to worry about me."

He nodded, but only slightly, and he wondered if his eyes mirrored the sadness he felt. After a moment, he said, "*Hau,* I will be free . . ."

Grey Coyote stared at her; perhaps, he thought, to memorize her features.

However, there was little more he could do to keep her with him. Thus, dropping her hand, he stepped away from her and said, "*Ito,* come, Little Sunset, let us prepare you for this journey."

"Little Sunset?" She tilted her head. "Who is Little Sunset?"

He shrugged. "It is what I have named you. For you, with your golden hair and eyes, remind me of that time of day. Do you remember the sunset we shared, there on the butte?"

She nodded.

"It was on that day that I gave you your name."

Her look at him was intense, and perhaps a bit somber. Breaking eye contact, she asked, "It is my Indian name?"

"*Hau.* You have an Indian name now. It will be with you always."

"Thank you." She glanced away from him, but after a short pause, she turned back and said, "I have another name, as well. An English name. I think you should know it."

"*Hau.* I agree."

"Funny," she said.

"Funny?"

"Yes, it's odd that I haven't seen fit to tell you my real name. We have been so close, one would think I would have said something about it before now. It's . . . strange . . ."

He inclined his head.

"Marietta. My English name is Marietta."

He frowned. *Marietta*? He had heard that name before. But where? When?

All at once, he felt odd, as though he were not a part of his body; a peculiar feeling swept over him. That name was connected with his tribe somehow, with him, with his mission . . .

"Do you not like my name?"

Grey Coyote's throat constricted, and he chose not to answer, calling back to mind the exact memory. It had been in the Minnetaree village, and he . . .

He could barely believe it. He had been with this

woman for days, and he hadn't known who she truly was. He hadn't put the pieces together.

But he recalled every single part of that puzzle now. It had been evening, he had been preparing to leave, and the wind had whispered to him . . . It had spoken to him, had called out this name. He had ignored the message at the time, and apparently, he had done so at his own risk.

The woman, it had said. *The woman, Marietta. She is the means.*

He was a fool not to have realized it sooner. This woman had something to do with him, with his people, with the riddle, with their freedom . . .

. . . And he had almost let her go.

"Please don't scowl at me like that," Marietta said, leaning in toward him. "It's a pretty name. Of course my full name is Maria Marietta Welsford. Can you not say it? At least once?"

"Marietta," he repeated softly. Then again, "Marietta."

Then he stared at her hard, very hard, because she was about to become *very* upset with him. And he was going to have to proof himself against her wrath.

He only hoped that when it was all over, she would forgive him . . .

CHAPTER 11

"Is something wrong?" Marietta queried, gazing up into his eyes. "You look . . . strange."

"Hiya," he said, "something is very right, I think."

What in the dear Lord's name did that mean? Frowning, she gazed up at him, and said, "I don't understand."

He nodded. "It is to be appreciated that you do not, but maybe some day you will. *Ito*, come. I have changed my mind about your journey. You will accompany me now."

At first Marietta wasn't certain she had heard him correctly, and she asked, "What did you say?"

"You will accompany me now," he repeated, his expression grave. "The decision is no longer yours to make."

What? What was this? She asked, "Changed your mind? But—"

He didn't explain. "You will gather up the meat and put it into bags," he commanded, "while I break camp. We will cache my robe and anything else you feel you cannot carry. We will leave at once."

"No, we won't," she said. "You can't just change your mind like that."

"I have a reason. A good one. Now prepare yourself for our journey."

"No. You can't do this to me. What's happened? One moment everything was fine, and then . . . What possible cause could have . . ." Gently, she shook her head. "Tell me this reason."

Though his gaze was subdued as he stared at her, his words were not, and he said, "I cannot speak of it."

"Cannot?" Shocked, Marietta could only stand before him and gape. After a few moments, however, she said, "You cannot speak of it? What does that mean? We talked. We communicated. We agreed."

"It does not matter. Something has changed."

She tossed her head, scowling up at him. "No, you . . . you can't do this."

"I can."

"Well, I won't . . . I won't go with you."

"Then I will make you."

"No. Let's look back at what we just discussed. You promised me to let me go."

"I did not promise."

"You said I could go. That's the same thing."

"It is not," he countered. "I said you could travel alone as long as you learned from me how to journey in the night. I choose now not to teach you."

She gasped. "No, no. This is not right."

"It does not have to be right. I have made up my mind. Prepare yourself and your things. We leave at once."

"Very well," she said. "I will leave with you—as long as we ride."

But he simply shook his head. "We have already discussed this. We will *not* ride."

"Then . . . I . . . I . . . " She stuttered. "You . . . you can't do this."

A muscle twitched dangerously in his cheek as he said, "An Indian husband speaks but once to his wife. Now, I am telling you, and there is to be no back talk. We are leaving."

"No, I won't go," she retaliated, back talking just the same. "And I will say whatever I want to you."

He ignored her, and bending, he commenced to break camp, smoothing over the ground, scattering the fire.

"What are you doing?"

"I am erasing evidence of our encampment, so that others who come behind us will not know that we were here. Now, return to the shelter, get any of the items you wish to carry, including the food, and be back here quickly."

Standing over him, hands on her hips, she said, "I will prepare myself to go on alone, back to the Minnetaree village. Nothing else."

But it seemed he had no sympathy for her, at least not now, and all he said was, "We leave here quickly. Either we go with your things, or we travel without them. The choice is yours. And remember this: A good woman does not chatter back to her husband."

"Well, in that case, I guess I'm not a very good woman, and Mr. Coyote, you are certainly *not* my husband."

"You *are* my wife. I *am* your husband and—"

She stamped her foot. "No, I am not. I refuse your proposal."

When he gazed at her incredulously, she simply raised her eyebrows and said, "This argument is pointless. It doesn't matter if I'm your wife or not. The essence of it is this: I will not go on with you," she said. "You gave me your word. And that is as good as a promise. I will hold you to it."

"You are right. This argument is meaningless. If you do not do as I say, I will force you to go with me."

She shrugged. "Fine. Then do your worst," she taunted. "You're obviously bigger than I am, and stronger, too. But I will not go into that dwelling—if you want something there, you can simply get it yourself."

"Humph!" he said, then added, "I will," before he continued speaking. "If you do not wish to bring your things," he said, "that is your decision. But I will then have no choice but to take you captive."

She squinted at him. "Do what you must," she said. "But I will be a very noisy captive."

"Then I will gag you."

"And I will run away at the first opportunity."

He shrugged.

"And how will you take me if we have no horses? Are you planning to carry me yourself?"

"No," he said. "You will ride."

Her relief was obvious, but short-lived, for he went on to say, "But *I* will not ride. I will walk the horse along behind me and hope that no one discovers us."

"But that means we would still be moving slowly, and I . . . Oh, Grey Coyote, don't you realize? I *must* do this. I *must* try. If I don't . . ."

Grey Coyote's expression didn't change, not one iota. As he stood up from his work, his features were tight, grim, and there was no understanding to be witnessed on his countenance when he said, "I have spoken. You are my wife, and you will do as I tell you, and I have no more to say on the matter. Do not question me further."

She glared at him. And though she didn't utter another word, when he turned away to attend to the other chores, she seized the brief moment to step toward their hideaway.

But she wasn't about to gather up her things. Indeed not. Perhaps it was silly, stupid—the whim of a mere girl—but she *had* to get away from him.

She couldn't meekly follow him. Who did he think she was? A person without spirit? Without pride?

How dare he treat her as though she were nothing more than a mere extension of himself, as though she were a lifeless entity with no personality, no dreams. Perhaps in Indian country this was how the men treated their women, but she would never forgive herself if she let him get away with this; she was made of firmer stuff.

So, while he was busy elsewhere, she would do everything within her means to escape. And if she were successful, she would find her way to the Minnetaree village, do or die.

She crawled into their shelter, scooted toward the very back of it, and digging out a hole through the shrubs that covered it, she slithered through it.

At last she was free, at least for a moment. True, he would most likely come after her, but she was certainly not going to cooperate with him. Let him do his worst, she thought. She would show her displeasure.

At the very least, she intended to be trouble. Lots of trouble.

Stooping over, she crept forward as fast as she could, until, after rounding a corner in the gully, she began to climb up to the level of the plains. Her feet skidded over sharp rocks, but she ignored the discomfort.

But, as she had predicted, Grey Coyote seemed to read her thoughts, and alerted to what she was doing, he easily caught up with her. Taking hold of her, he wrestled with her, until she was lying on her back on the harsh, rocky ground.

She lay beneath him, his hands holding her arms to the side. She tried to kick out at him, but she did absolutely no harm. Having placed one of his knees between her legs, he held himself up, slightly above her, but out of the line of fire.

He shook his head at her. "Why don't you simply obey me?" he asked, as though the idea of a man's orders going undone was beyond him. "There is a good reason why you must now come with me."

"If that is so," she said, "then tell me what it is."

"I cannot."

"Then don't expect me to do as you say. Believe me, if you do this, I promise that I will be an annoyance, and will create as much trouble as I possibly can."

He breathed out harshly. "You already are much trouble."

"Good!"

He sighed. "You realize that I will have to tie you now, don't you?"

"Do what you must," she said. "But *you* should be aware that I *will* escape. And if you find me, I will try again."

His voice was calm when he said, "Then I will have to ensure that you are never again successful."

She let out a harsh breath but otherwise remained silent, although if a glance could have done injury . . .

She kicked out at him, and in response to her fidgeting, he sent her a carefully contrived look of boredom.

Seeing it, she threw another fit, thrashing about, twisting and kicking at him. But he was prepared.

He lay over her, holding both of her hands away from her body as she wiggled and squirmed beneath him.

"*Tula*, lie still."

He might as well have kept silent, however. She lashed out at him all the more, but the effort had taken much energy, or so it seemed. At last, she lay still. Then, sucking in her breath, she opened her mouth, and he didn't wait to find out what she was intending.

He reacted the only way that seemed logical. He covered her mouth with his own. It wasn't a kiss. It wasn't meant to be.

It was simply a means to keep her silent, and yet, with the first touch, he was at once transported. His body stood alert. After the last few days, he practically knew this woman's body by heart, and it was only with the most extreme control that he did not press the matter further.

But her wriggling against him was having the opposite effect than the one she most likely intended, and as her teeth bit at his tongue, thoughts of other things, much more pleasant things, came swiftly to his mind.

He deepened the kiss and was rewarded to hear her low-pitched moan.

Still, she twisted in his arms, flailing about as though she believed he might intend her bodily harm. But instead of fighting her, he kissed her more fervently.

She groaned again, and the sound of it tore at his self-control. But he didn't change his tactics. Indeed, he deepened the kiss.

His mouth slanted over hers, his tongue searching out her own, dancing with hers, tasting her, then delving even deeper into the moist recess of her mouth. At last the struggle seemed to wear itself out, and gradually, he let go of one of her hands, if only to determine what she would do.

But she did nothing. In truth, her hands came up to hold onto his shoulders.

And gradually, so slowly, he barely recognized it for

what it was, she responded back to him in the sweet way he loved so well. She returned his kiss, running her hands down over his back. It sent him quietly out of his mind.

He then performed the most natural thing in the world. He made love to her, right there, right on the side of the gully.

There was no leading up to it, no waiting, no honeyed words. She might be furious with him, she might think him an unworthy beast, but she opened her legs to him, as if she could barely tolerate the distance between them, too.

It was lovemaking at its rockiest. It was taking, but also giving. It was rough, yet gentle. And they bore against each other over and over, straining together as if each thrust were another well-argued point in their disagreement.

The release was heavenly, yet earthy at the same time, and they came together in a madness of thrusting hips. The pleasure went on and on, as if each clung to the moment, as if each understood that the pleasure was fleeting.

At last it was over, and both were breathing heavily as he settled down over her.

Inhaling the scent of her spicy femininity, it was on the tip of his tongue to apologize, to explain himself, to tell her everything, even though he knew he dare not.

Pushing against him, she said, "Please get off me. If it be your intention to humiliate me, you have certainly done so."

"I?" He came up onto his elbows and looked down into her eyes. "But . . . I thought . . . you wanted it, too . . ."

However, if he had hoped to finagle a confession out of her, he was to be disappointed.

She said, "I suppose you think this is the way to quiet my rebelliousness."

"*Hiya*," he said. "Truly, I thought you wanted this as much as I did."

"I did not. I do not. I am angry at you, and I did not, I do not want your attentions."

He stirred uneasily but moved to the side of her, though he kept hold of her around the waist.

She sat up, settling her skirts down around her ankles and said, "I need to wash."

"I will take you to the stream, and then we will leave here."

She glared at him, and he could barely hold her glance as she said, "As far as I'm concerned, you have broken your word to me, and I will not go anywhere with you willingly. Though my protest may be fruitless, for you are obviously stronger than I am, believe me, that will not stop me. I promise you, I will hound your every step."

His sigh was very long and deep. Finally, he said, "I know. I even understand."

"Humph!" was all she said in return. With a brief nod of her head, she rose up to her feet and headed toward the stream.

Though he had no choice but to follow her, he did so at a very great distance.

In the end, Grey Coyote had tied her hands in front of her and had placed her on the pony in a straddle position. He had also gagged her.

True, Marietta had screamed at him, as she had promised she would. In that way she supposed she had a reason for what he did, but she wasn't particularly interested in giving Grey Coyote quarter at the moment.

However, they had been underway for no more than a few minutes when Marietta discovered that it was possible to squirm and shift about until, the good Lord willing, she could throw herself from the pony. Though such an action could be deemed childish and would only serve to irritate him, it was all she had at the moment.

So she did it. She twisted about until she could feel herself sliding off, but instead of falling to her feet as she had intended, she found herself hurtling toward the ground, face first.

"Do you mean to hurt yourself?" Grey Coyote scolded as he raced toward her, catching her before she made contact.

She didn't respond and merely glared her dislike at him.

But from that moment on, Grey Coyote had tied her feet together, and without a single word of apology, had positioned her face down, arms over her head, and like a sack of potatoes, had thrown her over the pony's back.

It was not a comfortable position. Blood drained to her head, and her stomach muscles were tired from the constant need to tighten themselves against the movement of the pony.

She squirmed, pressing her elbows into the flanks of the animal, and lifted her head in order to prevent the constant rush of blood; she tried to cry out, but mostly she hurt only herself.

At last, after what seemed like hours, Grey Coyote stopped.

They had been traveling through the night, their pace slow, and she wondered if Grey Coyote meant to taunt her. They had also been keeping their trek to the gully. She supposed that Grey Coyote was afraid to range out onto the open plains, even though, in her opinion, there was little light by which to see them. At present there was only a sliver of a moon, as well as the multitude of stars.

Stepping back toward her, Grey Coyote pulled her off the pony and carried her to a large, flat rock, where he placed her upon it, seated. Though she couldn't say a word, her fiery gaze expressed her anger at him.

Grey Coyote didn't speak, returning instead to the pony, where he hobbled the animal, petted it, then reached up to grab hold of a bag. She recognized the bag at once as being one that was filled with their food.

Still silent, he returned to sit directly across from her, and to her utter chagrin, ate his snack in front of her, never once taking his eyes from her. He even quenched his thirst from another pouch that was filled with water, looking as though he were enjoying himself thoroughly.

Hazy moonlight shone down on him, casting his features in stunning shades of grey light and shadows. And though she marveled at his handsomeness, at the moment, she would have rather died than admit it.

In due time, he asked, "Are you hungry?"

She refused to answer. Instead, she glanced away from him.

"Very well, we will travel onward, then." He stood to his feet.

"Hmm . . ." It was the only sound she could make.

"Did you say something?"

She rolled her eyes but then realized he might not be able to see it.

"Know that we are in enemy territory," he cautioned as he stepped toward her. "War parties generally have a scout that accompanies them, and these men cross the prairie at night, also, so do not think that you are free to scream. If I remove this gag, you must promise me that you will not screech or yell. Do you promise?"

She nodded.

Carefully, he untied the gag, and as he did so, it seemed to Marietta as though he took pains to avoid touching her.

At last, the gag was gone, and he squatted down before her. He asked, "Shall I feed you, or can I trust you to your word that if I untie your hands, you will not attempt to leave?"

"I will not attempt to leave." She said it resentfully, hatefully. But she said it, nonetheless.

He nodded and reaching around behind her, carefully untied her hands and her feet. He offered the pemmican and the water to her, and she reached out for them both greedily.

As she ate, he sat back across from her to watch.

After a while, her thirst and hunger satiated, she said, "I will repay you for this indignity."

He inclined his head but didn't speak.

"I notice that we are traveling south and west."

"That is a good observation, and it is so, we travel south and west," he responded. "The forest that I seek is in *Paha Sapa*, the Black Hills. They are slightly west of where we are now."

"I do not know of them. But tell me, where is the trading post in relation to where we are?"

"It is almost due south. We do not travel so much out of our way."

"Oh," she said and looked elsewhere, anywhere but at him.

He asked, "Are you finished?"

"I am."

"Then we will continue."

"Don't throw me over the horse," she commanded. "It is uncomfortable."

"Then you must promise me that you will not try to jump down from the animal and squirm about. Do you promise?"

She set her lips together, and he shook his head.

"You make this difficult for me."

"That's *your* problem."

He grinned at her slightly. "That it is. But it is also yours. Still, there is another position that might be more comfortable for you, my wife."

"Don't call me that."

He frowned. "Do you want others to think badly of you?"

"I don't care what others think of me . . . here. Besides, I have no acquaintances in this land—except for you, of course."

"And it does not bother you what I think?"

"Why should it? Why should I care what a man who has the audacity to throw me over a horse should—"

"I placed you gently upon its back."

"You *threw* me," she contradicted. "So why should I care what you think?"

"I do not know why."

She shrugged. "Well, I don't care."

"Yes, you do," he said. "You care very much."

"Humph!"

"Indeed, so much do you care, that you are furious with me for not allowing you your freedom."

"Stop it, do you hear? Stop it." And jumping up suddenly, she ran to the pony, vaulting onto it. She had almost attained her seating, too, when, having followed her, he reached up and pulled her to the ground. He held her by the wrists.

"You are breaking your promise," he spat at her. "You gave me your word that you would not try to escape."

"And you have broken your promise to me. We are even."

"We are not even. I did not promise."

"Let me go! Do you understand?" She wiggled out of his grip and turned, as if to run. But he caught her. "Let me go!"

"I cannot."

They fought then, in earnest, she twisting and squirming, he trying to hold her steady. They struggled against each other, and at last he became the victor, but only after he had wrestled her once more to the ground.

She lay face up, the dry grass and rocks scratching her backside; he adjusted himself over her, holding her hands above her head.

"You *did* promise," she accused.

But he chose not to dignify her allegation with a response.

After a while, she demanded again, "Let me go." And she glared daggers at him.

They were both breathing heavily, but she wasn't about to make the same mistake she had done the last time by attempting to scream; she pressed her lips together, making herself resistant to any form of a kiss.

He said, "I will release you if you give me your word that you will not run away. But you must keep your word. If you don't, I will tie you and not let you go again."

She gaped up at him silently, his handsome features—made more so by the shimmery moonlight—swimming in her line of vision. She said, "I will never promise you anything. Do you understand? Never. If I am to be a captive, it is your problem to keep me with you and contain my struggles."

"Then I cannot release you."

She didn't respond.

He said, "Here we are, on this balmy night. Though you fight me, I think that you are the most beautiful creature I have ever seen. The moonlight is, indeed, your friend, my wife."

She remained silent, but when he didn't move, and didn't make an effort to say more, she repeated, "You can get off me now."

He raised an eyebrow. "Did I hear you promise me that you would not run away?"

"I will not promise you anything."

"Then I would be foolish to remove myself."

She turned her head away from him, tears of frustration pooling in her eyes.

He must have seen them, for he asked, "Do you cry?"

"Of course I am crying. I am disheartened."

"And that is the only reason you cry?"

She bit her lip, refusing to say more.

He sighed and rolled to the side of her, though he kept one arm and one leg thrown over her. At last, he said, though with some reluctance, "You have made your point."

"Oh? Really? And what point is that?"

Again, he sighed. "I will do it."

"What? What will you do?"

"I will take you to the trading post instead of going on to the forest."

Instantly, she went still. "I don't believe you."

He shrugged. "You don't have to."

She hesitated, then, "You will?"

He nodded, but she could barely see the gesture. "However," he added, "we will not be able to take the pony, for our safety will rely completely on my ability to move across the prairie undetected. So that I can do that, you will have to learn a little about the prairie itself, for you must become a scout."

She nodded.

"And if I do this, if I teach you how to scout, I must have

your promise that you will use every bit of your power to learn these skills—and quickly."

"I will," she said at once. "I promise."

"And there is one more thing."

"Oh?" Cautious, she raised an eyebrow. "What is that?"

"You must swear to me that you will obey me, no matter what I say, and at once. For if there is trouble, I will not have the leisure to explain myself. Do you agree?"

She hesitated. "Whatever you say?"

He breathed out heavily, as though she did much to frustrate him. "If there is trouble."

"Oh, very well, then. I agree."

"It is well," he said. "I will make a camp here so that I can fashion a few weapons from stone, and begin your instruction in how to become the spirit of the wolf."

She stared at him, simply stared at this man's uncommon handsomeness. But only for a moment.

At length, she said, "Spirit of the wolf?"

"Hau," he replied. "In an Indian village, this is what we call our scouts."

"I see," she said, and then she did the unexpected. Without a single word, she threw her arms around Grey Coyote and cried.

CHAPTER 12

"To be a scout," he instructed,. "you must become accustomed to the wilderness. You must begin to think of it as your home, and you must feel as comfortable here as you would in your England."

She nodded.

It was early morning. The sun was up in the eastern sky, but barely; its pinks and reds diffused across the barren landscape, welcoming in the new day with color. Both Marietta and Grey Coyote were seated in the gully, on the ground. There was no fire between them, but a breakfast of dried meat had appeased their hunger.

Her first lesson had begun, and she was instructed to learn it well, for she and Grey Coyote would begin their travels that very evening.

"Mother Earth will provide everything for you," Grey Coyote was saying. ". . . all of your needs, be they food, medicines or weapons. But you must open your heart and your mind. You must become one with all existence."

"Become one with existence?"

He nodded. "There is a oneness with nature. A feeling of belonging, of being part of it. It is true power. We are, all of us, connected. Every living creature is part and parcel of every other living creature. When you can feel that aliveness, that oneness with all life, you have then truly become a scout."

"But I don't understand."

"Close your eyes," he said, "and tell me, what do you see a mile away from here?"

She chortled. "I can't see a mile away from here."

"Yes, you can," he encouraged. "Keep your eyes closed and feel the life that is around you."

She tried to do as he said.

"Can you sense that boulder?"

Heaven forbid, she *did* perceive something. And she asked, albeit a little shyly, "Is it to my left?"

"It is. I am proud of you. You can do this."

"But that was very close to me."

"It does not matter," he responded. "How far away something is, is not important. It is not the distance that matters, it is one's feeling of belonging to all life. Now, tell me, what do you perceive in the far distance from here?"

She tried to look. She tried very hard, but at last she shook her head. "Nothing," she said. "I can't do this."

"You can," he responded. "But it is, perhaps, too soon. You must practice. You must sit here. You must close your eyes and feel the life around you, for there is much activity here. You must permit yourself to become part of it, become one with it. We are all of us connected. You need only perceive that connection, and the rest is easy, for all your needs are provided by our Mother, the Earth."

"But—"

"It is why it is important to take care of the Earth." He expanded on the thought. "All life needs her, as she needs us. We are all joined by the life that flows through every living creature. That is why you must remember that to destroy something beautiful in the Earth is to destroy something beautiful in yourself."

She sat for a moment in thought. "I understand. You reap what you sow."

He nodded. "That life force that one uses to destroy another is *one's own* life force. It comes from none other than oneself. That energy exists as surely as the air you breathe, and it will come back to you, for you are the one who emanated it. And so it is that what one receives is good, or is bad, according to what one puts out into the world."

She gazed up at him. Her throat constricted, as though she were experiencing deep emotion. In some way, some how, what Grey Coyote was saying . . . touched her.

"How have you managed to become aware of all this?"

"My grandfathers," he replied. "And they learned from their grandfathers before them. But come, there is more you should know." And holding out his hand, he pulled her to her feet.

"The first thing that one must keep in mind when he is scouting is that one must avoid all man-made and animal trails. In truth, a scout avoids all trails. And a scout never uses the same path twice."

As Marietta stared at Grey Coyote, she tried earnestly to understand. After all, she had promised him to learn all she could as quickly as possible. However, she had a few questions, and she asked, "But if you avoid all trails, how do you know where you're going?"

"There are other landmarks one can use to tell one's

way," he said. "The sun is used during the day; the seven brothers at night, for they will point you to the Star that Stands Still, the North Star."

"Seven brothers?"

"The white man calls these stars the Big Dipper. But the Indians call it the seven brothers."

"Really? Why seven brothers?"

"It is from an old Cheyenne legend," he said. "In the legend, seven brothers escaped into the sky to avoid death. It is an excellent legend, and perhaps it is because of this that many of the surrounding tribes have come to adopt the name for this group of stars."

"I see." She nodded. "Will you tell it to me?"

"Hau," he said, "but perhaps at a later time. For now, I will give you lessons on how never to get lost."

"Really?"

He simply smiled at her. *"Hau, hau.* It is easy to find the seven brothers in the sky," he began, "for they are always in view unless it is cloudy. And from the brothers, one can gain not only direction, but can ascertain how early or late it is in the evening, for the brothers rotate around the Star that Stands Still."

"Yes, yes," she said. "I do know that."

"That is good," he acknowledged. "Now to find your way, you have only to take the two stars at the very end of the cup, and make a straight line upward from them. The first star that you will come to is the Star that Stands Still."

"I didn't know that."

He inclined his head. "Then it is good that we have discussed this, for you should never be lost again. Tonight, when we are on the trail, I will have you trace this path in the sky so that you can see how easily it is done."

"I would like that," she answered with a smile.

"Remember that once you can determine north—for the Star that Stands Still points north always—you have only to set your course accordingly until at last you come across landmarks that you know."

"Ah," she said. "That's how it's done. Well, I must say, this is a good thing to know." However, she wrinkled her brow. "But," she continued, "what if it's a cloudy night, and you can't see the stars? Do you simply not travel?"

"There is always a means to find your way," he responded. "When it is cloudy, one notes the course of the wind, which, depending on the season, comes from a particular direction. One can set one's path by this.

"The wind?"

"*Hau*," he said. "The wind. Now," he continued, "when we leave here tonight, I will tell you the direction we must go, and you will lead me."

"I? But—"

"It is the only way to learn." He peered at her as though he were trying to read her mind. However, after a short pause, he continued, "But there is much time before evening, and there is yet one more skill that you must know, a very important skill."

"Oh?" she asked. "And what is that?"

"How to travel as a scout. Because a scout must remain invisible to be effective. A scout must set his mind to traveling through the most difficult regions of the plains."

"What do you mean by difficult regions?"

"The swamps, the bushes, the places no one would think to travel. On the prairie, only men in great numbers can afford to keep to the easier paths. A scout goes where no one else wants to go, where no one else would think to go; thus he remains invisible. So that you might understand this further, it is a subject of shame for a scout to be seen when he is on a mission for his people. A scout is powerful, and his skills are only valuable to others and to his tribe when he remains undetected."

"I think I begin to understand," she said, bobbing her head slightly. "But how can one become invisible? It isn't as though a person *is* invisible. And a scout must walk, or crawl . . . he must exert some motion. Can't that be seen?"

"This is a good question," Grey Coyote validated. "Yet a scout must, for all practical purposes *be* invisible, and there are several ways for him to do so," he said. "One is to blend into the environment—to take on its color and aspects so well that it would be hard for another to distinguish the scout from the land. Another is to camouflage oneself as an animal; an animal that is often seen on the prairie."

"Ah," she said. "Like a buffalo? You make yourself up to look like a buffalo."

He shook his head. "It is the wolf," he said. "Wolves are a common animal on the plains. Few warriors, even when they see them, pay attention to the wolf, or kill them, either, for there is a saying that a bow that shoots a wolf will never shoot straight again."

"Hmmm . . ." She furrowed her brow. "So are you saying that in order to make ourselves invisible, we'll become like wolves?"

"*Hiya*, no," he said. "We cannot because I have no means to make us appear as wolves. A wolf skin is often kept for this purpose, but I have none with me. Nor do I wish to kill a wolf that I might take its skin. Instead, we will disguise ourselves in another way."

"Oh? What way is that?"

He pointed off to the small stream that gurgled merrily through the gully.

"We're going to wade in water?"

He smiled gently, shaking his head. "Come," he said. "I will show you."

Taking her hand in his own, he led her to the water.

They squatted next to the stream, and Grey Coyote, picking up her hand, directed it to the different textures of the soil, asking her to identify each one. He said, "What do you feel here?"

"Mostly sand," she replied.

"That is true," he said. "There is much sand, and sandstone. You see it in the cliffs. But is there anything else?"

"Hmmm . . . Well, there's dirt and clay."

"*Hau,*" he said, "there is dirt and clay. And do you see that the clay is the same color as the soil, and that this is also the same shade as the dry, golden grass?"

"Hmmm . . ." she murmured, hesitating. "Yes, I can see that."

"This is good," he replied. "We will paint our bodies with this clay." He eyed her with a fair degree of wariness, as though he expected her to suddenly burst into flames. But when she did not, he went on to say, "I cannot emphasize enough that a scout must remain as invisible to his environment as possible. Now the first thing you must do to make yourself invisible is to strip down to only the barest necessities of clothing."

At first Marietta laughed, certain that he was taunting her. But when he remained solemn, she said, "Surely you jest."

"I do not," he assured her quietly. "You must strip away

most of your clothes. I will do so also, although I do not wear as many as you."

"But—"

He held up his hand. "Consider this," he said. "When scouting, one will be trudging through swamps and valleys, bushes and brambles. Clothing can snag, can tear, and if your clothes are also excessive, they will burden you. If you continue to wear a dress as big as this one," he touched its cloth, "it will hinder you. It might also catch on branches or pricks, and will leave a trace of you behind that even a neglectful warrior may see and follow."

"Oh," she replied, "Of course. I begin to understand." She looked away from him awkwardly. "But there is one thing you have failed to consider . . ."

He raised an eyebrow.

"And that is that everything I am wearing is a necessity."

His look at her was amused, but when he spoke, all he said was, "Perhaps these things are so in the white man's world, but they are not here on the prairie, and particularly not if you wish to look as though you are a part of the environment. Come, it will be a great pleasure to help you remove your clothes one by one—and we will discover what your basic necessities are. That is unless you wish to go naked." His grin at her was full of humor, and he added, "It is not something to which I would object."

She wagged her finger at him, smiling, and she started to respond in kind, but suddenly Grey Coyote froze midaction, brought up his gaze to scan his environment, and before she could say a word, he placed a finger over her lips. Motioning her to silence, he bent, came down on all fours, put his ear to the ground and lay there for a good few minutes. She followed him down, resting on her knees.

Before long he sat up, looked at her, and said under his breath, "A war party approaches."

Instantly, her eyes went wide; her stomach dropped.

She didn't doubt him. Why would she? If the man were attempting to teach her how to perceive things at a distance, it would surely follow that he must, himself, have that ability.

She asked quietly, "How far away are they?"

He didn't answer.

Marietta quickly scrutinized their little gully, looking for a possible escape. However, what had once seemed a haven, now appeared a prison. This land was dry, barren. The cliffs were of sandstone, with little to no vegetation; there wasn't even a good cave in them. Literally, there was no where to hide.

True, there were bushes and scrub brush along the little stream, but most of these were small, and those that were of a larger variety were full of thorns. Worse, it was the early part of the day; there wasn't even a shred of darkness to conceal them.

She glanced toward Grey Coyote, but though he seemed alert, he did not appear to be frightened or concerned. On the contrary, he looked vigilant, determined.

Because they were still on their knees, he motioned her to crawl in close to him. But while she would have preferred to plunge forward, he coaxed her to approach him as slowly as possible.

"Movement can be sensed by an alert scout," he explained.

She gave him one brief nod, then carefully moved toward him. When she was well within his ability to reach for her, he took her in his arms.

Placing his lips to her ear, he whispered, "No matter what happens, you are not to cry out, do you understand? We must hide. It will not be a comfortable spot that I have chosen, but it will be a good cover, and it should be effective. Are you ready?"

Too frightened to speak, she nodded.

"We will hide in the bushes." He pointed toward them.

She looked. "Are you crazy?" she whispered at once, turning her attention back to him. "Those are wild rose bushes. They are full of thorns and stickers."

"Exactly," he said. "We will be well hidden."

"Exactly? But—"

"You must take off your dress now, quickly, for it is too full. I will not be able to prod you into and out of those bushes easily while you are wearing this. Worse, you might get stuck. Hurry."

"Prod me?"

"You will not be hurt."

She didn't even think to contradict him. Quickly, she reached her arms around behind her to undo the buttons, but the clasps were small, material-covered, and difficult even under the best of circumstances. Her fingers fumbled over the tiny objects, and she was almost crying, when she said, "I can't do it."

"*Hokahe,*" he said. "I remember these well. It would take more time than we have to undo them. Therefore I am going to have to cut the dress off you. Do you understand?"

Did she understand? "Rip it," she said. "Just rip the thing off me. I'll repair it later."

"*Hiya*, I cannot," he said, "The air around you is much like water—it carries waves. If I rip this dress, it will send out swells, much like the circles you see in the water, but these are in the air, and if this party has a scout within it that is alert, he will sense it. Hold still, it is not a difficult task to cut it."

She held still, and he cut it away at once, peeling the garment from her and leaving her standing in only her chemise, corset, drawers, hose and slippers. The chemise came off next, though more easily, and soon, it, too, fell away. Without a word, he wadded up both dress and chemise in his hands.

"Quickly," he said, "follow me."

She did, and they crept toward the bushes as fast as possible, half running in squats, half crawling. All the way there, however, Marietta eyed those bushes . . . Yes, they were beautiful; true, they smelled sweet . . . but she feared them. And she wondered which was worse: to die by getting scratched to death by thorns, or to meet the war party?

Clearly, Grey Coyote considered the former the better alternative. But did she?

However, it didn't appear she had a choice.

Having reached the bushes, Grey Coyote turned to her, and beneath his breath, said, "I chose this particular spot for our training because we *can* hide in these bushes. They will conceal us."

Bending down, he pulled up the branches of the rose bushes. Good Lord, there *was* room enough beneath those branches, enough to hide. Odd that she had never realized this about the rose bush. It would be a tight squeeze, true, but they would still fit.

Grey Coyote had shoved his robe up under those bushes, and pulling it out now, he opened it. For a moment, she stared at him aghast.

In anticipation of such an event, he had planned an escape route ahead of time. Her fear of these bushes had been groundless.

However, Grey Coyote was in motion, and pushing her cut-up dress and chemise into the top of the robe first, he turned to her and said, "You must crawl within the buffalo robe and pull it around you like a cocoon. Come, lie down on it, and make sure it is wrapped around you firmly."

"But—"

He interrupted her. "You will then scoot up under the bush with all your might while I will push you. Do you understand?"

She didn't say a word this time, just nodded and did as he instructed.

"One moment," he directed, bending forward to pull the robe up over an exposed spot. "Now go, scoot up as far as you can."

Without another thought passing through her mind, she did as he instructed, using her forearms and every muscle available to her to push herself under that bush. Meanwhile, Grey Coyote assisted by shoving at her.

At once, fragrances of rawhide, all mixed up with roses, dirt and the woodsy scent of bark assailed her, and combined with the scent of her own fear, the smell was distinct. But the one thing that she had dreaded most didn't happen. She wasn't pricked. The robe had cushioned her against it.

At last it was done, but she was yet again surprised when Grey Coyote didn't follow her.

Not only that, she heard him moving away. Instinctively, she called out in a whisper, "Aren't you coming in here with me?"

"I will be back. But first I must erase our tracks from the earth. If I do not return, you are to stay here and keep silent. No matter what happens, you are not to say a word

or indicate in any way that you are here. Do you understand?"

"Yes," she whispered, and the next thing she knew, he
was gone, leaving her alone with her thoughts.

CHAPTER 13

Marietta could hardly recall a time when she had been more frightened; her stomach twisted painfully, and adrenaline pumped into her blood, awakening every nerve and muscle. Tales of horror, of torture and worse, flooded her mind, and she shuddered. Thank goodness Grey Coyote had been insistent about letting the pony go.

To think, if this had occurred yesterday, all might be lost. They had only set the animal free last night.

If she survived this, she promised herself, she would not question the man again. Well, she amended that thought, she would not do so in matters concerning scouting and wandering over the plains . . .

Trying to dampen her thoughts, she waited. And she waited; then she waited some more for Grey Coyote's return. Where was he? Was he safe?

What would she do if he didn't come back to her? She didn't even want to consider the possibility.

Then she heard something—was it the enemy? No, it was the low whisper of a voice, one she recognized. It was Grey Coyote, and he said, "I am here."

Grey Coyote was scrambling into the buffalo robe, scooting and worming his way up to her.

Soon it was done; he was level with her, his head slightly higher than hers, and without another word uttered, he pulled her into his arms.

At once, she was engulfed in the earthy aroma of dirt, sweat and masculinity. Never had anything smelled so acute, so good, and although the two of them weren't safe by any means, Grey Coyote's presence beside her did much to calm her.

She turned her face toward his so that she could whisper in his ear, and she asked, "What do we do from here?"

"No more talk," he murmured. "If you must say something, place my hand over your lips, so I can feel them move. Try also to put all thought from your mind, for if you think too much, an alert scout can sense this."

She nodded, but did so very slightly.

"We will wait here until they are gone," he said. "It could be as long as a day, or as short as a few minutes. But hopefully the war party will pass us by quickly and without notice."

"Yes," she said, settling down, trying to remain as still as possible, while she attempted to think of nothing. However, this last was not an easy thing to do, she discovered.

Suddenly, she heard the enemy. They were riding. However, it wasn't the sound of their horses that she recognized. Not at first. No, it was their whooping and hollering.

There must have been twenty or thirty in their party, she estimated, and they were certainly noisy. What did that mean? she wondered. Didn't Indians usually cross the prairie more quietly?

Either they were very bold, she decided, or they were

within their own territory, giving them a great degree of security. If this be the case, and the enemy were in their own territory, then because she and Grey Coyote were heading south and west, if she remembered her geography correctly, this war party would most likely be either Lakota or Crow.

Interesting that she had arrived at that deduction. Perhaps in the short time period that she had been with Grey Coyote, his manner of thought was starting to influence her.

However, Grey Coyote appeared to need her attention, for he was very slowly inching his hand in toward hers. Reaching for her palm, he took hold of her fingers, brought them directly to his lips, where she *felt* him say, for there was no sound, "Breathe slowly—blank your mind of all thought."

She nodded slightly, then she strove to forget everything.

But it was nearly impossible. Two of the war party had dismounted, had stepped right up to their bush. She could hear them speaking to each other, laughing. And what they did—

Dear Lord. She heard the patter of something wet before she smelled it. The two warriors were clearly answering a call to nature—and unbeknownst to them, they were doing so right near Grey Coyote's buffalo robe.

Grey Coyote placed his hand over her mouth, as though he sensed that she was about to gasp, and he mouthed, "Make no move."

Too frightened to do anything at all, she neither fidgeted nor spoke. Instead she eased into Grey Coyote's embrace, and closing her eyes, she attempted to blank out the immediate environment.

Then came a voice that Marietta had thought she would never hear again. It was a feminine sound, and it scolded and rebuked some unknown source. But though Marietta could little understand the words, she recognized exactly who that person was . . .

It was Yellow Swan, her former maid.

Slowly reaching out for Grey Coyote's fingers, Marietta placed them over her own lips and mouthed, "I know the woman with this party. She is a friend of mine."

Grey Coyote nodded.

"Is she in danger?"

Again, Grey Coyote inclined his head, but slightly. "I understand the words of these people," he said with lips alone. "The woman has been captured, and they are arguing over who will lie with her first."

Marietta's eyes rounded. "They mean to rape her?" she whispered, but she did so without making any noise.

"*Hau*," he answered in the same way. "Unless one of them claims her as his future wife, they will each have a turn with her. But even then, her fate may be sealed."

"That's horrible."

He shrugged minutely. "It is the way of the the warrior and warring parties. Men are killed, women are mated, but if they survive and do not take their own lives, they are later adopted into the tribe."

"You sound as though you approve."

"I do not approve. It is only that it is the way of the warrior."

"Perhaps you may excuse this," mouthed Marietta indignantly, "but I cannot lie here and let this happen to her."

"I understand," Grey Coyote lipped. "I will rescue her."

"No," Marietta uttered softly, making no sound. "*We* will rescue her. After all, she is my friend."

Grey Coyote didn't respond. At least not at first. However, after a brief pause, he mouthed, "It will be dangerous work. We would be required to go into the enemy camp."

"That's why *we* must do it together," she said, though her words still had no sound. "Because it will be perilous, I must try to help. I would be of some assistance to you . . . Wouldn't I?"

"You could be, if you do exactly as I say."

She nodded very slightly. "I feel responsible for her. The truth is that I brought her here. It is possible that she wouldn't even be in this situation now if I hadn't hired her to accompany me."

He nodded, the movement minute, then they spoke no more. And Marietta—though perhaps her ideas might be considered naive—began to envision different rescue strategies.

At the sound of a high-pitched scream, Marietta jumped. But Grey Coyote held her close, soothing her. He murmured in her ear, "We must wait until it is dark, and then we will rescue your friend. Until then, we must do nothing, unless we, too, desire to become victims. And then I fear that we would be of little use to your friend."

Marietta bobbed her head imperceptibly. She did understand, but she didn't like it.

They waited until evening. Sometime during the late hours of the day, Marietta must have drifted off to sleep; she awoke to find herself alone.

For a moment she panicked.

But then, resolving to remain calm, she strove to listen to her environment. Surely there would be a clue as to what might be happening, and as to where Grey Coyote might have gone.

But it was useless. All she could discern was the noise of the babbling brook, which she knew to be no more than a few feet away from her.

Without warning, something grazed her feet and startled her.

Marietta almost let out a scream, but she caught herself at the last minute. Then came a dear voice; she heard Grey Coyote murmur, "It is I."

She sighed deeply and said, though in a whisper, "You scared me."

"I am sorry. *Ito*, come. I am going to pull you out of there. The war party is now at a good distance from us, and it is again safe for us to talk. I have located their scouts, who because of their success, I would assume, have been careless and have left traces of themselves. But none of them are close to us. Now, are you ready to leave your little refuge?"

"Yes," she said.

With one quick jerk, it was done. She was free. She sat up, looked behind her at the rose bush—which, she realized, had been their sanctuary—then threw open the wrap and came up onto her knees. Her attention was on the buffalo robe, however, and without looking at Grey Coyote, she said, "We will have to wash this covering of yours because of those warriors who—"

She looked up and gasped.

"Do not scream."

"B-but you look . . ."

"Like a piece of the earth?"

"Yes."

He grinned at her. "And so will you."

Gazing intently at him, Marietta wasn't certain this was something she wished. Grey Coyote appeared rather scary.

He was coated in clay mixed with tufts of dry grass that stuck out at odd angles all over his body, and he resembled a sort of monster; a monster, however, that did look exactly like moving earth.

But Grey Coyote gave her no chance to contemplate her fate, for he was saying, "*Ito*, we will save your friend. But first, as I do, so must you, too, look like the earth."

Marietta grimaced and said without thinking first, "If I do this to myself—make myself into a sort of earth monster—will you still love me?"

She said it jokingly. However, no sooner had the words been spoken than Marietta grew warm as a flush of emotion stole over her face.

Grinning at her inanely, Grey Coyote said, "I will never stop."

For a moment, Marietta stood as though thunderstruck. Did he love her? Did *she* love him?

No. Impossible. To be in love with this man would be to invite heartache, since love would create its own problems. Were she in love, she would eventually desire to remain here; she knew she would. Her own dreams would be for naught, and might she not forever be haunted by "might have beens"?

Indeed, to her way of thinking, to love this man was a problem.

But she had made beautiful love with Grey Coyote. Could it be that she had feelings for him, deeper feelings than she had at first thought? Perhaps.

But not love.

Still her thoughts were clouded, and Marietta gazed up at Grey Coyote, as though she would query him on the matter. She saw at once that this had been a mistake.

Darn the man, she thought, shaking her head. In addition to the clay covering his body, he wore a brazen smile over his countenance, a look that screamed at her, an expression that said he was aware of each and every one of her considerations.

However, he uttered nothing. Instead, he turned away from her and stepped toward the water.

But Marietta didn't follow him. She stood like one frozen, incapable of doing anything. After a time, however, Grey Coyote glanced over his shoulder, and as though aware of her predicament, he retraced his steps.

Still, he said nothing. Taking her hand in his, he gently led her to the stream.

"How did you manage to leave our little shelter under the rose bushes without my knowledge of it?" Marietta asked a little while later.

Even now, she was avoiding staring directly at Grey Coyote. Mostly, because so profound were her thoughts, it had taken a moment to regain her equilibrium. She resolved to think of more important matters, such as how they were going to survive, for one; how they were going to rescue Yellow Swan, for another.

At present, Marietta was squatted on the ground, reposing next to Grey Coyote, who had settled in a position by the stream. He was answering her question, saying, "I believe I was able to leave without you knowing it, because you sleep soundly."

"Not necessarily."

"Then perhaps," he suggested, "I am skilled in getting in and out of tricky situations."

"It would appear to me that this is more likely the case," she agreed, watching Grey Coyote as he mixed together clay, along with dry, golden grass. Carefully, she avoided watching his hands as he worked. Still, and quite involuntarily, images of what other things those hands could do, and had done, to and with her, came vividly to mind.

She shivered, but it wasn't due to her thoughts. It was because that *muck* he was concocting would be going on her skin. And there didn't seem to be a thing she could do about it.

This thought brought another to mind, a question that was more to the point, and she asked, "How am I to assist you with Yellow Swan's rescue?"

"You will watch the enemy camp for movement or for any sign that they have become aware of me. While I am in their camp, you are to observe closely, and if you see motion, particularly toward me, you are to inform me of it by giving me a signal."

"Ah. What sort of signal?"

"An animal call is what is usually used, but we could also employ the sound of a cricket."

"Oh, I see. I understand," she acknowledged. "In other words, if I see trouble, I will imitate the call of some animal?"

"*Hau.*"

"What sort of cry will we use, then?"

He smiled at her. "I do not know that yet. We will have to see where your talents lie."

"Ah, my talents," she repeated. Then she gazed up at him.

Big mistake. Despite being covered from head to toe in mud, he was gazing at her with a half smile that suggested he was very well aware of exactly where her talents lay.

But she was not going to rise to the bait, and she smiled at him, saying, "If I may suggest it, I have always been told that I have a high voice. Perhaps I could yip like a coyote, for their cry is often high-pitched."

"*Sece*, maybe," he said, returning his attention to the matter at hand. "In the meanwhile, I have brought something for you. A trophy from the enemy camp."

A trophy? What sort of prize would this man likely bring from an enemy camp?

Then it came to her, and she cringed. He hadn't taken a scalp, had he? Somehow the unreality of this, and the possibility that it actually could be, seemed to enforce the fact that she did not, she could not, love this man. They were too different.

But it wasn't a scalp that he'd brought her, after all.

Instead, he set before her three different bows and four assorted sets of quivers full of arrows, plus a knife sheath.

Weapons? Indeed, these were trophies!

Dear Lord, how had he managed to steal these things from under the warrior's nose?

Shaking her head, she smiled up at him. "This is quite a feat, Mr. Coyote."

"Mr. Coyote?" He raised an eyebrow. "How have I managed to slip back to being Mr. Coyote?"

"Never you mind," she replied, but there was humor in her voice. "How were you able to obtain these?"

His look at her became noble, quite grand actually, and as he raised his chin, he said, "All my life I have trained as a scout. I am expected to do these things and more. Besides, these braves are convinced that they are safe because they are in a region that they, themselves, guard. Therefore, they are not as alert as they might be were they in hostile territory."

"I see," she said. "This is truly a great deed. But I have one question."

"*Hau?*"

"Well, since we are determined to save Yellow Swan, and since you were able to steal all these weapons without detection, was it not possible to do something about Yellow Swan as well?"

"That is another good question," he said. "While it is true the enemy feels secure, making them unaware of their environment, they are not careless with their prisoner. In truth, she is very closely watched. Besides, our rescuing her is not as easy to accomplish during the day as it is in the evening. But come, she is faring well now, and these warriors have made their camp not too far from ours. They are celebrating their victory over some enemy—perhaps the woman's husband. But, as I have said, they are not at present on their guard, so they are not alert. That is how I have been able to take and hide many of their weapons. More than these."

"Have you really?"

"*Hau,*" he said. "Their weapons are cached, and the enemy will be embarrassed, indeed, when they reach for their defenses, and none will be there."

"Well, well," Marietta said, grinning at him, "you're a very tricky gent."

It was odd, she thought. Despite his mud-covered appearance, his smile was so handsome, yet so innocent; she found her gaze clinging to his, if only to drink in his splendor. Gradually, she forced herself to look away from him. She said, "What you did was very admirable."

Casting him several surreptitious glances, she could have sworn that he seemed to swell with dignity. All he said, however, was, "Come, we must plan our evening well. Let me tell you what I have been able to ascertain."

"Yes, that would be good."

He nodded. "There is but one guard on duty. I already know where he will be stationed. It is also lucky for us that the warriors have sent their scouts on ahead to their village, perhaps to announce their homecoming. Their scouts, I fear, would have been harder to fool than the warriors themselves."

Marietta inclined her head. Indeed, she thought, if their scouts were anything like this man, they would be very hard to deceive.

"*Ito*, come, we have much to do. And I would ask you to stand now. Part of the plan is to paint you well. I must give it much attention."

"All right," she agreed, though even she could hear the reluctance in her voice. She continued, "Somehow putting mud all over me is not something that appeals to me."

"*Hiya*," he said, "I suppose not. But come, it must be done."

"Yes, all right," she repeated. It was an odd sensation, however, standing before Grey Coyote as she was. In truth, she felt almost naked, and perhaps she had good reason. For she wore only corset, drawers, slippers and hose.

"Ah, that I had more time." He shook his head, reaching out for her and running his hands down her torso. "But we have very little of that, and this must be done right, so let me begin. The first thing I will have to do is to cut off and cache much of these leggings that you wear."

"Leggings? You mean my pantalettes?"

"Is that what you call them? To me they are leggings." He pointed toward them. "But look at how loose they are. *Haiye*, they are too full, and I fear that they will snag if I do not cut them."

"Cut them?"

"And I must cover their color, also. Pure white is not necessarily a common hue on the plains at this time of year."

"But," she said, drawing slightly away from him, "if you cut away my clothes, what will I wear to cover my legs?"

"Clay."

"Clay? That's all?"

He nodded while she sighed. However, perhaps because she had already resigned herself to such a necessity, all she found herself saying was, "It is a good thing that we refer to ourselves as being married. For if we did not, I am afraid I would be required to do something to save my honor. Indeed, were I at home, you would have long ago been slapped quite soundly, I expect."

"*Hokahe.*" He chuckled. "At last you see the advantage in our being married."

Marietta didn't answer him right away. In truth, she couldn't. Something had lodged in and caught in her throat.

Feeling silly for being so emotional, she exhaled, then said, "Do what you must."

And he proceeded to do so. The first cut he made, she drew in her breath.

"You have beautiful legs," he said, caressing her thigh.

"Thank you, but the rule of fashion is that no one is supposed to *see* a woman's legs. A properly dressed woman is not supposed to have *legs*," Marietta recited, as though she were a couturiere for a fashion house. "A woman, once dressed, should appear to *float* as she walks."

"Float?" He grinned.

"That's right."

He shook his head. "It is little wonder, then, that I have found the white woman's style of clothing to be . . . strange."

"It is not strange," she defended. "A woman's legs are supposed to be kept hidden from all but a husband's view."

Grey Coyote chuckled again, good-humoredly. "Perhaps it is good, then, that I am that to you."

Her response was little more than a grimace. "That doesn't make what I am doing right," she said. "Look at me. I might as well be naked."

"I am looking. And I like it."

She rolled her eyes.

"*Haiye,* I understand that you are upset," he said, "but this has to be done."

"I know," she responded. "I know. But it doesn't mean I can't protest."

"*Hiya,*" he said, "you are right. Protest all you like." But he didn't stop what he was doing, and he continued cutting at her drawers, repeating the same procedure to her other leg.

Dear Lord, she thought. Even in her sleep, she wore more than this.

For a moment, if a moment only, the yearning for her own society became almost more than she could bear. But she suppressed the feeling. This she would endure, she promised herself. If only because she had to.

"I am sorry," Grey Coyote said after a moment. "I realize that this is difficult for you, for I am certain you do not wish your form to be this amply displayed. But come, you are being very brave. Now let us be even more courageous."

Again, she sighed.

"However," he said, looking up at her, "there is one thing I feel compelled to say."

"Oh?"

"You are perfect, my wife. Perfect, indeed."

The compliment made her smile, and he returned the gesture, adding, "I thought you should know."

Suddenly, within her, there was a need to do something further than simply stand before him. What she really wanted, what she really needed, were his arms around her, and hers around him. In truth, she leaned in toward him.

As though she had spoken aloud, Grey Coyote answered her need. In a rush, he undressed her completely, and Marietta, standing nude before him, had never felt naughtier, nor so sexy.

Quickly, he washed his hands in the stream, and soon after, his fingers unerringly found their way to and into her femininity. She welcomed him, moving her hips against his touch, desiring more . . . all of him . . .

He said, "I don't believe I have ever witnessed anything so perfect as you. And I don't think I have ever wanted anyone more."

She gasped, then whispered, "Nor I."

They fell into one another's arms, fitting perfectly. Despite having been together for no more than six days, they each one seemed to grasp instinctively what the other required. Perhaps it was because they had made love so often these past few days, or mayhap it was some other source. After all, terrific danger faced them yet this day. Whatever was the cause, every nerve ending she owned screamed at her, and she was ready for him. Now.

And he knew it. Grabbing hold of her bottom, he scooped her up off her feet, holding her against him, and said, "Wrap your legs around me."

She didn't even think to hesitate.

No sooner had she complied, than he was there, pushing himself into her until he was firmly sheathed within her warm folds. Gratification was intense. In truth, she could not recall being pleasured more.

She reached her pinnacle almost at once, and he, coming down to his knees, gently lowered her to the stream's bank, though he, himself, remained kneeling in front of her, as though she were an altar, and he her worshiper. Her legs he placed around his shoulders, and as he thrust into her, once, then again, over and over, she couldn't help but rise up to her pleasure once more.

The ultrasensitive sensation didn't die, either. It went on and on, lasting so long, that in due time, while she was still reeling in the grandeur of it all, she felt him shudder, and she welcomed his final push into her as he spilled his seed.

For a few moments, neither one of them moved, neither said a word. It was as though the experience was too flawless to disturb. Then, rising up slightly above her and looking down into her eyes, he uttered those words that she had little realized she had been longing to hear.

"I love you," he said.

She gasped, but he continued, as though once started, he was compelled to say it all. "My feelings are powerful," he whispered, "my intent toward you earnest. Know that though we must eventually part, I will always love you."

She smiled at him. So great was her joy, especially as it was, coming at the end of such a close moment, that had she been able, she might have returned the sentiment.

But she didn't.

Unfortunately, she couldn't. Though she rejoiced to hear his confession, in truth, she, herself, was still more than a little confused . . .

So much so that her silence seemed somehow deafening.

CHAPTER 14

The shadows of evening were closing in around them, as Grey Coyote carefully covered her body with mud, clay, grass and guck. Already, the air around them was awash with the sounds of insects and the steady howl of the wind. It was scented, too . . . with the sweetness of sage and roses, and was so fragrant, it almost covered up the more balmy smell of dirt and clay, the one that seemed to have permanently lodged inside Marietta's nostrils.

Grey Coyote had been at his task for a while now, his care obvious. However, after a time, it caused her to ask, "My husband, does disguising oneself always take this long to do?"

"*Hiya*, no," he replied. "It is only that I am being very careful, for there should be light and shadow on your body, and my work must match the earth exactly. It is also required that there be tufts of grass placed on you at intermittent spots, so that your disguise alone will keep you invisible. I know it is not easy to stand still for so long a time, for you are unaccustomed to it, but these details are very important."

"But why are they important?"

"It is because I have not yet taught you how to travel like a scout," he said. "Nor do I have the time to do so. So understand, if I do not paint you well, others might see you. And if this happens, it is not your fault. It is mine. An error that I would regret always. But come, I am almost done. I have left your face and hair for last."

Rising up onto his feet, he came to his full height and stared down into her eyes. Bringing up a hand, he ran his fingers gently through her hair, causing her to sway slightly toward him.

"Hmmmm, that feels good," she said.

"*Hau, hau*, it does. But alas, we have not the leisure to do more," he said.

She turned her face into his touch, sighing.

"I have observed," he said, "that you have scars on one of your arms, and your leg. How did you come about them?"

She didn't answer his question at first. Instead, she asked, "Do you think that they are ugly?"

"Not at all," he was quick to say. "Such beautiful perfection should have a little fault." He smiled. "But it appears to me as though you were at some point in your past hurt badly."

"And so I was," she said. "I was thrown from a carriage . . . very long ago, and for a while, I couldn't walk. But I recovered."

He bobbed his head. "But it has also left a scar on your spirit, as well as your body, has it not?"

She bit down hard on her lip. Darn the man. He was so observant that she could not hide body or soul from him.

She said, "My uncle sold me into the service of another."

"Like a slave?"

"Hmmm, somewhat, but not quite a slave. However, I

have thought that the reason my uncle did this to me was because he feared I would be a difficulty to him all my life."

Again, Grey Coyote nodded. "Is this one of the reasons why you are so intent to rush to England?"

She didn't even ask how he had put this all together. The man was perceptive, indeed.

"It is," she said. "Among others."

Again, he shook his head. "I understand," he said. "I do understand. But come, we have work to do."

"Yes," she said. "Let us rescue Yellow Swan from a similar fate."

He grinned. "And so we shall. Now, I have only your face and hair left to paint," he began, "and while I do this, let us discuss what will take place tonight, and the rules that you must follow, the rules that guide the scout. They are few, but are themselves important, so much so, that I must obtain your promise that you will obey these rules."

"Yes, very well," she said. "What are they?"

"The first is this: You must not let others see you; you must do everything you can to avoid this. Next, at all times while we are scouting, you must do exactly as I say. There will be no allowance for argument, and in truth, a disagreement might cause us to be discovered by the enemy. Do you grasp this?"

"Yes."

"You must also say nothing. Scouts communicate through the use of signals and the gestures of sign. Since you do not know these, you must resign yourself to the fact that you will have to keep quiet, unless you are giving me a warning. But we will say more about how you are to alert me in a moment.

"But most of all," he continued, "once I have placed you

into position, you are not to move. As long as you stay still, it will be almost impossible to see you or detect you, because you will look exactly like the landscape."

She nodded.

"*Waste*. Good. Now, the last rule of the scout is that, unless absolutely necessary, we kill no one. We can embarrass the enemy, we can cause them to look silly, stupid, but a scout does not harm those people on whom he spies."

"Really?" This seemed odd to her, and at variance with rumor, and she said, "But I thought Indians—"

He cut her off. "You will be acting as a scout. Unless directly attacked, a scout harms no one."

So firm was his tone, that she knew she dare not dispute him.

"Now," he went on to say, "we will practice what your signal to me will be. Let us start with the cry of the coyote, as you suggested, for it is almost that time of evening when they begin to howl. Here is what they sound like."

He gave several yips, ending in a wail. "Now you try it."

She did, imitating him almost exactly.

He nodded at her, his look pleased. "You are very good," he said.

She beamed. "I have been told that I sing well. Perhaps that is why."

"*Hau, hau*. Now do it again, only this time bark four times before the longer howl." He demonstrated.

Again, she duplicated it, causing him to smile at her. "It is good," he said. "It is very good. I am impressed. Now, listen well. Once we are in the enemy camp, if you see someone coming toward me, and you fear I am unaware of him, you are to give me this signal. Do you understand?"

"Yes."

"Once I have freed your friend and have her within my

grasp, we will leave, but we must not flee their camp in a rush. To do so, would be as to put ourselves at a disadvantage. It is another dictate of the scout: He should be even more careful in departing than he is in coming."

"Very well," she said. "I understand."

"Good. There is one more thing."

"Yes?"

"Even if I leave you for a moment," he said, "you are not to stir until I come for you. I have told you before that you are not to move, but there is more. I must obtain your complete word of honor that you will not budge or try to find me, for I may have to hide your friend, then come back for you. There may be other plans I might make instantly. And I cannot worry about you doing something I have not envisioned."

"I understand."

His eyes narrowed at her. "Ensure that you do. If there is anything that gives you uncertainty, you should ask me now. For once we are in the enemy camp, there is no leeway for error. Even if their warriors begin to spill out of the camp, and they are seeking me, you are not to move. Your inaction in this will be your salvation, for they will not see you, unless they step on you, which is unlikely."

"All right."

But he further added, "Even if I am attacked. Do you agree?"

She hesitated. "Actually," she said, "I think that's expecting a lot. I mean, even if you're attacked? What kind of friend am I if I don't do something?"

"A very good friend, for I am compelled to ask you, how could you, alone, fight off twenty warriors?"

"That's not the point. If you're in danger, I might want to—"

"It *is* the point. I am a scout. I know how to hide, I have been trained all my life to slip in and out of hostile territory, and I would get away. Rest assured that I can do this. But I cannot worry about you, or have my attention on you or what you might try to do. Therefore, I require your promise that you will obey me in all these things."

She exhaled forcefully, though she said, "Very well."

"And you promise? I must hear you promise."

"Fine," she said. "I promise."

He nodded. "Then as soon as I complete the painting of your face, we are ready to go. Almost."

"Almost?"

He nodded. "There is one more thing I am obliged to do."

"Oh? And what is that?"

He kissed her.

She grinned. "Is that what you had to do?"

"*Hau*, plus I am going to make a doll out of grass and buckskin."

"A doll?"

"*Hau*. But I will need to borrow some of your clothing. Will you let me?"

"Of course. But what are you going to do with it?"

"You will see," he said. "You will see."

Her smile at him widened. To her surprise, the danger of what they were about to do seemed . . . thrilling. In truth, excitement coursed through her.

As though he sensed it, he smiled back at her.

Crawling, slithering across the dim moonlight, they spanned the prairie toward the enemy's camp, moving slowly, fluidly, making no sound. But it was very slow going.

Dear Lord, she thought. Did all scouts possess the patience of a saint? It would seem to her as though they must.

With every motion taken forward, Grey Coyote dropped
back to cover their footprints . . . constantly. Because he
was also leading their small party, and because he carried a
large, grass doll on his back, as well as his own and another
bow, the continual need to backtrack soon became tedious
and tiresome.

Marietta was not used to being crouched into a rolled up
position for any length of time, nor was she accustomed to
squatting, for that matter. She soon found her calf muscles
spasming.

But she refused to give in to the impulse to stop, or to
turn around and go back the way she had come. She had
said she would help; she meant to help.

They had probably crawled over a mile or more when at
last they came to a ridge.

Grey Coyote turned to her, brought her hand to his lips,
and formed the words, "The enemy is over that crest. I will
put you in a position so that you can see into their camp.
Scan it, keep alert, but also train your eyes on me."

She gave him one brief nod.

"Over there"—he pointed to the west of the hostile
encampment—"is where your friend is tied and guarded.
When you look for me, watch for earth that moves—that
will most likely be me."

Again, she inclined her head.

Carefully, he guided her into a place slightly lower than
the crest of the ridge, taking much pain with the exact position. Only her eyes and the upper portion of her head
were above it.

At last he seemed satisfied. Briefly, he placed the fingers of one hand over his lips, bringing those same fingers
to her lips.

It was his way of kissing her.

Then he was gone. He had disappeared over the summit of the ridge and was even now slithering down into the enemy camp. For a moment, Marietta watched him, yet so fluidly did he shift over the land, that after a while, considering how the wind blew about the earth and grasses, he literally did disappear.

Nevertheless, she was determined to watch, and every now and again, she thought she caught sight of him, but she was never certain . . .

Grey Coyote left, feeling secure in the knowledge that Little Sunset would be safe. To the naked eye, she would simply look like a rock on the ledge.

Though he was aware that she hadn't liked many of the conditions he had forced on her, he'd had no choice but to procure her promise. A scouting mission was a very dangerous affair; it was not something that allowed for error.

Slowly executing a belly crawl, so that it was without sound, he slid down the slight incline toward the enemy. As he did so, Grey Coyote also recited his plan in his mind.

He would skim around the outer line of the enemy camp, even though this area lay exposed and open to the eye. Because no one would expect an attack from that quarter, their guard's attention would likely be elsewhere.

Inch by slow inch, carefully, Grey Coyote slinked across the ground, edging toward the west, where the woman was held. There was but one sentry posted over her, and this man seemed alert, as though he anticipated an attack.

That this would cause Grey Coyote some difficulty was obvious, since the man would be hard to fool. However, it was not impossible.

Grey Coyote at last crept up behind the guard, and there

he paused for a time, watching the man, observing him to see if there were a pattern in his defense. If there were, that pattern would be the man's weakness.

However, this sentry was alert, and there were no flaws to catch, except for one odd detail: Not once in many moments had the man glanced at the woman he guarded. Indeed, it was almost as though he expected an attack from within the camp.

And maybe he did. Perhaps he had claimed the woman for his own, and this was his way of protecting what he had decided was his.

The woman was tied, hand and foot; she was also asleep, and the guard most likely assumed that she would remain so. Grey Coyote did not make a sound as he slowly crept up to the woman. She was not gagged, so he placed his hand over her mouth to muffle any intake of breath. But this woman was Indian, well-trained to expect the unexpected—as Indian women often were—and she did not cry out. However, her eyes flew wide open.

Grey Coyote touched her on the shoulder, then showing her his face, signaled to her that she was to remain quiet. Slowly, he shook his own hand once to show he was a friend. She inclined her head in understanding, but the movement was very minute.

Carefully, so as not to disturb the air with the telltale evidence of his presence, Grey Coyote gestured toward her, telling her to keep still. Again she answered with the slight bending of her head.

Then came the lengthy process of untying the knots that bound her. Placing his knife in his mouth, Grey Coyote stole toward her feet. The ties were tight and would require much too long to undo. Taking knife in hand, he made one clean slice, and her feet were free.

He crept back up toward her hands. Another cut, and those bonds also dropped away.

She was now free, but in securing their flight, of necessity they would both have to be very careful. At present, the guard was keeping his vigil and had not looked this way, but any sudden movement would send his attention toward them.

With a slow gesture—his right hand moving down under his left—Grey Coyote gave the woman to understand that she was to come with him, and that she was to hide. He had already selected the place for her, a small cave by the canyon's edge. It was hidden from even a trained observer's eye, obscured by no more than a profusion of common rabbitbrush. She would hide while he returned to the camp to wage his own subtle battle with the enemy.

Carefully, as though they had all the time in the world, the woman rose up to a crouch. Luckily, the guard's attention had been drawn toward his comrades' encampment, where a dance had commenced. Whooping and hollering, as well as a steady drum beat, split through the air.

Good. This would do well to cover over any mistakes the woman might make.

Yellow Swan followed Grey Coyote and slipped into the small cave easily. Using hand signals again, Grey Coyote gave her to understand that he would return for her momentarily.

She nodded.

He set off. Slowly, he crept back to where her captors had tied her. Noiselessly, he slipped both doll and one of the bows from across his shoulder. The doll he set on the ground and tied the woman's former bonds to it. In the doll's lap, he placed the bow. Leisurely, he smiled, taking a moment to admire his handiwork.

It was, indeed, a good joke. For when at last this was discovered, the owner of that bow would be blamed. At least it would be so at first. Shortly, however, many of the men would discover that their own weapons were also gone.

Then, and only then, would these men know the shame of being too easily lulled by complacency.

Grey Coyote was beginning his backward exit from the camp, when the guard happened to gaze at the place where the woman should have been. At first the ploy worked, and it looked as if the man saw nothing except what he wanted to see.

But then, his eyes narrowed, and cautiously, he stepped toward the doll.

Grey Coyote froze, lowering himself to the ground. Then gradually, one smooth motion after another, Grey Coyote backed away, slowly covering his tracks as he moved. No panic, he reminded himself. A calm mind would see him out of this camp alive.

Suddenly, the alarm was sounded. Grey Coyote's ruse had been discovered.

The drumming ceased, the whooping stopped, although the night air still rang with the noise; excited warriors, one by one, ran to the place where Yellow Swan had once been tied. Their combined voices contributed to the confusion. However, there was little to do except scold the one whose bow had been stolen. So they took out their frustration in the only way possible—on the doll, attacking it, pulling it apart.

A name was called—probably the name of the owner of that bow, and a few of the enemy hurriedly left to find the man responsible. However, one warrior, a young lad—perhaps a scout in training—spared the doll but a glance.

Instead, his gaze roamed over the immediate area,

searching for what the boy knew had to be close at hand—
a scout. Alas, the lad unsheathed his knife and started toward Grey Coyote.

But Grey Coyote was prepared. He stopped all movement, letting his body become a part of the earth while he
wrapped his fingers around a stone. Quickly, with as little
motion as possible, he threw the rock in an opposite direction from where he lay.

Luckily, the lad was still a novice, and he fell for the
trick, changing his direction.

Grey Coyote, meanwhile, continued his exit, slowly,
methodically backing toward the cave where he had hidden
Yellow Swan. At last, he stumbled back into the cave, certain that for a moment, they were safe.

Outside of this cavern, however, the enemy camp was a
riot of confusion, and Grey Coyote grew concerned. Would
Marietta remain hidden, as she had promised? Or would
she panic?

True, she had given him her word, and he was certain
she would try to keep it. But sometimes things could startle
one, and a person would react involuntarily. It would be
that response that could cost her.

He resolved that he had best see to her at once.

Yet, though anxiousness for her welfare tore at him,
Grey Coyote knew that for himself to panic would create
disaster.

Using the Plains system of hand signs once again, Grey
Coyote gave Yellow Swan to understand that she was to
follow him. Without complaint, she nodded, leaving Grey
Coyote to conclude that she must have desired greatly to
leave the camp.

"You must do exactly as I do," he signed with his hands,
since to speak would be a catastrophe. "Their confusion

and anger will be their weakness. We must use that," he
went on to sign. "Do you understand?"

Again, she nodded.

They left the safety of the cave. On stomach and elbows, they slithered across the moonlit landscape, ignoring
the pandemonium in the enemy encampment.

But he could not lead their party and also erase their
trail. Giving Yellow Swan the sense of the direction they
should take, Grey Coyote followed her, correcting her
course now and again.

It had been a wise thing to center their trail over the
open and defenseless ground. Not one warrior, not even the
lad, thought to check in that direction.

At last, he and Yellow Swan climbed over the crest of
the ridge, where Marietta still lay in wait. She gasped as
they came into view, but he forgave her that—in truth, he
could see the panic in her eyes.

Signing toward Yellow Swan, he gave her to understand the general direction they were to take, and again,
he let her lead their party. Silently, they crept away from
the encampment.

They stole across the prairie, slowly, carefully, cutting a
circuitous path back to the area of the rose bushes. Then, at
last, they trailed into their own little gully. The distance between this and the enemy's location was not as great as it
might be, so Grey Coyote would not permit open talk.
Slow gestures, fingers to one another's lips if necessary, he
cautioned.

However, he couldn't stop Marietta throwing her arms
around Yellow Swan and hugging her, nor could he keep
Marietta from whispering, "It's Marietta, my friend. Remember me?"

"English . . . friend? Save . . ." There were tears in the Indian maiden's eyes.

"Yes," said Marietta. "It's me." And it seemed to Grey Coyote that Marietta almost wept, too.

But he would allow no more talk, and with slow, sweeping gestures, he gave Yellow Swan to understand that she was to disguise herself, much as he and Marietta had already done.

"I will help you to do this," whispered Marietta.

Yellow Swan nodded slowly, and Marietta led her friend to the stream where, only hours ago, a completely different couple had made magnificent love.

Watching them, Grey Coyote wondered if, somehow, the stream would retain their presence . . . forever. Indeed, for him, this spot would always remain sacred.

But enough wasted time. Every moment counted, and Grey Coyote set about making preparations to abandon camp. After all, no matter how unlikely, the enemy might yet possess one amongst them who could track a scout . . .

With a loud bang, the beast, half man, or perhaps half bear, threw the wolf pelts onto the trading post's counter. He grunted.

"What'cha give me fer these here pelts?" growled the beast.

The proprietor, a Mr. LaPrenier, approached the trading post's platform, but he did so with some misgiving. Though he was accustomed to the wild look of the trappers in general, there was something about this particular man that seemed too wild, as though he were more creature than man.

Perhaps it was the brute's smell, or maybe it was his size.

Or mayhap it was the man's clothing. So greased were the beast's garments from wear and use, what had most likely been a buckskin tan color was now an ugly black. Worse, so stiff was the hide of these, from perhaps sweat and other unmentionable things, the clothing looked more like a sheet of metal than that of an animal skin.

Still, LaPrenier was a businessman, and in as friendly a fashion as possible, he came to stand before the beast, the trading post's counter between them.

"Been wolfin'?" asked LaPrenier pleasantly.

The creature didn't answer, simply grunted, showing yellow, crooked teeth.

Carefully, LaPrenier lifted up the skins one by one, setting them out before him. Without appearing to do so, he studied each one before he said, "These is good wolf pelts, *monsieur*," he said. "What do ye have here, thirty-five, forty?"

"What's t' matter with yer? Can't ya count?"

"Of course, *monsieur*. Of course. Is only that the customer usually tells me how many he bring. I trust to their honor."

"Does ya now?" grunted the beast. "In that case thar's fifty pelts here. Thar's right. Fifty."

LaPrenier eyed the trapper warily, and, fearing the man lied, the proprietor commenced to rapidly sort through the merchandise, counting each fur covertly.

As he had thought, there were only thirty-eight pelts. Mentally deducting the difference, he said, "I can give ye one dollar a fur."

The brute snarled unpleasantly. "If'n I take 'em upriver, they'll give me four."

LaPrenier shrugged. "That is all I can give ye. Wolf pelts not in high demand—not like beaver."

The beast grumbled but said nothing.

Then, still of a mind for pleasantries, LaPrenier asked, "Will ye be wanting anything from the store, *monsieur*? We have good assortment of hunting knives, traps, whisky."

"Whisky, coffee, flour, sugar, tobacco," said the beast. "Them things I need fer my outfit. But give me whisky first . . ."

LaPrenier nodded, and turning, reached for a bottle of spirits. "That's five dollar a pint."

"Make that two bottles of whisky, and keep it comin'."

Again LaPrenier turned to do the brute's bidding, but fearing the man—especially under the influence of drink—LaPrenier laced the brew with laudanum. It wasn't long before the beast fell to the floor, sprawled out like a giant bear. But the creature was not so unconscious that what manner of liquid could not be kept down, soon came up.

"Mr. Acme," cried LaPrenier to his partner, who had kept to the back of the store during this exchange. "Come, help me roll this beastie to the water. Mayhap after a bath, we may be able to tolerate his stench. Come, help . . ."

Mr. Acme, braver now that the beast lay asleep, hurried forward to do his duty.

CHAPTER 15

"Husband . . . heap . . . good scout."

Marietta gave Grey Coyote an affectionate glance, as well as a warm smile, even though he wasn't at the moment gazing directly at her. So deeply was he involved in setting up their camp, he took little notice of the two women.

All night the three of them had set their wits against the warriors. By keeping to an irregular path, crawling through bushes and shrubs, and constantly paying attention to erasing their trail from the land, the three of them were still alive.

At last—it was early morning—it appeared as if the enemy had given up, and the three escapees had stopped to set up camp, each enjoying a good bath and scrub.

A narrow coulee would be their home for the day, providing them with shelter as well as a few amenities. Nearby ran a shallow stream that played host to a solitary live cottonwood tree. There were, however, several dead tree stumps scattered over the ground, looking as though they had been lifted up by their roots and thrown about the earth, perhaps in some long ago battle between God and the elements.

There were also several thorny shrubs and bushes that grew close to the water, as well as short bunches of green grass. The walls of the coulee were lined with sandstone, and several of the rocks that were heaped up next to the stream were of this same sandstone. It was near these boulders that Grey Coyote worked, and Marietta could tell that he was taking pains to set up their temporary dwelling so that it would fade into the environment, becoming invisible to all but those who knew it was there.

After a while, Marietta said, "You are right, my friend. Grey Coyote is a good scout, isn't he?"

Yellow Swan held her right hand up, forefinger up. Twisting her hand slightly, she brought that finger down in a flash—Indian sign language for "yes." She said, "Him embarrass enemy . . . warriors all."

"Yes," said Marietta. "And he's teaching me a little about scouting, too."

"Humph!" said Yellow Swan. "Wolf Clan . . . secret . . . hmmm . . . club. Him risk . . . much . . . telling you . . ."

"Does he really? He dares the wrath of his own people by showing me how to scout?"

"Clan of . . . scout . . . secret . . . even to own . . . tribe. Many not . . . know who . . . are. If warriors know . . . how scout . . . track . . . scout not . . . safe. Them keep . . . all secret."

"How very interesting. I didn't know that."

Yellow Swan nodded.

It was still early in the morning, and as yet, the sun hadn't appeared on the horizon. Still, in the east, the sky was starting to come alive in shades of silver-gray and navy-blue. Not a cloud marred the heavens, Marietta noted, and, in her opinion, it was looking to be a beautiful day.

Not that they would see much of it. For all intents and purposes, they would be asleep inside their hidden shelter.

It would be a well-deserved sleep. They had traveled far through the night, and this continuous skulking over the landscape was becoming wearisome.

They had fled over a midnight prairie as though they were lengthy shadows touching the earth. It had been a beautiful night, but Marietta couldn't recall ever being more exhausted.

"Tell me, Yellow Swan," said Marietta as she turned her attention away from Grey Coyote and to her friend. "What happened to you? How did you come to be with that war party?"

Yellow Swan nodded, then began. "When white . . . friend's other . . . husband—"

"Mr. LaCroix was not my husband," Marietta corrected.

"Oh," said Yellow Swan, "that right. It hard . . . for Yellow Swan"—she pointed to herself— "to . . . understand. But I . . . try." She smiled at Marietta. "When white man who act like husband . . ."

Marietta sighed.

"When him lost . . . white woman . . . to him"—Yellow Swan indicated Grey Coyote—"white man . . . took Yellow Swan . . . as wife. Travel far. Go down . . . Big River. One night . . . war party come . . . kill him . . . take me."

"That war party that had captured you—they killed LaCroix?"

"*Han.*" Yellow Swan nodded.

"I'm so sorry. I didn't know."

"It . . . bad   thing . . . but . . . *waste* . . . good," Yellow Swan continued to say. "You go with . . . this . . . scout." Yellow Swan inclined her head toward Grey Coyote.

"White friend—avoid . . . bad . . . things. You go with . . . white man . . . you . . . captured . . . too."

"That's true. I hadn't thought of that. But tell me," Marietta continued, "I never did understand exactly why you were traveling south with me, and I never asked. Were you, by any chance, going that way in order to reunite with your tribe?"

"*Hiya*, no," she said. "Yellow Swan . . . travel south . . . to find . . . own husband. Him gone . . . long time . . . go south . . . get ponies . . . Him gone . . . too long. I go . . . look . . . for him."

"Dear Lord," said Marietta. "I didn't know that was why you had agreed to make this trip with me."

Yellow Swan nodded. "I . . . find him . . . soon. Be . . . happy."

Marietta stared at her friend for several moments, and though she doubted that Yellow Swan would ever find her husband alive, she kept this opinion to herself. Instead, she said, "Then it is good that we rescued you. And since we are proceeding south, perhaps we may find your husband along the way."

"*Han*," said Yellow Swan. "*Sece*, perhaps. White friend . . . good friend."

"I try to be," said Marietta. "I do try."

At that moment, Grey Coyote approached them both. He appeared to have finished his chore, but it seemed that he needed something else. With several hand signals, he instructed Yellow Swan to do something for him. At least it looked that way to Marietta, since Yellow Swan arose and stepped toward the water.

Marietta started to arise and follow in her wake, but Grey Coyote placed his hand over Marietta's, keeping her seated.

Curious, Marietta asked, "What did you tell her?"

"I asked your friend to get us water."

"Oh," said Marietta. "Not that I'm complaining or any-thing, but it would be nice if you would speak in English, so that I could understand you, as well. Otherwise, I feel rather . . . left out."

He nodded. "I will try to correct this," he said, "but per-haps also my wife might think to learn the language of sign, for it is the way all tribes talk to one another."

"Yes," she agreed. "Although"—she cast Grey Coyote a veiled glance— "since I won't be in this country very long, there seems little reason to learn it."

He didn't comment, but his look at her was long and solemn. At length, he said, "I came to beg a moment alone with you."

"Oh?"

He nodded. "Come, I have found something I want to show you."

"Very well," she said, following him up and treading across their camp. He led her to a log that had fallen across the stream, perhaps in ages long past. At least it seemed that it must have been long ago, because in spots, the log was hollowed.

Then, without warning, Grey Coyote squatted down, poked his hand into its trunk, and pulling back, he came away with something . . . alive. A tiny, little masked crea-ture . . .

Marietta gasped. "Is that a baby raccoon?" she asked. Then, "Oh . . . It's adorable." She reached out to touch it. "It's sweet, isn't it?" she asked. "But where's its mother?"

"She is nearby," answered Grey Coyote, "perhaps gath-ering food, or maybe watching us. Her tracks are here." He pointed toward them. "And they are fresh. But the baby does not yet know fear, and she has a few brothers and sisters in this hole with her."

"Oh . . . Can I pet her?" asked Marietta, reaching out for the tiny animal.

Grey Coyote gave her the sweetest of smiles, nodded, and said, "It is why I thought I would show her to you. But we cannot keep her. You know this."

"Of course I do," she said. "But I have never seen a baby raccoon." She returned his grin. "How can you tell it is a girl. I mean, she's so small."

"In the age-old way," he said, pulling up its tail. "She may be small, but it is not impossible to distinguish male from female, even at this young an age."

"I see," she said, bestowing Grey Coyote with a good-natured smile.

At that instant, he laughed with her. But it was more than the gesture of a simple smile. Somehow, in some way, this moment between them was special. It was as though, because of a tiny, little raccoon, they shared an instant unlike any other. Love and affection flowed like a current between them.

She should tell him, she thought. After all, he had confessed his love for her. She should at least admit that she had . . . feelings for him. She took a breath, glanced up at him, opened her mouth . . . but whatever she had meant to say died on her lips.

Behind him, standing at the peak of their little coulee were two coyotes. Seeming neither friendly nor fearful, they appeared rather misty, as though they stood in shadow.

Marietta said, "Mr. Coyote, look there." She indicated the spot with her head.

Grey Coyote turned, nodded slowly, then gazed at her in a curious fashion. Though he said, "You see them," his look at her was puzzled.

"Of course I see them," she said.

Then unexpectedly, the oddest thing happened. The coyotes were howling, yipping, with one answering the other, but there was more. Gradually, so that she was never certain when it happened, their barking turned into talk . . . human talk . . . English . . .

Was she loosing her mind?

"The one you seek is near," said the male coyote. *"Your chance approaches.*

"Neither small nor large, nor wide, nor narrow, the white man possesses a thing that will propel you toward freedom. Though he will think it is possessed by him and though you must possess it, and it will possess you, only when you are free from it, yet act as it, will your people be released from the mist.

You alone must solve this, you alone must act on it, and if you do, your people go free. Fail to settle the riddle satisfactorily, fail to act, and your people remain enslaved. Further, if you err, and do not resolve this, you will live the rest of your life forever knowing that you did not prove yourself worthy."

But there was more.

The female coyote yipped, then spoke, saying, *"Woman, do not be deceived. You are now, and have always been, a part of this.*

Then in unison, they said, *"We have spoken."*

Slowly, the images disappeared, fading, as though they were no more than a mirage. For a long moment, Marietta could neither speak nor look away from the spot where they had been.

But when she shifted her weight from one foot to the other, the spell dissipated. She shook her head. "That was . . . odd."

"Indeed," Grey Coyote responded.

Marietta blinked several times. "I . . . I could have sworn . . . no, it couldn't have been."

Grey Coyote was glancing at her strangely, and he asked, "Couldn't have been?"

"Oh, it was nothing. I just . . . I thought . . . did their howling seem peculiar to you?"

"What do you mean, peculiar?"

"I . . . I . . ." She chortled. "I could vow that they"—she hesitated—"spoke."

Grey Coyote nodded. "Indeed, they did," he said.

"Then I am not mad?"

"You are not mad," Grey Coyote affirmed. "The small wolf is my spirit protector, and often speaks to me in vision. What I find curious is that you heard the coyotes, you saw the coyotes, as well as I."

Slowly, she nodded. "Was that a riddle?" she asked.

"It was."

It all seemed a bit much, and placing her hand on Grey Coyote's arm, she lowered herself to the ground.

"Please, sit with me," she entreated, as she attempted to pull him down beside her. He complied easily enough and came down to squat next to her. She said, "Tell me. Tell me what is going on. What does this mean?"

She watched as different expressions flitted over Grey Coyote's countenance. At last he said, "I hesitate to tell you everything, and yet if you have seen this vision—"

"Was that a vision?"

"*Hau*," he said. "We have shared a vision. This is rare, indeed."

"Yes," she said. "I would assume so."

"In all this time, I have thought that I, alone, must bear this burden, must solve this riddle, but somehow now you are a part of this. I know not how, so I cannot explain your role in this."

"I see," she said, though she was uncertain she really did. She continued, "Tell me what you know. What is this?"

"*Hau, hau.* You will find it difficult to believe. Even my adopted people, the Assiniboine, would think I had been in the sun too long if I were to speak of the entirety of my life, and that which I must accomplish. And the Assiniboine are a spiritual people, given to belief in the mysteries of the universe."

"Yes," she said, repeating herself. "This is why you have never related to me what the deed is that you must accomplish? Because it is fantastic?"

"That is partly true," he confirmed. "But perhaps you might recall that a part of the riddle said that I alone must solve it."

"Yes," she said nodding. "I do recollect that."

He inclined his head. "And so it is that I have believed that to share my problem with anyone—be it you or even a medicine man—would be as to betray my people, not the Assiniboine, but those who are trapped in the mist."

"In the mist? I don't understand."

"Nor should you," he said. "I will explain. The Assiniboine are my adopted people. The people of my birth are of the Blackfoot tribe; they are the Lost Tribe, the people of the mist. Because of a great wrong they committed to the children of the Thunderer, they were cursed by the Creator to live forever in the mist. Their existence is but a half existence, neither dead, nor real. But once in each new generation, a boy is chosen from each band of the tribe. He is charged with the duty to go out into the world, to learn of the environment around him, and to undo the curse, if he

can. This is my purpose. The riddle you heard is my clue.
The man I seek possesses something that should help me
end this spell. And once I find him, to undo this riddle, I
must correctly guess what this thing is that he possesses. I
must act on what I find, and if my deeds are done in the
right way, I will end the curse for my people."

Marietta didn't move, didn't say a word. Of course, it all
made sense now. All his actions, all the things he had done.
It explained much. However, it left her with questions.

"That one coyote, the female, said that I am now a part
of this. Is that true?"

He paused. "It is the first time I have heard that piece of
the riddle. It has never been stated before. I can only tell
you that, for my people, a vision is that which gives a
man—or a woman—purpose, that which shows one what
he must attain to in his life. If you ask me whether or not a
vision shows truth, I can only say that a vision is the Creator's way of communicating to you."

"I see," she said, nodding. "And of course if that is so,
then it would be truth."

"*Hau*," he said. "However," he continued, "I do not
know what part you are to play in this."

"Nor do I," she said. "Nor do I. But I can say that I begin to understand you a little better."

"*Waste*, this is good," he said. "And now I think I can
tell you that the night that I won you in the game of chance,
the wind whispered your name to me. But I didn't put that
name to you until you told me what you are called in English. I knew then that I could not let you leave me. I regret
that I caused you pain."

"Oh," she said, "thank you." But she frowned. "Tell me,
the male coyote stated that the enemy is near, and that the
time to end the curse is at hand."

Grey Coyote bowed his head. "Yes, I, too, have ascertained this, because my dreams of late have been filled with the image of the man whom I seek. It is why I must journey to the trading post as quickly as it is safe to do so."

"Then we should hurry there," she said.

"*Hau*, we will hasten to go there—but we must never forget that we cover the ground as scouts."

"Which means we will go about it very slowly . . ."

"Perhaps," he said. "You should remember that I am also in hostile territory. Come, let us return this tiny raccoon to her brothers and sisters, and then we will rest. If all goes well, we should arrive at the trading post within the next few days."

"This is good," she said, nodding. "But I think you should know that I have not, I cannot give up my plans to return to England. I will help you as best I can. But I, too, have a dream to follow."

He didn't respond, merely looked at her.

And in defense, she said, "Those dreams are all I have."

He nodded, one brief bob of his head. Then turning, he was gone.

Something was not right.

Grey Coyote realized it as soon as he was within a half day's journey of the LaPrenier and Acme Trading Post. There was no noise in the air, no motion, no ever-expanding circles in the atmosphere to indicate movement. Of which there should be.

He frowned. Worse, the closer he came to the locality of the post, the less sound accompanied them. No twittering of birds overhead, no quick rustling of the animals in the undergrowth.

True, the wildlife stayed away from a white man's post as a rule, but the LaPrenier and Acme Trading Post had been here long enough that there should be some hint of animal life. At the very least, Grey Coyote should hear the cooing of doves.

But there was nothing, no sound, save the wind.

It was not a good sign.

At present, the day was only beginning. In the east, though the sun had not yet risen, a pinkish light was slowly advancing toward the earth. Soon, the cloak of darkness would no longer shield them.

The three of them had been winding their way through the night and had come to this place, which was a slight rise in the prairie. On the other side of this hill lay the trading post, a site that usually held many of the white man's unusual provisions.

It was a spot that gave the red man much interest, and he had thought to entertain his wife here. But not today. Grey Coyote could not allow either of the women to go farther, not when he sensed that something was not right.

What he needed was to find shelter for the women, a hiding place. He scanned the prairie in all directions, seeking cover, but saw little except expanding fields of dry, yellow grass. However, he noted there were bushes that surrounded this hill.

It would have to do.

As he searched for the best hiding place, he realized that he must proceed cautiously. Very, very cautiously.

Perhaps it should be noted that a man is not the only creature alive who seeks adventure. Even in a woman's heart, there is a thrill associated with any new undertaking. And

so when Yellow Swan discovered a means by which to
view the trading post—without revealing themselves—
Marietta had pounced on the chance.

True, Grey Coyote had left them here, that he might
scout around the post. He had also disclosed that he suspected foul play, thus the women were to remain con-
cealed. But as long as they were properly hidden . . .

As it was, the shrubs extended around the perimeter of
the hill. If the two women scooted far enough along the
line of bushes, they could position themselves so that they
could see the trading post, without being seen.

Having arrived at one such spot, Marietta gazed out before her. It was quite a small affair, she noted. Little more
than a camp, it had no palisades to ward off attacks, or bastions to defend it. From her location, the place looked as if
it consisted of no more than three log buildings and a
medium-sized corral.

The odd thing was that there was no activity there. None.

At length, Marietta whispered, "It doesn't look to be
much of a going business, does it?"

"Something . . . wrong," said Yellow Swan. "It not . . .
as I remember it. Long ago . . . it . . . cheerful . . . place."

Marietta nodded and stared out at the post from as many
different angles as she could manage without exposing herself. There was no sign of Grey Coyote.

How long would he be gone? she wondered. He had
left hours ago. Still, she reckoned, since he was on a
scouting mission, if he were doing his job well, she
wouldn't see him.

Returning her gaze toward the trading post itself, she
frowned, then said, "I think that you are right, Yellow
Swan. Something about that place is unwelcoming."

"Han."

"I guess we'd better wait here."

Yellow Swan didn't speak, but she bobbed her head briefly. Then the two of them settled in to wait.

Death lived here. Grey Coyote had sensed it, had smelled it.

It must have happened within the last few days, he determined. Otherwise there would be more animal activity in and about the place.

But what had happened?

Slowly, Grey Coyote crept up to and around each of the post's buildings, three in all. The horses were gone; the corral gate hung open with the wind blowing it back and forth.

Grey Coyote examined the parched ground around the corral, trying to piece together what had taken place. A large man, a very large man had been here . . . about three days ago.

Bending down, Grey Coyote examined one of the moccasin prints. The particular shoe, he determined, was made from one piece of rawhide that had one seam that ran from ankle to heel.

These were not Indian prints. These were the white-man-turned-Indian tracks. Those of a trapper.

Was the trapper still here?

Carefully, Grey Coyote listened, sniffing the air, trying to perceive any ever-expanding circles that would indicate motion . . . or life—in any direction.

There was nothing.

Coming down onto hands and knees, Grey Coyote studied the footprints, seeking other signs that would tell the tale of this post. Placing his fingers into the print, Grey Coyote felt it for subtle differences. The man walked like a beast, dragging his feet, he concluded. This would be a big man, overweight, but strong. There was more: The man was irrational . . . perhaps mad. It could be seen in the frenzied pattern of this print.

But what of the two men who ran the post? Where were they?

None of their footprints were here . . . If his guess was right, it indicated that they had never left. Again, Grey Coyote sent out sensory perception, feeling the air for a sign of movement.

But once again, there was nothing. Nothing but the natural motion of nature all around him.

He would have to investigate.

Abandoning the footprints, Grey Coyote crept toward the buildings. Out of the corner of his eye, he caught motion in the bushes next to the hill. A careful observation showed it to be the two women, hiding behind the shrubs. He didn't admonish them. He could understand their curiosity.

With a wave of his arms, Grey Coyote gave them to understand that they were to stay where they were and keep out of sight.

It was Yellow Swan who acknowledged him.

Giving a slight nod, Grey Coyote turned back to the task at hand, and coming around to the entrance of the building, he slipped inside. The stench of death greeted him, and he followed the smell until he found one of the two proprietors.

Slowly, Grey Coyote crept forward toward the body. He recognized the man at once. It was Acme, and he lay face down, sprawled on the floor. Moreover, on his back were several knife wounds. Whatever, or whoever, had killed this man had hacked away at him long after it was necessary.

There had been little struggle, suggesting that the trapper had crept in on the man unaware.

But where was the other trader? The one called LaPrenier?

Once again, Grey Coyote extended his perceptions into every corner of the post. Slinking forward, Grey Coyote stole into an inner sanctum. There was a door, and he guessed that this would be where LaPrenier would be found.

Though he still didn't sense any signs of life, he opened the door carefully. As the entryway flung wide, he at once saw LaPrenier.

The man had been stabbed twice, maybe three times. He lay slumped over a table, and clutched in one hand was a quill.

Had LaPrenier been trying to write something?

Though Grey Coyote was not acquainted with writing, many times he had witnessed his brother-in-law working over papers and books very similar to these.

Taking a few steps forward, Grey Coyote moved LaPrenier's body slightly. Sure enough, the man had written something before his death. But what?

Though he could make no sense of what the marks meant, sitting behind some bushes, out there on the hill, was someone who very likely could.

Moving LaPrenier's corpse farther to the side, Grey Coyote grabbed hold of the book, and placing it under his arm, very carefully slipped away from this place.

"*Ito*, come," Grey Coyote said to the two women as soon as he was within speaking distance. "Let us go back to the far side of the hill, where I originally told you to wait. It is a better location for hiding than this one is. We must talk."

Yellow Swan scooted in the direction he pointed, and Marietta made a move to follow her, but Grey Coyote caught her by the arm.

My wife," he said, "I have need of your talent."

"Me?" She turned back to him, her look slightly puzzled. "What do you mean? What talent?"

Grey Coyote held out the book to her. "Can you tell me what the white man's scratches mean?"

Mystified at first, Marietta stared at the book, then accepted and opened it. At length, she said, "Yes, I can read this writing. Where did you get this?"

"From the spirit of the men who traded at this place," he said.

"Spirit of the men?"

"They are dead. But there is something in this book that drew me to it."

"Oh no," she said, "the men are dead?"

Grey Coyote nodded. "Three days. One man was stabbed many times in the back. One man was stabbed three times. But this man held a quill clutched in his hand, and he had been making white man's writing. Some of the scratches I see are different from the others. I do not know what these mean, but I wonder, did he leave a message?"

"I don't know," Marietta responded. "Let's go back to our hiding place and I'll have a look."

Grey Coyote inclined his head and led her there.

CHAPTER 16

"This is a book of record," said Marietta. "One hundred pounds of beaver pelts at three dollars a pound, two hundred pounds of buffalo robes. It's a journal of their day-to-day business."

Grey Coyote nodded. "But is there anything special about what was written three days ago?"

"I don't know," she said. "Here, let me flip to that page." She turned to the last entry—not a pretty sight. There was dried blood, and Marietta made a slight face. "Do you know why these men were killed?"

"I do not," said Grey Coyote. "I am trying to determine that."

Marietta swallowed hard. "It's not the last entry that is important, but what is written on its adjoining page—here." She pointed. "The man was dying as he wrote this. You can see it from the style of his penmanship."

"*Hau*, yes, this I know. But what does it say?"

" 'The beast,' he writes, 'brought in wolf pelts to trade, got drunk.' "

Marietta stared up at Grey Coyote. "He then writes that

he and his partner drugged the man because they were afraid of him. The beast awoke; he was insane."

She pointed to the writing. "They shot at him, but like a bear, the beast could not be killed. The two partners holed up in the back of their house, hoping the beast would go away, but he didn't."

"These things he wrote before the beast burst in on him. But look, his last entry is a description of this thing he calls the beast: half man, half animal. Long, dark straggly hair. Black beard, mustache. A big man, more bear than human."

"Humph!" said Grey Coyote. "This is familiar."

"Familiar? About the beast?"

"*Hau, hau.* Please read it again."

"Long, dark straggly hair. Black beard . . ."

But Grey Coyote heard no more. It was he, the man that Grey Coyote sought. And he was only three days away. At last, Grey Coyote was on the right path.

Glancing up, Grey Coyote observed that, in the west, storm clouds were accumulating fast. It was hardly surprising. Nor did it astonish him that above him came a rumble of thunder. Indeed, such phenomena were a part of his namesake. These were signs, mere signs.

The chance to end this curse was near . . .

Fort Pierre was designed in a square, with a garden at its southwest section. Much more fortified than the Acme Trading Post, Fort Pierre's main building was surrounded by pickets of large logs that were taller than the fort itself. Bastions jutted out from the fort's northeast and southwest corners, causing Marietta to wonder if there were a reason for such defense.

Was this western land really that dangerous?

Regardless, in her view of it, the fort represented civilization. But instead of the enthusiasm that this thought should have brought, a sense of loss swept over her. Strange.

She, Yellow Swan and Grey Coyote were at present lying on a cliff, overlooking a scene that stretched out over a level expanse of dry, brown prairie. They had traveled there through the night, having burned the trading post to the ground as a burial ceremony.

They had then set their trail to intersect with the beast, following his tracks . . . to this place.

Marietta had to admit that Fort Pierre sat amongst a great deal of beauty. Perhaps two hundred or more graceful Indian lodges were pitched in the fort's vicinity, their aesthetic, conical shapes adorning the landscape. Close to the fort flowed the Missouri River, its muddy currents rushing by at a fast pace. Hills rose up on the western side of the fort, and in the far distance were the hazy, dark shapes of even taller mountains.

Marietta frowned. This, of course, was her chance. There swirled the Missouri River, so near, she could almost reach out and touch it. There lay her ticket to St. Louis. Indeed, at this place she could hire a guide, then follow the river all the way back to St. Louis.

But she was not the same person she had been only a week ago. There were other things to consider now.

Could she leave Grey Coyote? Could she do it when his destiny seemed so close at hand? Moreover, hadn't his vision, and hers, expressed that she should follow him?

But what about England? What about Rosemead, the family estate? Didn't she have her own dream to follow?

After all, if she did not appear in the solicitor's office in a timely manner . . .

Before her adventures with Grey Coyote, Marietta had been fairly certain of what her future might hold were she to survive the journey. And it had been a happy prospect. Could she really disregard it so easily?

However, there was now a another consideration. What if she *did* leave and Grey Coyote didn't end the spell . . . because of her? Would her decision to leave be a source of distress to her for the rest of her life?

Most likely it would be so, which was not a pleasant prospect.

Yet . . . her hopes, her dreams, her duty to her family . . . Truly, in this regard, Marietta stood divided.

Grey Coyote, who reposed on his stomach between Marietta and Yellow Swan, was happily unaware of Marietta's thoughts and had begun to speak, "The Indian camps here—those that are raised around this fort—are of the Teton and Yankton Lakota. And though these tribes are cousins of the Assiniboine, we are at war with them."

Marietta tossed him a quick glance. "Does that mean that it will be difficult to approach the fort?"

"Difficult, it will be," he acknowledged. "But not impossible." Carefully, he turned over, stared up into the sky, and said, "I may find myself dressing in the fashion of the Lakota."

"Dressing like the Lakota?"

"A scout," Grey Coyote said, seeming amused, "must effect many different disguises."

"Ahhh," said Marietta, beaming at him. "That is a very good idea." However, glancing down at herself, she frowned. "But we have a problem, Mr. Coyote," she said.

"Beneath the mud and grass that I have been forced to wear, I am practically naked."

"I know," he acknowledged, a half smile pulling at his lips. "Your lack of dress has been of much inspiration to me."

She shook her head at him. "No, you don't understand. I can't approach the fort or the Indian encampment like this."

"*Hau*, this I understand, and it is too bad that your manner of dress—or rather undress—will have to change," said Grey Coyote. "But, alas, it has to be. Therefore, I think we will pause here while we bathe and change clothing."

"Ah, how I would love to get rid of this mud and clay," said Marietta. "But there is still a problem." She pointed to herself. "I don't have any other clothes. I didn't save so much as a simple chemise."

"*Hokahe*," said Grey Coyote. "Have I not taught you to observe better than that?"

"What do you mean?"

"Have you not noticed how greatly this parfleche bulges?" He pointed to the bag strapped around his shoulder.

"No, I have not, and I . . . You don't mean that you . . ."

He nodded. "I have brought your dress with me."

"You have? Why that's wonderful." Her enthusiasm, however, died quickly, and she said, "Still it's not good. Remember? You cut my clothing off me."

"And can you not repair it?"

"Oh, yes, yes, of course I can," she said. "But is there time? And do we have the materials that I will need, that I might sew?"

"We will take the time. And we have sinew for sewing. Perhaps you could see what you can do to it today. We can rest here while you make the repairs. Then tonight we will find a deserted stream and wash this mud from our bodies so that we might clothe ourselves appropriately. Once done, we may then approach the fort in the early dawn tomorrow morning."

She nodded. "That sounds like a good plan."

"*Hau*, I had hoped that you would like it. Come, let us make a shelter that we might complete our work without worry."

Grey Coyote turned over again, back onto his stomach, and coaxing the women to follow him, they scooted down from their overlook.

The sun hadn't yet put in an appearance on this bright, new day, when a party of three stepped toward the fort's gate. Two of the group were Indian, a man and woman. The third was a white woman.

Perhaps it was because of this woman that the three presented such an unusual sight. Maybe, too, it was their "new" clothes that seemed to cause speculation.

Somewhere, somehow during the night, Grey Coyote had managed to count *coup* on some Lakota clothing, as well as a few trinkets from the surrounding Indian camp. It was a good masquerade they had effected, for Grey Coyote had not only donned the clothes of the Lakota, he had parted his hair down the middle so as to reflect the appearance of that tribe in every way possible. Yellow Swan had done much the same.

Thus, the three of them had walked safely through the Indian encampment toward the fort. There had been curious stares, yes, but they had arrived at the gate with impunity.

"Who goes there?" called the gatekeeper after they had asked for admittance.

"You must answer for us," whispered Grey Coyote.

Nodding, Marietta at once called out, "I am Maria Marietta Welsford, an English lady. I have arrived here with the two Indians you see beside me. They have seen fit to accompany me here."

"Yer a white woman?"

Marietta didn't reply at once. Instead, she said, "Have you no eyes, man?"

"What'cha waiting fer?" came another male voice from over the wall. "Are ye blind? Open the gate."

"But a white woman? Here? It's hard ta—"

"I was traveling with a party from Europe," Marietta interrupted, "but I became lost from them," she added. "These Indians found me and have brought me here."

No reply followed this. However, the gate slowly swung open, and after a few moments of hesitation, Marietta stepped into the inner sanctum of the place called Fort Pierre, followed first by Grey Coyote, and then by Yellow Swan.

On her left and right, she was greeted by the sight of rows and rows of log houses, though directly in front of her stood a larger, more magnificent home, with a smaller building to its right. No grass grew here, she noted. It was all dirt, though there was an American flag raised on a pole, which waved at them from the center of the parade ground.

There, however, the pleasantries ended. Far from being the refreshing scene that Marietta had envisioned upon her return to civilization, she cringed.

There wasn't a single head that wasn't turned her way. Moreover, men of all sorts and sizes were rushing at her from every possible direction of the fort. Some were pulling on pants as they ran, others shirts and coats.

All shared one common trait. They gaped at her. None approached her, however.

Doubtfully, Marietta said to those who had assembled, "Is there anyone at this post who can help me? As I have already said, I became lost from my party, and these Indians found me and brought me here. But I search for a man . . . a trapper. I need to speak to someone."

No one answered her. In truth, it was as if the shock of her presence had momentarily startled them out of speech.

At last, a short, balding man came rushing toward her. From his waistcoat and vest, to his brisk, no-nonsense manner, Marietta fathomed at once that this man was most likely a clerk.

He said, "The bourgeois, Mr. Laidlaw, has requested I bring you to him, miss. Follow me."

"Yes, thank you, Mister . . . ?"

"Smith," said the man.

"Thank you, Mr. Smith," said Marietta.

Mr. Smith spared a glance over his shoulder and smiled at Marietta. But espying the Indians, he said, "The Injuns cannot come with you, Miss . . . what did you say your last name was?"

"Welsford," replied Marietta. "And it is Lady Welsford, sir. But there is a problem."

"A problem?"

"Yes, you see, Mr. Smith, these Indians are with me. I would ask that they be allowed to accompany me everywhere I go. Mr. Coyote, here, saved my life."

"Saved your life, did he?"

"That's correct, sir, he did," said Marietta. "Surely in light of that, you might understand my position on this matter. Besides, Yellow Swan is my maid, and I will require her attention."

"Well . . ." the man hesitated, "all right. Just this once I reckon we can forgo the rules. Follow me."

Marietta, picking up her skirt, prepared to do exactly that. Ignoring the stares from all around her, she and her party paraded across the grounds to the house of William Laidlaw, Fort Pierre's bourgeois, a title that, in this land and at this time, was much like a king.

"That was lovely, Mr. Laidlaw," said Marietta, patting her lips with a white linen napkin. Sitting forward in the dining chair, she continued, saying, "It has been a long while since I have been treated to real butter and cream. I assume this comes to the table via that large herd of cows I saw when I first approached the fort."

"That it does, lass," said Laidlaw, a fair-headed Scotsman who seemed to favor long sideburns and whiskers. "That is does."

Marietta nodded, and Laidlaw continued, saying, "Now tell me, lass, what has happened to ye? How have ye come to be here in these western plains?"

Marietta placed both hands in her lap, paused briefly, and said, "I traveled here originally with members of royalty, led by Princess Sierra, heir to the throne of Baden-Baden. There was a fire aboard our steamship, the *Diana*, and I became parted from the princess."

"Terrible things, those ships," said Laidlaw. "'Tis a wonder ye are here in one piece, lass, for 'tis a savage land, these western plains."

"True," said Marietta, "yet this land is also a country of beauty."

Laidlaw frowned but appeared to have nothing of import to add to this last comment. Instead, after a moment, he said, "Come, ye are safe now. Whatever ordeal ye suffered is over."

"Thank you, Mr. Laidlaw. I appreciate your kind words." Marietta lapsed into silence, then said, "However, I have need to ask you for information, if I might. I search for someone, a man."

"Do ye, lass?"

"Yes, sir," she replied. "He is rather beastly. Of large frame and ill-temper, he is of haggard appearance, long, dark hair, beard and mustache. Have you knowledge of this man?"

"And why would ye be lookin' for him?"

"It is . . ." Marietta hesitated. "It is personal, sir, but of one thing I can say. We suspect that this . . . beast has killed many people."

"We?"

"Mr. Coyote, Yellow Swan and myself."

"Ah," said Laidlaw. "The Indians."

"Yes, sir. The Indians. The Indian gentleman saved my life. The woman is my maid."

"Troubling company, ye be keepin', lass . . ."

Marietta placed her napkin beside her plate—an item that was made of the finest china. Trembling slightly, she thrust out her chin and said, "Forgive me, Mr. Laidlaw, if I seem impertinent. Though I understand your house rules, and though I respect your right to entertain whomever you choose in your own home, I do not agree with you on the subject of Indian character. I have found Mr. Coyote and Yellow Swan to be true friends. In fact, I would not be here now were it not for Mr. Coyote. And I am disheartened that he must wait outside whilst you entertain me with breakfast."

"A necessary precaution, lass. Very necessary here in a fort like this."

"Perhaps so, and I do not mean to tell you your business," she said. "But I am disappointed."

Laidlaw responded with no more than a severe look in her direction, and Marietta decided it might be best to change the topic of conversation. She said, "Perhaps we should discuss the matter at hand, sir. Have you knowledge of the man I seek?"

Laidlaw drew his brows together in a frown. He said, "I must ask ye again, lass. Why do ye search for him?"

Marietta set her glance to Laidlaw's, staring straight into his hazel eyes. Could she trust this Scotsman? Perhaps. But dare she chance it? She asked, playing for time, "Do you want the truth, or a lesser version of what has happened?"

"I'll take the truth, if ye please."

"Very well," said Marietta, biting down on her lip. "I have . . . lost a family heirloom, sir, and I have reason to believe that this man either has it or has knowledge of where I might find it."

Laidlaw raised his brow, squinting at Marietta. "An heirloom?"

"Yes, sir."

"And what is this heirloom, lass?"

"A . . . a . . ." Marietta—who rarely had cause to tell great fibs—glanced quickly around the table, her gaze alighting on a diamond-and-gold napkin holder. "A brooch, sir," she said.

"A mere brooch?" Laidlaw frowned.

"It is an uncommon one, Mr. Laidlaw. It is"—she hesitated—"made of gold and . . . diamonds." She smiled.

"It must be an uncommon one, for certain," said Laidlaw, "if it brings you here in search of it."

Marietta gulped, glanced down at her lap, and said, "It is all that I have left of my family, sir." Amazed at her audacious behavior, she drew a deep breath and continued, "This man either has my brooch or knows where it is. And so you see, I have great need to find him."

"I understand," said Laidlaw. "Then ye dunna seek him to take his life?"

"No, sir, I don't," said Marietta, "although I am not certain that he doesn't deserve to die. We believe that he killed the bourgeois and company at the LaPrenier and Acme Trading Post."

"LaPrenier and Acme are dead?"

"Yes, sir," said Marietta. Reaching down beside her chair, she took one of the parfleche bags that she carried, and pulling it up, extracted from it the LaPrenier and Acme Post's journal. Opening it to the last entry, she handed it to Laidlaw. "This was Mr. LaPrenier's last words. As you can see, I believe this beast killed him."

Several minutes passed as Laidlaw examined the book. After a while, he said, "So it would seem . . . so it would seem. But come, lass." Laidlaw gazed up at Marietta. "This be something for the likes of me to handle, not a young woman."

Marietta smiled. "Yes, sir. However, I still seek the man. After all, it is my family heirloom that is in his possession, I believe, and I would have it back."

Laidlaw nodded. "I hear ye, lass. I hear ye. But how did ye lose such a fine possession?"

"I"—Marietta thought fast—"had it in my possession at one of the Indian villages. I went to sleep with it within my grasp, but when I awoke, it was gone. Others say this man was seen leaving, and in his possession was my brooch."

Laidlaw nodded. "Fair enough," he said. "But lass, I think now I'll be needin' to know how ye came to be in such bad company that ye be sleeping in Indian villages."

"Bad company?"

"Aye, lass. How is it that ye came to be travelin' with the Indian and his squaw?"

His squaw? Oh, yes, Laidlaw was referring to Yellow Swan, of course.

But Laidlaw was continuing, ". . . and what have these two to do with yer adventure?"

Marietta cleared her throat. "As I mentioned earlier," she said, "they found me when I was separated from my mistress."

"And what have these two to do with your brooch?"

Marietta swallowed. "Why nothing, sir. They merely escorted me here."

"Nothing, ye say? And yet I know that an Injun never does anything 'lessen there's somethin' in it for himself. What is it ye've offered that young fellow? And don't tell me nothing, for I know them well."

Marietta gulped, at a loss for words. Had she been found out in her lie so soon? She said, "I don't know what to tell you, sir. I have not much to offer him."

"Then the Injun wouldna have followed ye here. Come, now, lass."

She sighed dramatically. "Very well," she said, as though resigned, "you have found me out. And I suppose I must tell you the truth. In return for his escort to St. Louis, I have promised him my favor, sir, though I do not intend to keep that promise."

Laidlaw paused, then laughed heartily. "Ah, lass, ye are a smart one. Now *that* I understand. And think nothin' of it, lass. Ye did what ye had to do. We all must lie sometime."

Yes, we must, thought Marietta, who was keeping her gaze carefully trained on the floor.

"Now," said Laidlaw, "let us talk about more pleasant matters."

Marietta smiled faintly.

"While ye are at Fort Pierre," continued Laidlaw, "I insist that ye stay here in this house. It will give ye more comfort. I'll send for—"

"But about this man that I seek, sir?" Marietta interrupted. "Have you knowledge of this man, the beast?"

"The truth is, lass, that I do. But I dunna want ye worrin' about him. I will send out one of my own men to find him and bring him in. Will that set your mind at ease, now?"

"It most certainly would, sir."

"That's fine then, lass. That's fine. Now, I will have one of my Indian maids make up a room for you."

"Thank you very much, sir. That is kind of you."

Laidlaw bunched up his own linen napkin and threw it on his plate. He said, "Now, if ye will excuse me, lass, I have work to do."

"Yes, Mr. Laidlaw. But I have one more question, sir."

"Aye? And what be that?"

"It concerns the Indian, sir. I am thankful that you are giving myself and my maid lodging. But what about Mr. Coyote? Though he be troublesome, and though I have confessed my duplicity in his regard, the man has, on several occasions, saved my life. Have you nowhere to house him?"

Laidlaw frowned and raised an eyebrow, giving her a considering look. He said, "I dare say that the Indian can take care of himself, lass. He can stay with the other Indians gathered round the fort."

"But that's where you are wrong, sir," said Marietta. "He cannot remain with those people."

"I beg your pardon?"

"He cannot be sent to those Indians, sir. I realize that he looks Lakota, but he is, in reality, an Assiniboine Indian, and as you know, those tribes are at war."

Laidlaw raised *both* eyebrows. He said, "And of course he saved your life."

"Yes, sir," said Marietta, "several times. I would be much beholden if you could arrange quarters for him, here within the fort. It might save his life."

Laidlaw frowned at her. "Ye seem a right too concerned about this man. Are ye tellin' me the truth?"

Marietta felt the blood rush to her face. "The truth?"

"Ye dunna intend to keep your promise to that Indian, do ye, lass?"

"No, sir, I don't, but," she hesitated, "when someone does a person a favor, it is customary to return it. He may be Indian, but I owe him much. Perhaps not what I have promised, as you say. But much."

Laidlaw nodded. "It is a fine quality ye possess, lass, to worry about another. Dunna fret. It will be done. I will give him quarter."

And Marietta, catching the bourgeois's glance, smiled.

CHAPTER 17

An accordion and a banjo accompanied the dancers. The traders, dressed in their very best, were lined up, one after the other, each awaiting a chance to claim a dance with the newest person to their post, Marietta. In a corner of the same room, several other men were engaged in a game of cards, while another few were engrossed over a chess match. On the dance floor were several dancers, engagés and their Indian wives. One, however, was Marietta, who was stepping around the dance floor in the arms of one of the traders.

It was evening now, but earlier in the day Marietta had extracted some gold from her purse and had bought a ream of green satin from the trader's store, as well as some cotton fabric. These had gone to make a new dress, chemise, petticoats, and drawers. Plus, she had purchased a brand-new corset. In truth, she was astonished at the riches contained at this post, and it had been a pleasure to shop at the storehouse. She and Yellow Swan had spent the day making the dress that Marietta wore this very evening.

Grey Coyote was not in attendance, since it was being held in the house of the bourgeois, who dictated a firm rule that no Indian could ever be admitted. In truth, since arriving at Fort Pierre, only two days ago, Marietta had neither seen nor heard from Grey Coyote.

Mr. Laidlaw had informed her that Grey Coyote had been given a bed with the engagés but Marietta had not been able to confirm this as true.

At best, she suspected that Grey Coyote wasn't here, that being a scout, he had found a way to leave the fort as easily as he entered it. Perhaps he had gone on to find the trail of the man he sought, leaving Marietta safe behind the walls of the fort.

But this thought caused her to brood. Did she *want* to be safe behind these walls? In truth, the more she contemplated it, the more she realized that she longed to be out there on the prairie, with Grey Coyote, instead of stuck in here like a much-cherished pet.

Besides, wasn't she a part of that vision? Didn't she have a right to accompany Grey Coyote? Indeed, it was fast becoming her consideration that Grey Coyote was being insensitive . . . if only by excluding her. The more she turned over the thought, the stronger the feeling became.

At last, the music ended. As the musicians debated over their next song, Marietta took advantage of the break to disengage herself from the gentleman with whom she had been dancing. She smiled up at the man and said, "I thank you for the dance, sir."

The man was not a particularly handsome fellow, but he seemed kindly enough when he asked, "May I get you anything, Miss Welsford?"

Marietta immediately responded, saying, "Yes, if you please. A glass of water would be most welcome."

"Yes, ma'am," he said. "I'll get it at once."

"Thank you," said Marietta, and the gentleman departed. Briefly, Marietta waved a handkerchief in front of her face, trying without much success to dispel the cologne that the man wore. It was odd, she thought, that the men at this post wore so many scents.

Perhaps, she thought, it was to cover their body odor, which unfortunately seemed an almost impossible task. Though she knew daily bathing was not part of the American way of life, she couldn't help comparing these men unfavorably with Grey Coyote, who seemed to relish his early-morning bath.

"May I have this next dance, Miss Welsford?"

Marietta smiled up at the next trader. "Yes, that would be nice," she answered, "though someone is bringing me a glass of water. Could we wait until I've had some refreshment?"

"Of course," said the man gently. "Should I go and find him? Perhaps hurry him?"

"Yes," agreed Marietta. "That would be most welcome."

With a stiff bow, the man departed, leaving Marietta alone for the first time all evening. She truly did wish for that glass of water, however. Since she hadn't sat down all evening, she had worked up a bit of perspiration.

"Here we are, Miss Welsford," said the gentleman, at last returning with her drink.

Marietta spun around on her seat, and taking the glass in hand, she said, "I thank you kindly, sir."

"My pleasure, Miss Welsford. Is there anything else I can do for you?"

Gazing wistfully out the open window, Marietta said, "I would love to take in some air. I am afraid I have been dancing for the past hour, and some fresh air might do me good."

"Very well," said the man. "I can accompany you, miss."

"Yes," agreed Marietta, offering the gentleman her gloved hand. "I would like that, Mister . . . ?"

"Adams, miss. Allen Adams."

She nodded, and ignoring the pointed looks from the others, Marietta left the house on the arm of Mr. Adams.

Once outside, she inhaled deeply, and gazing up at the sky, immediately located the Big Dipper, which of course led her gaze toward the North Star. Briefly, she recalled Grey Coyote's instructions about direction and she smiled.

Odd, how she missed the out-of-doors. Though the bourgeois's house was nice, she felt strangely stifled. But here she seemed to feel . . . at home . . .

The man at her side broke the silence and spoke, saying, "It is a beautiful night, isn't it?"

"That it is," she agreed. "Listen," she said, frowning, and lowering her voice. "Something is wrong, Mr. Adams. Do you hear that?"

"What, miss?"

"The quiet."

"I don't understand, miss. Hear the quiet?"

"Yes," she said. "These past few nights have been filled with noise—the Indian drumming and singing from the camps. It's gone on all night. But not tonight. Listen. There's not a wolf howling, nor even a nighthawk squawking. It's quiet. Too quiet." She turned to the man. "Do you know the cause?"

"No, ma'am, I don't."

"But you should, Mr. Adams," she said. "There should be sounds. Indians, nightlife. Something." She glanced around the deserted courtyard. "Sir, could I beg a favor of you?"

"Yes, miss. Anything."

"Could you please return inside and inform the bourgeois that I fear something is wrong?"

"But—"

"Please?"

"Of course, Miss. I will do so at once."

"Thank you. It will set my mind at ease."

After exchanging a polite smile, the man turned to do her bidding.

Again, Marietta inhaled deeply. Ah, how good the night air felt in her lungs.

"The Indians have broken camp," said a low voice behind her, as Grey Coyote stepped out of the shadows. "That is why it is so silent, for the animals have run away at their approach."

The wind rushed into her face, yet she turned quickly, and without preamble, she said, "Where have you been?"

"Looking for the man we seek."

"And have you found his trail?"

"I have."

"Good," she said. "Good. When do we leave?"

Grey Coyote paused. "Then you are ready to go?"

"Of course I'm ready to go. Why wouldn't I be ready to go? The sooner we get this thing over with, the sooner I can depart for England."

He shrugged. "I had feared that perhaps the lure of your own civilization might be too much, that you would not wish to travel again. At least not as a scout."

Marietta jerked her head sideways. "Then you feared incorrectly. I said I would help. I will help."

He grinned at her, and reaching forward, ran the back of his fingers over her cheek. Fleetingly, she closed her eyes, leaning into his touch. It felt so good.

She said, "I have missed you."

He nodded. "I, too, have missed you."

Music from the house filtered out over the courtyard, softening the atmosphere, and Marietta swayed to the rhythm. She said, "I have been dancing all night."

"I know," he replied. "I have been watching you."

"Have you?" She grinned up at him. "Why?"

He smiled back at her. "I think that I find you beautiful. Perhaps that is the reason. Maybe also I am a little jealous of these men who have the honor of holding you in their arms, when I can only stand in the shadows and observe."

"Well," she said, "that can be remedied immediately."

He raised a quizzical eyebrow.

"Do you dance, Mr Coyote?"

"Certainly, I dance. I have danced since I have been able to walk."

"Ah yes, of course," she said. "But can you dance the white man's dance?"

"I have done so in the past. You forget that my brother-in-law runs a trading post."

"Yes, yes. I should have remembered. But which dance do you do, Mr. Coyote?"

His glance at her was surprised. "There is more than one?"

"Undoubtedly, there is more than one. This one they're playing now is a waltz. Do you waltz, Mr. Coyote?"

"I can try," he said, stepping toward her and taking her outstretched hand in his own. "Will you teach me?"

"It would be my pleasure, Mr. Coyote." Grinning up at him, she fell into his arms.

It was heavenly to touch him, to be touched by him, and he danced as though he had been born to it, keeping time to the three-quarter beat as easily as if he were walking. The moonlight shone down on them tenderly, silhouetting them against the shadows of the night.

What was it about moonlight that cast this man in such a handsome image? He had braided his hair tonight, she noted. It was the first time she had seen him with it thus, for he usually left the length of it long and unbound, and more recently, he had fixed it with clay all through it.

Dear Lord, she thought, he was probably the handsomest man she knew.

As they twirled round the shadows of the parade grounds, it was as though this place were their own private haven. Glancing up at him, smiling up at him, watching him, Marietta spun into a self-evident truth that she should have admitted to herself long ago.

She loved this man.

She had probably loved him for quite a while now. She had suspected it days ago, but she hadn't been willing to acknowledge it . . . not until now.

Lord help her, she felt compelled to ensure that he knew it, so she said, "Mr. Coyote, I have a confession to make."

"Do you?" he replied. "And what is that?"

"Mr. Coyote, I am in love with you."

His smile was pure admiration directed toward her, and he said, "I know."

"You know?"

"*Hau.*"

"How do you know?"

"Because of who you are," he said. "You permit me liberties. And you are not the sort of woman to do that without having love in your heart."

She chortled, half laugh, half sigh. She said, "I guess there's no fooling a scout, is there?"

"One can try," he acknowledged, with a grin.

Shaking her head at him, she inquired, "When do we leave to find this man?"

"Tonight," he replied. "Prepare Yellow Swan, and we

will quit the fort as soon as the others here are settled in for the night. I will slip into your room for you."

"Can you do that?"

He simply smiled at her.

"If you can do that, you should have come to me each night, Mr. Coyote. I have a bed. Do you understand? I have a *bed*. We could have made love on a bed."

"And alerted the household to what is between us," he completed the thought. "Have you not noticed that the bourgeois of this place does not think well of the Indian? Beware, my wife, the bourgeois here is not a stupid man. As it is, even dancing as we are, I fear we flaunt the customs of this place. He watches us even now."

"Does he? Where?"

"From the veranda." Grey Coyote nodded toward it.

"Very well," she said, as they stepped around their dance floor of dirt and rocks. "I will say no more on it. But I will also be ready to leave with you this night."

"That is good, but be very careful. It is possible you will be watched."

"I will be careful."

"Good." He grinned at her. And she couldn't help herself. She beamed right back.

William Laidlaw stepped onto the veranda for a breath of air and a smoke. Striking a match, he cupped his hands around the flame, leaning his cigar down into the glow. That was when he detected movement to his right, in front of the clerk's house.

Glancing that way, he looked, not certain about what it was he was seeing. He gazed that way again.

Good Lord. What was this?

It was the lady, Marietta, and the Indian . . . whatever his name was . . . They were dancing, smiling and speaking to each other as though they were of long acquaintance. Though Laidlaw understood that the two were, indeed, of some association, it did not also follow that they had a right to fraternize. Not in *his* fort.

This fort was not a republic, though he knew the surrounding country considered it such. Fort Pierre was his domain, his kingdom, and he the king of all he surveyed. Nothing happened here without his approval.

The Indian was clearly overstepping his bounds.

And what was the lass doing, dancing with the savage? Allowing him to touch her?

It was possible, he supposed, that Miss Marietta felt beholden to the Indian—if the man had saved her life as she said. But even if this were the case, Laidlaw could little understand her actions, unless . . .

Had the Indian already lain with the maid?

Aye, it had to be. Look at them.

The thought made him burn. An Indian with a white woman? Why, this was a crime; an example would have to be made.

He would hang. Truly, the Indian would hang.

"Where ye goin', man?" asked Laidlaw.

"Oh, pardon, sir, I didn't see you there, and I have been looking for you."

Laidlaw nodded. "What is it ye need, Adams?"

"I have a request from the lady, sir."

"A request?"

"Yes, sir. She fears there is something wrong, because it is too quiet. She has asked me to tell you this."

Again, Laidlaw nodded. He said, "There is a great deal

wrong, but 'tis not because 'tis quiet. Gaze out yonder, man." He pointed.

Adams did so and inquired, "That is the Indian that brought Miss Welsford to the fort, is it not?"

"That it be, Adams. That it be." Laidlaw rubbed his chin. "But I fear the lady is confused."

"Sir?"

"Look at them, Adams. They be too familiar."

However, Adams, a clerk for the company, was not to be so easily persuaded. He said, "But it's only natural that they should speak to one another. I would think they would have been together many days, sir. After all, 'tis not an easy trek they undertook."

"Aye," said Laidlaw. "Aye. But I think the lady needs reminding of who she is. She has asked me about boats to St. Louis. It seems she has great need of traveling there."

"But, sir," said Adams, "there are no steamboats going that way for another year."

"Aye," said Laidlaw. "That is why I think that yerself and a few other men should accompany the lady by canoe, or perhaps by mackinaw, to St. Louis. Mayhap along the way, she will remember who she be, and perhaps also she might recall the rules of privilege that she was born to."

Adams nodded. "When would you like us to accompany the lady?"

"Tonight, I think," said Laidlaw. "After the party. Take her maid, as well. Do ye think ye can accomplish it?"

"Yes, sir. Where does she stay, sir?"

"The last room on the north side of my home. Take her clothes. Do it up well so that she is not overly taxed. But take her. Tonight."

"It will be done," said Adams. "And what 'bout the Indian?"

"Kill him, and hang him from the nearest post."

"Aye, sir."

"An example must be set."

"Aye, sir."

"Oh, and Adams, take whatever supplies ye need from the general store. Charge it to the Company."

"Aye, sir," said Adams, and with nothing more to say, but a great deal to do, Adams turned and stepped away from Laidlaw, heading in the direction of the warehouse.

CHAPTER 18

Marietta was sitting up and awake, awaiting Grey Coyote, when the four men burst into her room.

She screamed. Yellow Swan screamed. Marietta kept screaming.

Fiercely, two of the men gagged the women, effectively silencing them. One of the brutes threw a sheet over Marietta, wrapping her in it, then tying it with a belt. She kicked out at her assailant, but very quickly her feet were bound, as well.

What was going on? This couldn't be the work of Grey Coyote. He would never approve such manhandling. Soon, however, the smell of tobacco and rum gave away the identity of the men.

They were white men. But that knowledge only confused her more. White men? Treating her as if she were a common criminal?

"Got her?" one of the men asked.

"Yep," came the reply. "Got the Injun, too."

"Then c'mon. Let's get 'em to the mackinaw. Adams has it tied up and waiting on the river."

"They're goin' by mackinaw?"

"Fastest, cheapest way. Better than a canoe."

Marietta listened to the conversation. What was amazing, she thought, and perhaps telling, was that none of these men were disguising their voices. No low whispers. No attempt at secrecy.

The bourgeois knows, she realized, and he approved—likely he gave instruction for this act.

One of the men hoisted her up over his shoulder, the action interrupting her thoughts. He said to some unknown source, "Did'cha kill the Injun?"

"Nope," came another voice. "Not yet. Couldna' find him."

Kill the Indian? Were they speaking of Grey Coyote?

"Well, find him, man," said the one carrying her. "If ye dunna kill the savage, chances are he'll come after these two women. Especially if he considers 'em both his squaws. Don't know 'bout ye, but I dunna want to meet up with some warrior out to save his women. Don't think any of our scalps would be safe."

"Ye'll be safe enough," said another unknown voice. "Four against one?"

Would they? wondered Marietta. She wasn't so certain.

Briefly, she said a prayer of thanks. *Thank the Lord they couldn't find him. In truth, they would probably never find him.* Chances were, he had probably sensed the presence of the men seeking him long before they had ever come close to him.

But what had happened? Why was this occurring? And why now?

As though in answer to her question, Grey Coyote's words from earlier this evening came to mind, haunting her. *"As it is, even dancing as we are, I fear we flaunt the customs of this place. He watches us even now."*

Quickly, Marietta pieced together what few facts she knew and realized. Laidlaw had probably not liked what he'd seen this night. It was the only explanation that made sense.

Odd, she had heard that the men who ran these trading posts considered themselves to be something like kings. She had simply not given the matter proper thought . . . unfortunately.

All at once, the man who carried her threw her down, none too gently. Furthermore, whatever she had landed on was hard, though it rocked.

They must be aboard a boat of some kind. What had one of the men mentioned? A mackinaw? Although she wasn't certain what kind of a boat this was, one thing was clear, it was wet. Already, her dress was soaking up water like dry cotton.

"Who's goin' on this trip?" came one of the voices.

"Jenkins, Adams, you and me," answered another man. "That's all. A bit of cargo for St. Louis, but not much, since we just sent some down with the *Yellowstone*. Mostly we're supposed ta play host ta the women."

Raunchy laughter accompanied this bit of news.

"There's Jenkins now," continued the voice. "We're set to go, but where's Adams?"

"He went lookin' fer that Injun."

"Well, go get him," said another voice. "We're supposed ta set this boat off now. The bourgeois said there was ta be no delay."

Aha, thought Marietta. She had been right. This was Laidlaw's work.

"But he said ta kill that Injun, too."

"Ah, you know we'll never find the savage. Damned Injuns. No one hides better'n they do. You go tell Adams

that, hear? We need ta get this boat off now, before that Injun finds us."

Yes, thought Marietta. *I'd be worried about that, too, if I
were you.*

"Ah, here's Adams now. C'mon, man, get aboard. Laidlaw wants this mackinaw ta set off now."

The boat pitched back and forth as someone stepped
onto the boat—probably Adams—nice, friendly Allen
Adams.

"Did'cha find that Injun?"

"No," came the voice of Adams. "But you're right—we
best not waste any more time looking for him. Let's get
going."

And Marietta, still covered in a sheet, felt the boat set
off from the shore.

The mackinaw turned out to be a cheaply made flat-
bottomed boat about forty feet long and pointed at the bow.
A long rudder extended out of the back, or the stern of the
boat. It required at least two oarsmen to guide her and was
steered by a man who sat on a high perch astern. At the
bow of the boat was the hold, which, in this particular
mackinaw, had been set aside to house the women and an
odd assortment of cargo.

At the moment, however, the entire crew, as well as the
women, sat on a flat, grassy bank. Evening was descending
on them, and as was custom along the river, the crew had
rowed the boat ashore.

A large fire sat in the center of their small circle; an iron
pot was extended over it, cooking their supper of vegetables and pork. The crew was an odd assortment of men,
Marietta had decided. Two of them wore red bandannas

tied around their heads; another sported a black hat with the brim turned up. This man was Adams, and as she recalled from the previous evening, Adam's face bore a mark of kindness.

All of the men or bullies, as they were called, wore buckskin breeches and buckskin shirts that looked as if they'd seen better days. Three of the men sat smoking T-stemmed pipes, while a fourth man worked on the boat, securing it.

An overhanging growth of cottonwood and willow trees sheltered their little nook, creating a sort of "park." It was a picturesque spot, and under most any other circumstance, Marietta might have been content to simply sit and enjoy the scenic beauty.

But she wasn't content, nor was she inclined to relish the idle chatter of the men. Not at the moment. Truth be told, she was boiling mad.

Interrupting one of the men, she said, "You shouldn't build such a big fire."

All of the crew except Adams laughed at her. One of the bullies said, "And what would *ye* be knowing about it?"

"Apparently more than you," she replied, but it was said more under her breath than aloud.

"What was that?" asked the man.

"A large fire can be seen from far away," explained Marietta, "and its scent will warn any Indians traveling in the area that you are here. It's better to build a small, smokeless fire."

The man snickered. "Ye been travelin' with that Injun too long, I expect, ma'am."

"Perhaps," said Marietta, "but at least I felt safe under his protection."

"Don't ye worry, ma'am. Ye're safe with us. If'n them Injuns choose ta surprise us, we can get away in our boat."

"Get away in the boat?" Stunned at the stupidity of the statement, Marietta stared at the one who uttered it.

"That's right," said the man.

"I beg to differ, sir," she replied. "But by the time it would take you to run to the boat, you would most likely be dead. Besides, don't you realize that any Indian could follow you? You do know that they can swim, don't you?"

For a second, the bully looked ridiculously blank. After a brief pause, however, he grinned at her. "Them Injuns aren't brave enough ta follow us," he said. "'Sides, they'd flee before our guns."

"Maybe," said Marietta, shaking her head and looking away from the man. "Thank heavens your guns are big enough to make up for your lack of brains and skill."

"What was that, miss?"

"Nothing," said Marietta, though she caught Yellow Swan's gaze, and the two women shared a secret smile.

It was then that Yellow Swan raised her hands, making hand motions—with her palms facing each other, she drove her hands forward in zigzag motions. It was the sign for "follow." Then she formed the sign for "husband."

Marietta nodded.

"What did that savage say?" asked one of the crew who wore a bandanna.

"I don't know, sir," lied Marietta. "But I have heard that all the tribes use this form of language. It might do you well to learn it."

"Like hell ye don't know what she said," the man cursed. But when Marietta remained silent, he appeared to take out his frustration another way: He leaned over to one side and spit.

Marietta, momentarily repulsed, looked away.

With the exception of Adams, these men were as different from Grey Coyote as they could possibly be, she thought, her heart warming to the subject. Grey Coyote, who at all times had presented a pleasant manner, would have never spit in her presence. Not like that.

To give the crewman his due, however, she considered that perhaps Grey Coyote *could* act as grossly as did these men. But if he had ever done so, she wouldn't know of it. In her presence, Grey Coyote had always been a gentleman.

She sighed. Dear Lord, she missed him. Traveling as they were, without him, wasn't the same, wasn't nearly as interesting, exciting or as beautiful.

For one, she missed Grey Coyote's constant reference to the different natural phenomena of the plains, his pointing out things that she had neglected to see, his educating her of the grasslands, his showing her how and why the wilderness was not really "wild."

Perhaps to abate the feeling of loneliness, she decided to try to converse more intelligently with her captors, and she said, "Excuse me, sir," she spoke to Adams. "Your name is Allen Adams, isn't it?"

He beamed. "That's right, miss."

"Mr. Adams, tell me, did you say that you are charged to return myself and my maid to St. Louis?"

"Aye, ma'am. That we are. We carry some cargo downriver, too. But our main purpose is to get you to civilization."

"Thank you, sir. It is considerate of you to do so."

He smiled.

"It would be even more considerate had I not been dragged away, a sheet forced over my head, and my hands and feet tied."

"I understand, miss," said Adams, "but Mr. Laidlaw thought this way was for the best. I suspect he was afraid you might protest."

"I see," she acknowledged. "How fortunate for us that Mr. Laidlaw can think for us all, without ever having to consult us. Heaven forbid we tax our own minds."

Adams grinned, and Marietta was certain that, if the man had grasped the sarcasm underlying her words, he chose to ignore it.

He said, "You should get yourself ready to turn in, ma'am. I'm sorry that we'll have to bind both you and your friend, but it'll be for the night only."

Marietta frowned at him. "I hardly think that's necessary."

"I'm sorry, miss." And he truly did look sorry. "But it's Laidlaw's orders," he said. "Guess he felt you might try ta steal away."

Marietta pressed her lips together, drawing in her brows. "And dear God in heaven," she said, "spare us if we should think to disobey Mr. Laidlaw's orders."

Adams smiled at her. "I'm sorry. Just get ready to settle in. We'll be up early in the morning to get started again. Me and the men are goin' to go secure the boat now, but you and your maid should get yourselves ready to sleep."

Despite his good nature, Marietta might have replied to that with even more sass, but at the moment, one of the other men, the one who had been securing their cargo, stepped into their camp. In his hand, he held a small tree he had uprooted, and with an inane grin, he said, "Look what I found—this little sapling'll make a good whip." And he swung the tree round and round his head, using the sapling like a lash as he did a little dance. The men all laughed, even Adams.

As Marietta watched, she recalled another time, another set of saplings, another man and another set of values. She wondered, did this voyageur know that he had disturbed the "oneness" of nature?

Probably not. Only days ago, she wouldn't have known any differently, either.

But now she did and wondered, would the voyageur ever come to realize that all life was precious? That the life you took from another could detract from your own immortal soul?

It was then that it happened. All at once, Marietta slammed into a realization: She had changed. Her viewpoint on life had changed; it was completely different than it had been. Indeed, England seemed very far away, in many ways. Not at all connected with the here and now.

Odd, she considered further, it was as though all this time she had been living in the future, forgetting that there was a present.

But not now. At this moment in time, she was very aware of the presence of things. In truth, she felt the urge to become a part of every living creature—to attain that "oneness" in nature, and to experience the beauty of it to its fullest extent.

Dear Lord. How had it happened? When had it happened?

Somehow, in some way, her spirit and Grey Coyote's had merged, had become kindred; they were connected by something more real than this material universe. Perhaps the very spirit of the land had entered into her soul.

If it had, it was a good thing, a very good thing. For it was a wonderful feeling.

She inhaled deeply. Though less than a month had passed since she had begun traveling with Grey Coyote, she was a different person. *This* was now her home; Grey Coyote, her man.

She would escape. Luckily, thanks to Grey Coyote, she had a good idea of how she might accomplish this.

Glancing toward Yellow Swan, Marietta curled her fingers into fists and crossing her hands over each other, she jerked them both to the side, slightly upward, opening her fingers at the same time. It was the sign for "escape."

Very subtly, Yellow Swan nodded, making the gesture for "tonight?"

Marietta inclined her head, and Yellow Swan replied with the sign for "good."

Together, the women smiled.

Gazing up at the Seven Brothers, Grey Coyote realized that dawn was only a few hours away. It was the time of night that he had awaited; soon the darkest hour would be upon them. It would be then that he would rescue the women.

Grey Coyote had followed the boat carrying his wife. In truth, he had dogged its progress for two days. He had watched it; he had waited. But he had not acted to take Marietta away, mostly because in his own mind, he had realized that perhaps this was the opportunity his wife had awaited. Hadn't she talked often and long enough about returning to St. Louis?

Indeed, if this were what she craved, Grey Coyote would let her go, for it was not in his nature to hold her against her will. And if the curse were to be more difficult to break because he had allowed her to leave, then so be it.

But in watching their camp closely this night, he had witnessed Marietta make the sign for escape—tonight. Seeing those gestures, Grey Coyote's heart had broken free. In truth, it had soared.

He understood: His wife would rather flee than continue down the path that would take her to St. Louis, even though, for the length of time he had known her, she had talked of little else. Had Marietta finally come to realize that, no matter the circumstances, they belonged together?

Silently, he acknowledged that it appeared to be so.

Shrewdly, Grey Coyote had set his plans, had awaited his moment to act, though he had certainly not been idle in the time intervening. Stealing up close to each man this very evening, Grey Coyote had taken their weapons, one by one. It had been a necessary precaution, but it was also a form of revenge.

Now, advancing noiselessly toward his wife, Grey Coyote placed his hand over her mouth, a safeguard in case he startled her into crying out. Bringing his face to her face, he settled his lips over hers.

Immediately, her eyes popped open. She stared, and he couldn't help but grin at her, watching as her countenance slowly changed from surprise to enchantment. Ah, how he loved this woman.

Raising up barely, he placed his finger to his lips, then taking out his knife, he slipped its blade between the ropes that bound her hands. He did the same with her feet, then repeated the procedure with Yellow Swan.

Quite naturally, both women rubbed their wrists, but Grey Coyote, with a sharp sign, cautioned them to cease all action. Movement, he reminded them with a frown, would send out those ever-expanding air waves. And if he were to secure their escape, they would need to effect their desertion with as little motion as possible.

Marietta nodded.

Then, taking her hand in his and bringing it to his lips, he kissed her fingers gently and mouthed, "You must remove your dress and petticoats if we are to leave here without notice."

Again Marietta nodded, and without even a small comment or protest began to undo the buttons of her dress.

Next, Grey Coyote crept toward Yellow Swan, and with a series of signs, asked her to help Marietta.

But Marietta seemed to have misunderstood, for she reached out for Grey Coyote's fingers, and bringing them to her lips, she mouthed, "Shouldn't Yellow Swan also remove her dress?"

Grey Coyote shook his head.

"Why not?" asked Marietta.

Taking up a handful of Yellow Swan's dress, Grey Coyote made the signs for "buckskin," "tear," then "resist."

Yellow Swan meanwhile had crept toward Marietta, and with two sets of hands working over Marietta's dress, the chore was soon done; his wife had shed her outer garment, her petticoats and chemise. That it left her sitting in no more than leggings, drawers and corset was becoming to him a common sight.

However, the dress was not cached or thrown away. The dress, the petticoats and chemise were all laid out over the ground. Taking up the ropes that had bound his wife, Grey Coyote tied them to the clothing.

This done, they gradually crept away from the camp. Once out of sight, Grey Coyote ushered the women into a grove of tightly packed willow trees. Here they would hide.

Once more, bringing Marietta's fingers to his lips, he mouthed, "You are both to stay here while I backtrack, so that I may erase our passage. You are not to do anything or say anything until I return. Do you understand?"

She nodded, and he kissed her again before he turned away.

Sneaking back into the river boat encampment, Grey Coyote took up the weapons he had confiscated earlier, arranging the arsenal into a neat pattern next to Marietta's dress. If that design gave all the appearance of creating the English word, "fools," so be it.

Noiselessly, Grey Coyote slipped back to the willows, where for a moment, he held his wife in his arms. Then, with one more kiss, they were on their way.

CHAPTER 19

On this day, dawn was a spectacular event. The eastern sky was tinted the palest peach, accompanied by the darker shades of silver and blue. Marietta and Grey Coyote were sitting together, arm in arm, reclining behind a stand of bushes. They faced east, gazing with admiration at the sky, land, and a herd of buffalo, which had come to feed over the low ground.

Earlier, Grey Coyote, as well as Yellow Swan, had welcomed in the day with prayer, Marietta watching them both. Then without a word being said, she dropped to her knees herself to pray, but in her own way.

At present, Yellow Swan had retreated to the low ground, to collect roots. As she worked, though she kept within view of the other two for safety's sake, she was for the moment out of earshot.

Leaning close toward Marietta, Grey Coyote said, "I followed you for two days."

"Did you? Then, why didn't you . . ."

"Understand, I did not act to rescue you, not at first," he said, "for I thought you might welcome the trip downriver. I know that in your heart is the need to return to your England."

"Yes, that's true," said Marietta, "but if I had gone there without the curse being lifted . . ."

"I thought that perhaps you might consider it was not your problem. Or that the adventure to return to your home might be more than you could easily resist. I was not going to intervene if this were so, for it is not in my heart to deny you."

"But—"

"And then," he continued, "I saw you make the sign for escape, and my spirit took flight, and I . . ." His voice trembled, and he ceased speaking, his lips caressing her on her forehead instead.

Marietta leaned into him, emotion rolling through her. Had she ever loved him more? She said, "Yes, I wanted to escape. I can never remember desiring anything more, not even returning to . . . my England."

Grey Coyote's arms tightened around her, and gazing at the soft look in his eyes, Marietta said, "Know this, my husband. I . . . I . . . have changed." She took a deep breath, and looking away from him, she continued, "I can't tell you when it happened, or even why. All I know is that when I am with you, I feel alive, as though every bit of me is a living, vital thing, as if the world around me is filled with mystery and enchantment."

Gazing back at him, her glance scanned his every feature, as though she wished to memorize each one. She said, "I am so in love with you, Grey Coyote. I don't wish to live without you."

"Nor I, you," he replied, and there was a tear in his eye that he did not attempt to deny or explain.

She felt so close to him, but there was more to say. "If that means that I never see again the shores of England, then so be it. I can live without that. I cannot live without you."

"Nor should you have to," he said. "For as long as I exist, I will love you, my wife. From the first moment I saw you, I admired you for your beauty, for it is uncommon. But then, when I came to know you more fully, I was touched at first by your kindness and your passion. Later, I was surprised, yet inspired by your courage in rescuing your friend, and your willingness to do things many women would never do.

"And then," he continued, "when you, too, saw the vision and decided to stay to help me . . ." He couldn't finish the thought, as his voice quivered overly much. But after a moment, he swallowed hard and said, "Know this, my wife, while I am committed to ending the curse for my people, whether I be successful or not, I am dedicated to you. And this I promise you, so long as I exist, I will love you."

Marietta cried. She simply cried, and throwing her arms around him, she said, "Love me, my husband. I know the time is not right. I know my friend is nearby. But I have never wanted anything more than to have you, all of you. Please love me."

Picking her up in his arms, he brought her to her knees in front of him, the two of them kneeling before one another. He whispered against her neck, "I will, my love. I will, and I do."

It took almost no effort to remove her drawers, leaving her corset intact—at least for the moment. Grabbing ahold of his buffalo robe, he positioned it beneath her, and gradually, he lowered her to the ground, opening her legs so that he could admire the beauty that was hers and hers alone.

He said, "Oh, that we had the whole day to love."

"But we don't, my love," she said. "I understand this, but we will still have this moment."

"*Hau*," he said. "*Hau*."

Before she could stop him, he bent toward her navel, tasting her, kissing her, gradually letting his range extend downward, until at last, he kissed her very femininity.

It was a wicked sensation, it was delightful, and oh, the pleasure, the rapture, to be loved in such a way by this very proud and wonderful man.

He murmured, "Open your legs more fully for me. Give yourself to me completely."

And she did. Over and over again, he made love to her. Indeed, he took her to the heavens and back again. When she thought she could take it no more, he rose up over her.

Bringing her legs to his shoulders, he knelt before her, his hands carrying her hips up to meet his. He then joined himself with her.

Never once did he look away from her; never once did she pull her glance away from him. Smiling at one another, they made love, building up to an apex, and then he let her come down.

She was ecstatically there again, tripping over the edge of pleasure, and at that exact moment, he thrust more deeply into her tight recess, spilling all of what he had to give, for her alone. Still, not once, did they look away from one another.

"I love you so much, my wife," said Grey Coyote, as he bent toward her, showering her with kisses.

"And I love you. So long as I exist, I will love you."

Smiling, she pulled him down to her, where she once more embarked upon the road to pleasure . . .

"Where are we going?" Marietta asked of Grey Coyote later that evening. The three of them were once again on their way, traveling over the countryside. For a time, they had stopped, as both Grey Coyote and Marietta seemed inclined to do of late. While they were halted, the two of them were to be seen sharing an embrace, a hug, or sometimes even a kiss. Luckily, Yellow Swan was more than content to look the other way.

"If my calculations are correct," Marietta continued, "we are heading north. You're not backtracking toward Fort Pierre, are you?"

"I am," said Grey Coyote.

"But why?" asked Marietta, as she turned to frown at her husband. "You must know that I don't want to go back to that horrible fort. What will Laidlaw do if he sees me again with you? Oh, and did I tell you that Laidlaw ordered Adams to kill you?"

"I did know that," said Grey Coyote. "But we are not returning to the fort. We go that way because I have some good news for Yellow Swan."

This statement had Yellow Swan, who had been reclining off to the side, turning toward the two of them. But she said nothing to Grey Coyote, as Marietta had come to learn was Indian etiquette.

Marietta had also discovered over the past few weeks, when in the presence of both Yellow Swan and Grey Coyote, that it was left up to *her* to intervene for the two of them. It was the only way that they would speak to each other.

Apparently, in Indian country, unless he had to, a man

did not talk to a woman who was not his wife. So Marietta asked, "Did you say you had news for Yellow Swan?"

"*Hau*," replied Grey Coyote, "it is so. Tell her," said Grey Coyote, as though Yellow Swan weren't there and couldn't hear his every word, "that while I was in the Lakota camp, I learned that many of the Lakota horses have recently been stolen. The warriors did try to track the man who took them, and they know that he who did it was Assiniboine. However, they were unable to catch him."

Yellow Swan's face brightened, but she remained silent.

Marietta asked, "Do you think the man who did it was Yellow Swan's husband?"

Grey Coyote grinned. "I suspect it was, for his description fits the manner of her husband."

At this announcement, Yellow Swan smiled, though she had cast her gaze politely downward.

So Marietta said for her, "Then we should journey to the north as soon as we trap the beast, so that we may bring Yellow Swan to her people."

"We could," said Grey Coyote. "However, if she does not wish to wait for this to happen, I have other news, perhaps better news. I found another Assiniboine woman in the Lakota camp. She is waiting for Yellow Swan, for she, too, wishes to go back to her own people. Together, they can return to Assiniboine territory, if she wishes."

For a moment, gazing at Yellow Swan, Marietta was uncertain if her friend was going to break out into laughter or tears, so varied were the emotions to be witnessed over her countenance. At last, however, Yellow Swan did neither.

Instead, Yellow Swan said, "Tell . . . scout . . . I thank him."

And she turned away. However, Marietta could have

sworn that before Yellow Swan gazed away from them, she had seen tears in her eyes.

"Will you be able to pick up the beast's trail again," asked Marietta, as she and Grey Coyote set out once more, after having introduced Yellow Swan to the other Assiniboine woman. It had been a warm meeting between the two women, for they knew one another; they were, in truth, cousins.

They had rested for a day, and then Grey Coyote had pointed both women in the direction of home, while Marietta had ensured they had plenty of food. Soon the women were gone.

At present, both Grey Coyote and Marietta were scouring the ground, looking for the beast's tracks.

"I will find his trail," Grey Coyote said. "It has not yet been a week, and it has not rained. The earth will still hold the impression of those who walk over her."

"Yes," said Marietta, "but how do you know where to start?"

Gazing up at her, Grey Coyote said, "There are some facts that we possess. One is that we tracked this man, the beast, to this post. Laidlaw must have seen him, for I am certain that nothing comes in or out of his post that is unknown to him. Yet, Laidlaw would not tell you where the beast went."

"That's right."

"Why?" asked Grey Coyote.

"I don't know."

Grey Coyote set his features in a frown. "It was the asking of that question that has caused me to believe," said Grey Coyote, "that the beast works for this man."

"The beast? Works for Laidlaw?"

"It is possible," said Grey Coyote. "It would explain why Laidlaw would not help you. It would also excuse why Laidlaw was intent on getting you as far away from the post as possible."

Perplexed, Marietta furrowed her brow. "But I thought he was trying to do me a favor."

Grey Coyote stared at her hard, then said, "It is possible that he was, but you must try to think like this man—if only for a short while. Could a man who would order the death of another, without thought, without conscience, be also a man of benevolence?"

"I don't know. Could he?"

"I do not think so. Men who require other men to do their killing for them, rather than confront the deed themselves, are not quite human. In my opinion, they are not social, are less than an animal, for such men have no concept that there are things in life that are right, things that help others and all creation. Such men deal in destruction, not creation."

"I've never thought of it like that before.

"Those are my thoughts. I could be wrong. But if it is true that Laidlaw hires others to do his killing for him, then he would not be above hiring the beast to work for him, also."

Marietta inclined her head. "I see."

"Therefore, we will most likely find the beast close to Fort Pierre. But if not, we should be able to discover his trail there and pursue him."

"Hmmm," she said. "But, still, is it safe to go that close to Fort Pierre? You realize that it's possible that if you are seen, you will be shot on the spot."

Grey Coyote nodded. "You are right. It is not safe. Therefore, we will be careful."

"Yes," said Marietta. "Let us be very, very careful."

* * *

It was dark when at last Grey Coyote was able to pick up the beast's trail.

"He is proceeding south and keeping to the river, where there is a good cover of trees," said Grey Coyote. "I suspect that he is enroute to each major trading post along the river, for I still think that he is accomplishing some duty for Laidlaw."

"But why?" asked Marietta. "What could he be doing?

Grey Coyote shrugged. "I do not know, unless it is to spy on other companies, and perhaps to create havoc. My brother-in-law has told me how the big companies spy on one another, for the jealousy between them is high. But come," said Grey Coyote. "I do not wish to confront this man at any one of these trading posts. Let us track him to his own hideaway."

"But isn't that a little too dangerous?" she asked. "After all, we know that this man is capable of murder. Are you certain you want to enter his encampment alone?"

"I do not intend to do that. Merely find it. And once I locate it, I will set mantraps all around it. And if I have to, I will do this each night until I catch the beast. Then from the safety of the trap, I will question him, until I can learn what he possesses that might end my people's curse."

"I see," said Marietta. "What is a mantrap?"

"It is a trap like any other used to catch animals," said Grey Coyote. "But a mantrap must be placed in such a way that a human being will not suspect it. However, unlike animal traps, a mantrap is not used to kill, merely to bring to bay. They have great value, for when one is in enemy territory, one can arrange mantraps around his own shelter as protection."

"Brilliant," she acknowledged. "But what are they? I mean, how do you outwit a man?"

"By the use of snares," he replied, "or sometimes pits are used, covered with a blanket of dirt so that they are invisible to the eye. The snare will catch a man's foot, causing him to hang by it. The pit speaks for itself."

"Oh, I see," she said. "So if I understand you correctly, you will make a trap, catch this beast, and then from a safe distance, question him?"

"That is my plan."

She thought a moment. "But what if he won't talk to you?"

Grey Coyote shrugged. "He may not. I can only hope that he will."

"Very well," she said. "I think it is a fine plan."

"*Waste*, good," said Grey Coyote. "We have only to follow his trail now, locate his hideout, and then I will set up these traps."

Marietta nodded and replied, "Lead on."

Immediately, they set out, following the earthen impressions, the two of them gliding ghostlike across the moonlit landscape.

It was raining. Above Grey Coyote, dark clouds ruled the the night while lightning streaked through the sky. The wind had become so strong that it rocked him almost off his feet, and thunder rolled menacingly through the heavens, as though to give warning.

But this was no omen. No, this was the Thunderer, perhaps even other gods, come to mock him.

However, the thunder and lightning, though annoying, did little to deter Grey Coyote. If anything, these things gave him encouragement. To his way of thinking, they confirmed that he was on the right path.

Only hours ago, he had located the beast's encampment. Though it was almost impossible to estimate the time of night, for there were no stars overhead, Grey Coyote figured that there were still several hours left before sunrise. Within that time, he must erect several mantraps.

Before he began his work in earnest, however, Grey Coyote had set up a temporary dwelling for Marietta, instructing her to stay within it. He had left her with plenty of work to do, as well—for she would fashion the ropes he would need for his snares. She had protested being left behind, of course, insisting that she be allowed to help him. But Grey Coyote had denied her. He was taking no chances; she would have no contact with the beast.

Though their shared vision inferred that they must both confront the beast, it did not necessarily follow that he should endanger her life. He would confront the beast first, tie him up, make it safe. Only then would he allow Marietta access to the beast.

"But how will you break the enchantment if I am not there?" she had asked. "Remember, I am a part of this."

"And so you will be," Grey Coyote had responded. "When the beast is tied, and I am certain he can do no harm, I will guess the riddle. You will be there then."

"Hmmm," she said. "But what if you require my help before that?"

"I will call you. This shelter is not far from his encampment."

With a sigh, Marietta had at last agreed.

Leaving Marietta to construct the ropes he would require, Grey Coyote had set to work forthwith, setting his snares, tying the lines to trees big enough that they would hold a huge man. When there wasn't a tree large enough for a snare at a particular spot, Grey Coyote had tied the ropes around two or three smaller trees.

Throughout, the rain pounded on him, and his fingers slipped over the knots he made, but he patiently kept on; he could not stop.

At length, he was satisfied with what he had done so far. However, he still had one trap left to set. When that was done, he would await the results of his handiwork . . . from a safe distance.

The storm, meanwhile, had worsened; it began to hail, and though dawn approached, the sky was as gray and as dark as night. A bolt of lightning crashed close to hand, shaking the earth, causing the trees to tremble, but Grey Coyote ignored it, certain it was the Thunderer, mocking him yet again.

Suddenly, he heard a scream, high-pitched and filled with terror.

A scream?

Marietta . . . She was in trouble.

How had he not foreseen this? Why had he not antici-pated this?

Jumping to his feet, Grey Coyote crashed forward through the undergrowth and trees, uncaring that such haste would announce his approach. It didn't matter. He had to get there . . .

Marietta sat forward, dragging with her the line she was working on. Something had made a sound out there—something besides the steady pounding of the rain. Coming up slowly onto her hands and knees, she pushed back a few of the branches that hid her shelter. She gazed out into the night.

She saw nothing. Had she imagined it?

No, something was wrong. She could feel it.

Suddenly, there was a burst of light, followed by an explosion that crashed through the air. The ground shook, but worse, she saw what looked to be a bear or something as large as a bear. And it loomed over her.

She gasped, then scolded herself, knowing instinctively that she should have kept quiet. Belatedly, she went completely still, wondering . . . had she given herself away?

Marietta saw a big man, the beast, and he looked her way. And without warning the beast burst in upon her.

He grabbed her, and she screamed again and again. Something hit her in the head, and looking up, she beheld a broken-toothed smile in a horribly scratched and bearded face.

With one last terrible scream, she fainted.

The beast held Grey Coyote's wife within its grasp. From where he stood, Grey Coyote could see it all.

Was Marietta alive? From this distance, he couldn't discern her fate. He only knew that she didn't move.

His heart sank. She *had* to be alive. She *must* be alive.

He realized he would have to kill the beast. Now.

Forget the riddle; forget that he knew not what the beast possessed, or that thing which he himself must possess. Never mind that by killing the beast, he would fail himself and his people . . . forever.

Nothing was more important than the safety of his wife.

Grey Coyote drew up his bow, but he hesitated. Could he really endanger his tribe? Throw away his lifetime of training? Could he live with what would assuredly be his failure?

But then, all other thoughts were swept away from him. The man-beast had pulled off Marietta's remaining clothing, not caring that she was getting hurt in the process.

He meant to rape her.

Casting all doubts and concerns aside, Grey Coyote went into action. With his bow already in hand he quickly positioned an arrow against it, and released it, followed by another arrow, another and another, one after the other; so quickly did he shoot them, the sky might have been raining arrows.

But the man had not been compared to a bear merely because of size. He was impossible to kill, and like a bear, Grey Coyote's arrows served to do no more than anger him.

Letting go of Marietta, the beast staggered forward, toward Grey Coyote. Though Grey Coyote had allowed himself a reserve of arrows, it was not long before he was fitting the last one to his bow.

Still the man-beast kept on.

"What is it you possess that I must have?" shouted Grey Coyote at it, as though the brute held all the answers.

But the man didn't answer, roared instead, "I will kill you."

Bow drawn back, ready for action, Grey Coyote yelled, "Though I would rather die than let you take my wife, it will not be *I* who dies this night. It is you, my friend. You."

"Never," said the beast.

"Come no farther," bellowed Grey Coyote, "for if you do, this arrow goes straight to your heart."

But the beast ignored him, came on, was almost upon Grey Coyote. Still, Grey Coyote hesitated.

If he killed this man, his chance to end the curse for his people would die, along with himself. If he didn't kill the man, his wife would die.

"Come no farther," shouted Grey Coyote again.

But his words were to no avail. The beast was close enough to take a swipe at him and did so, the action ridding Grey Coyote of any uncertainty he might have had. Grey Coyote let go his last arrow . . . into the creature's heart.

The beast screamed, stopped, then reeled forward. Grey Coyote jumped back and threw the last thing that he had at the man—his bow.

He prepared himself for a fight. But it never happened. The beast fell to the ground, dead.

Tentatively, Grey Coyote stepped toward him, using his foot to turn the man over. He expelled a deep breath.

It was done. It was over. As was his chance—

But he drove the thought from his mind. Marietta—was she alive?

Grey Coyote sprinted toward Marietta's side. Throwing himself to the ground beside her, he picked her up, feeling for a heartbeat.

It was there. Faint, but it was there.

Without a word, he nestled her into his arms, tears streaming down his face, and holding her against him, he began to caress her, running his hands up and down her back, over to the sides of her body, up to her neck, her head.

"Are you hurt?" he asked at last, not expecting a response. But he received one, nonetheless.

She shook her head, and he thought his heart would burst with grief, for there was horror, as well as tears, in her eyes.

"I am so sorry," he said. "Vision or none, I should never have brought you here."

But Marietta was crying, too, and between sobs, she said, "How can I ever forgive myself? It is I who have failed you. The beast is gone. How will you end the curse for—"

But before she could finish, the wind began to blow even more fiercely than it had during the storm. So strong was it, the very clouds above them parted, revealing one, single morning star.

The sun had started to rise. Suddenly, and almost at once, a golden ray of sunlight shone down, enveloping them within its beam. Within that circle of sunshine, figures of other people were beginning to emerge . . . misty images at first, but then, even as Grey Coyote watched, the forms became more and more corporeal.

"My wife," said Grey Coyote, and there was surprise in his voice. "I recognize these people. They are my own clan. How? What is happening?"

From the sky above them, came the vision of the spirit coyote, and as it drifted toward the earth, it sang a haunting refrain:

> "Neither small nor large, nor wide, nor narrow, the
>   beast possessed a thing that propelled Grey Coyote
>   toward freedom. Though the beast possessed her,
>   and though Grey Coyote possessed her, also, and
>   she possessed him, he sacrificed all that he was and
>   had ever been, or would ever be, because in his
>   heart, there was love.
> Grey Coyote has ended the curse."

He had broken the enchantment? Emotion, elation, grief, thanksgiving, flooded through him, overwhelming him. Not knowing what else to do, he bent his head so that his face was hidden within Marietta's golden locks, and despite himself, he cried.

CHAPTER 20

A great council was called that very night. All the important clan members were present, including Grey Coyote's own father. Within that circle sat White Claw, the tribal medicine man and Grey Coyote's grandfather. Grey Coyote reposed next to this man, and though it was not often allowed, Marietta was positioned next to Grey Coyote.

A pipe was lit, White Claw offering the smoke to the four directions and to the Above Ones. Then it was passed to each member of the counsel, including Marietta.

She, too, would smoke. For without her, the curse might never have been broken.

At last, when the necessities of council were dispensed with according to ritual, White Claw spoke. "We honor you, Spirit Raven, or as you are known to your adopted people, Grey Coyote. You have done what others before you failed to do. You have broken the curse that enslaved your clan. Your people will now be free to live the lives they were meant to live."

Grey Coyote nodded.

"We honor also the woman you have brought to us,"

continued White Claw. "We will sing songs praising her and you, so long as we exist."

Again, Grey Coyote nodded.

"And now," said White Claw, "I feel, Grandson, that you have questions. I will answer them to the best of my ability, but know that I cannot stay here long, for there are others who are still entrapped within the mist. And while this is so, I cannot rest. However, I am here now, and I will help you as best I can, so that you might understand."

"Thank you, Grandfather," said Grey Coyote. "There is something I would like to know. I heard the spirit coyote's song, I heard his words, but I do not understand how it was that I broke the curse. I thought I would need to guess the riddle correctly. Was this not true?"

"But, Grandson"—White Claw nodded sagely—"you did guess correctly. That you said not the words has no significance."

"But how, Grandfather. What did I do? In my own mind, I thought I was sacrificing myself and the tribe, for I acted against what I have been led to believe I must do to end our plight."

Again, White Claw inclined his head. He said, "Sometimes, Grandson, the best within us is shown, not with the head, but with the heart. You did discover what this man possessed . . . your wife . . . and you did act on it, despite what you thought was the right thing to do. Your sacrifice, Grandson, was completely selfless."

Grey Coyote nodded.

"And now," said White Claw, "you must answer a question for me."

"*Hau*," said Grey Coyote. "I will do my best."

"Tell me, Grandson, why did you commit such a selfless act?"

Grey Coyote took a moment to collect his thoughts before he answered, saying, "Because, Grandfather, I loved someone else more than I loved myself, even more than my duty to my people."

"Exactly," said White Claw. "There was love, and only love in your heart. Not revenge. Not duty. Only love. Perhaps that is the answer we all look for. To love someone so greatly that we do not even have to think to act. Remember that had our clan loved so well in the past, we would not now be enslaved."

Grey Coyote bobbed his head in understanding. "I think, Grandfather, that you are right."

"Perhaps so," said White Claw. "Perhaps."

"And now," said the old man, "may I speak with your wife, Little Sunset? For I would answer any questions that she might ask of me."

"Of course," said Grey Coyote.

White Claw, addressing Marietta, asked, "Have you something you would like to ask me, wife of Grey Coyote?"

Marietta cleared her throat. "Yes, sir, there is," she said. "Will these people, who have only now arrived here—will they continue to be real? Will they live their lives out here? Now?"

"Aaah, yes," said White Claw. "They are now very real. And yes, they will live their lives here, in this time and in this place. And you, Granddaughter, will be a part of them, since these are your husband's people. But he will also be a part of your world, too, for know this. There is still time to accomplish those things in your world that are most dear to your heart."

Marietta sat momentarily stunned. "You mean," she said, "that I still might be able to claim that which is mine? I might yet be able to restore Rosemead?"

White Claw nodded.

Pressing her lips together, Marietta turned away. There was a tear in her eye.

"Go now," said White Claw. "Go, knowing that happiness will be forever yours."

With this said, White Claw emptied the ashes from his pipe, saying, "This council is now over."

All rose to their feet, but White Claw alone stepped away from the others. Without looking back, he tread out of the circle and into the light of the morning sun.

Grey Coyote and Marietta watched him until he was no more than a tiny, misty shape. And then all at once, he was gone.

Grey Coyote turned to Marietta and bending, kissed her on the lips, whispering, "I will love you forever."

Marietta smiled. "And I will always love you, too."

So it was that the two passed into legend. But it is also a part of that legend that, as predicted, they did, indeed, live a happy life, both in England and in the American West.

GLOSSARY

The following list of terms is provided to assist in understanding and ease of reading:

Assiniboine Indians A tribe of Indians that was originally a part of the Dakota or Lakota tribe. The Assiniboine spoke the same language as the Lakota. The Assiniboine split off from the tribe many centuries ago, long before the white man came into Indian territory. They were to be found in the northwestern United States and Canada, and at the time of this story were a very powerful and numerous tribe.

cache A term meaning "to bury goods in the ground for safekeeping." Usually some symbol was left above ground so that the goods could be found again easily.

count coup A phrase used to describe an action of touching the enemy; a deed of valor.

ecenci A Lakota or Assiniboine term meaning "exactly so."

Gros ventre A tribe of Indians that was located in the Northwestern United States. Their land bordered the Assiniboine.

haiye Joy—perhaps upon learning good news.

han Lakota for "yes." Only used by women.

hau Lakota for "yes." Used by men.

haye-haye Lakota word for "delight," as in receiving a gift.

hiya Lakota for "no."

hokahe Lakota word used to signal action.

hehe, hehehe Lakota word for expressing regret.

hunhe-hunhe Lakota word that means "regret."

iho Lakota or Assiniboine word for "look, see."

ito Lakota or Assiniboine word for "come."

kakel Lakota word meaning "thus."

kitanla Lakota word meaning "a little."

kola Lakota or Assiniboine word for "friend." Usually used between men.

mackinaw A type of boat used during this period in history. It was a cheap form of transportation, and it often was to be seen on the Missouri River.

Minnetaree Indians Sedentary Indians with permanent mud huts. Their village was on the Knife River, and they grew crops and vegetables.

ohinni Lakota word for "always."

sece Lakota word for "perhaps."

tula Lakota word meaning "to be surprised."

waste Lakota word meaning "good."

THE ANGEL AND THE WARRIOR

KAREN KAY

Angelia Honeywell needs rescuing from her brother's latest scheme: impersonating a scout and leading a wagon train across the plains. But when a Cheyenne brave named Swift Hawk rides to their aid, Angelia can find no escape from his compelling gaze.

"Karen Kay's passion for Native American lore shines through."
—*Publishers Weekly*

"Karen Kay writes with such strong passion that it hooks her readers."
—*BookBrowser*

"Entrancing!"
—Cassie Edwards

0-425-20529-0

Available wherever books are sold or at penguin.com

Also available from
BERKLEY SENSATION

Master of Wolves
by Angela Knight
The *USA Today* bestselling author whose werewolf romances are "torrid and exhilarating"* returns with more werewolves—and a handler who's too hot to handle.

0-425-20743-9

Whispers
by Erin Grady
Not only has Gracie Mitchell inherited the Diablo Springs Hotel, and with it the curse that has haunted her family for years, but now the man she has tried to forget has mysteriously returned to town.

0-425-20890-7

Tempt Me
by Lucy Monroe
Lady Irisa Langley is at her wit's end. She has a secret that would shock even the world-weary denizens of the ton—and destroy any future she could have with her exasperatingly perfect fiancé.

0-425-20922-9

Wicked Nights
by Nina Bangs
In an adult theme park, the Castle of Dark Dreams is home to three extraordinary brothers who promise ultimate fulfillment for any woman bold enough to accept their sensual challenge.

0-425-20370-0

*Best Reviews

Available wherever books are sold or at penguin.com

Also available from
BERKLEY SENSATION

Duchess of Fifth Avenue
by Ruth Ryan Langan
The *New York Times* bestselling author of
"heartwarming, emotionally involving romances"*
brings the Gilded Age to life.

0-425-20889-3

The Penalty Box
by Deirdre Martin
From the *USA Today* bestselling author, a novel
about a hockey heartthrob, a stubborn brainiac,
and a battle of wills that just might end in love.

0-425-20890-7

The Kiss
by Elda Minger
After she finds her fiancé with another woman,
Tess Sommerville packs up and takes a road trip to
Las Vegas, ready to gamble—on love.

0-425-20681-5

Dead Heat
by Jacey Ford
Three beautiful ex-FBI agents have founded a security
firm—and their latest job uncovers a fatal plot against
America's top CEOs.

0-425-20461-8

Library Journal

Available wherever books are sold or at penguin.com